A Piper at the Gates

Book One of The Children of Hamelin

By
Stuart Orr

ABOUT THE AUTHOR

Stuart Orr began his writing career in Melbourne's independent theatre scene. His first play, *Telefunken*, a solo show which he also performed, was selected to open The Malthouse Theatre Company's Tower Theatre, where it won the inaugural Melbourne Fringe Touring Award. His second play, *La Rejectamenta*, another solo which he performed, was staged at La Mama Courthouse.

Since *La Rejectamenta*, Stuart has written three novels: *Ocean of Noise*, *A Piper at the Gates*, and its sequel, *The Piper's Apprentice*.

Stuart teaches English in The Macedon Ranges, where he lives with his wife and their two children.

To my father, who showed me the stars.

ACKNOWLEDGMENTS

Thank you, Jane Jervis-Read, my favourite writer, for reading…so many drafts, and helping me to understand how my characters feel on the page.

Thank you, Ant Brock, for sharing my story with your kids.

Thank you, Nick Levy, for all your invaluable advice.

Thanks to my students, who've taught me so much.

CONTENTS

DAY 1

1 Jack in a Box — Pg 2

2 Lucy and Her Mother War — Pg 11

3 Jangling Jack — Pg 14

4 Lucy Makes a Run For It — Pg 21

5 Jack on the Mountain — Pg 26

6 Lucy Punches a Hole in the World — Pg 35

7 Jack Goes Through the Mill — Pg 41

8 Monsters Inside and Out — Pg 48

9 Lucy Through the Looking Glass — Pg 58

10 Jack Voyager 1, Guitar Hero — Pg 64

11 Lucy Looks Over the Edge — Pg 76

DAY 33

12 Jack's Magic Theatre — Pg 86

13 Lucy Sneaks a Peak — Pg 97

14 A Piper at Jack's Window — Pg 105

15 Lucy, Mum and Dad Have a Nice Little Chat — Pg 118

DAY 57

16 The Secret Language — Pg 123

17 Lucy's Surprise Visitor — Pg 138

18 Making a Monster — Pg 143

DAY 64

19 Lucy Is Happier than She's Ever Been!   Pg 151

20 Debut   Pg 155

21 Lucy Remembers   Pg 167

22 Jack in the Sandbox   Pg 172

23 Open Mic.   Pg 179

24 Out of Step and Into Mystery   Pg 186

DAY 65

25 Lucy Hears the Light   Pg 195

26 Lucy's Loving Vengeance   Pg 201

27 Lucy in the Sky   Pg 222

DAY 177

28 Voodoo Child   Pg 230

DAY 180

29 Tokyo Rose   Pg 245

DAY 181

30 Playing in a Travelling Band   Pg 261

31 The Shadows   Pg 266

MORNING, DAY 182

32   Dragon's Gold Part 1.   Pg. 278

33   Dragon's Gold Part 2.   Pg. 291

34   Dragon's Gold Part 3.   Pg 295

AFTERNOON, DAY 182

35   When the Levee Breaks   Pg 305

36   Standin' On the Outside, Lookin' In   Pg 310

37   Dancing In the Street   Pg 316

38   Road to Nowhere   Pg 321

39   Down and to the Left   Pg 330

NIGHT, DAY 182

40   The Drain   Pg 342

41   River to the Shadowland   Pg 353

42   Duet   Pg 361

All the little boys and girls,

With rosy cheeks and flaxen curls,

And sparkling eyes and teeth like pearls,

Tripping and skipping, ran merrily after

The wonderful music with shouting and laughter.

- Robert Browning, *The Pied Piper of Hamelin.*

But we're never gonna survive, unless

We get a little crazy.

- Seal, *Crazy*

DAY 1

1. JACK IN A BOX

The airlock door was cold to Jack's touch, yet it hummed with a harmony of machines, footsteps, and voices. This trembling at his fingertips would be the last sensation he would ever feel of life inside *The Hamelin*. No more whisper of recycled air. No more whoop and roar of emergency drills. No more fleeting moments of laughter caught between his parents' shifts.

Jack didn't know what lay beyond these familiar walls of routine and duty, but he knew he could not stay.

Something was calling to him, somewhere Lucy was waiting.

He took a breath, turned towards the outer doors and crouched like a sprinter, ready to launch himself into the unknown.

"Airlock doors will open in FIVE…"

The frozen vacuum of space is deadly.

"…FOUR…"

All his life, Jack had feared it.

"…THREE…"

Now he was leaping into it…

"…TWO…"

..without a suit.

"…ONE. Doors opening."

Jack need not have braced himself to jump. In an instant, the silent ocean flooded the airlock and swept him out into its dark and fathomless depths.

He remembered his training. Don't hold your breath, cadet. The lack of pressure will burst your lungs. One long slow exhalation. Fifteen seconds was the record anyone had lasted in open space before blackout. And paralysis. Then it was only a matter of moments before the body froze and that was that. No more Jack.

Twisting, tumbling through the endless black, the boy pursed his lips, and with his last breath, he whistled.

Six months before he took that fateful step, Jack fell out of a nightmare into the tangled blankets of his bed and cried, 'Uroun!'

He sat up in the darkness of his bedroom and rubbed his arms against the cold. In air-conditioned cabins just like his, cadets throughout The Fleet would now be rising with that same word on their lips.

Uroun.

He pictured them readying themselves with flexes and stretches in preparation for whatever challenges the day might bring. This morning was the first day of the most important year of their lives, their sixteenth, the year their roles in The Fleet would be decided. Positions in Communications, Medicine, Engineering, and Food Tech were for the elite. Failing that, he would join the general ranks of Maintenance.

To everyone a place. To everyone a mission.

But Jack knew there was no branch in The Fleet where his skills would be valued. No exam could test and prove his particular talent. There was no rank awarded to dreamers.

Cool air from the vent above the bed blew across his sweaty neck.

With a shiver, he kicked off the blankets and left his quarters.

He kept the lights of the living room off. He didn't need them. He knew every inch of his family's cabin. Depending on where you stood, the ship's drone echoed differently. To his right, he heard the engines buzz and rattle softly through the polished metal surfaces of the kitchenette. To his left the sound was warmer, muffled by the couch, the carpet and the bookshelf. Between them was their cabin's single wall-wide window. Beyond that, lay the stars.

He stepped silently across the carpet, crouched by the window frame, and slowly lifted the shutter to admit the faint glow of starlight. Through the abysmal black of deep space, these points of light had traveled thousands, millions, billions of years to reach him. They shimmered within the silhouette Jack's messy mane of raven-black hair cast upon the glass. So many worlds, so many possibilities.

But only one destination: *Uroun.*

Ting!

A message appeared on the window, which doubled as a video screen. It was a note from his mother and father. Jack tapped the glass and read their words glowing coldly in regulation blue font amongst the stars:

'Happy birthday, Jack. We're sorry we couldn't see you off to Induction this morning. There's a fleet-wide alert on but nothing to worry about. We'll see you this evening and you can tell us about your first day of Year 16(!) Stand strong. Listen well. Make friends. We love you.'

Jack could tell his mother had written most of it and added *'Make friends'* to soften his father's *'Stand strong. Listen well.'*

He didn't mind that they weren't there. Birthdays didn't matter so much when everyone turned another year older on the same day. It was his parents' birthday too, but even if they'd wanted to celebrate, they couldn't take a moment away from their responsibilities. His mother, Xinjuan, was a Food Tech engineer, supervising the operation of the algae farms that fed all ten thousand of their ship's crew. Michael, his father, was a Communications Officer, a 'Net-Cop', overseeing the children of *HMAS Hamelin* as they studied and played in the online worlds of School and Sandbox.

Though Australia had been a small nation, its starship, *The Hamelin*, had pride of place in The Fleet. After all, it was an Australian, the tech-wizard Theodore Hamelin, who had invented The Gravity Shower. Life in the ships would be impossible without it. Through its interface, the children could escape their cramped cabins and enter an online world they could not only see and hear, but feel. In there, their muscles could flex, their sinews could stretch, their hearts pump from real exertion. Suspended in The Shower's well of vibrating atoms, they could do more than imagine they were an eagle soaring over the gameworld, they could feel each fine, strong feather slice through the wind.

Outside their parents' cabins, there was no room for play – no parks, no paths or promenades - and no child was permitted to step beyond those four walls until they graduated. Until that day, The Gravity Shower ensured that childhood was not a cramped and boring prison term. And every day their parents and teachers assured them that the years spent learning and playing in there would be the very best of their lives.

Yet Jack Voyager 1 spent as little time online as he could. He didn't hang out in the network clubs posing for selfies or trading insults and gossip. He didn't race or chase or kill in *Dragon Quest* or *Gangstar's Paradise* or any of the thousands of Sandbox games.

To Jack, his cabin was not the prison, his Gravity Shower was.

The first time he stepped into it, his first Induction Day, Jack was five. He had not seen other children before, except in videos. But here they were, together at last, looking back at one another's avatars, only slightly enhanced by their proud and anxious parents. Above their heads, The Admiral mounted the dais to welcome the children to School, where they would spend the next thirteen years together. Almost as soon as she began to speak, an irregularity in Jack's heartbeat was detected by his Shower's diagnostic resonator. Little alarms sounded and yellow triangles with angry black exclamation marks appeared all about his avatar. He tried to run, but everywhere he turned in the crowd the jangling symbols followed, as though he wore a jester's costume covered with loud golden bells. Everywhere he tried to hide, The Admiral's stern gaze found him.

Later, the ship's doctor had assured Jack and his parents that his heart's irregular beat was nothing to worry about - just a harmless genetic abnormality. His Shower had been reprogrammed not to embarrass him with any more alerts next time his heart skipped a beat. But the damage was already done and the memory of School and Sandbox was long. *Jack the Joke, Jester Jack, Jangling Jack* or just plain *Jangles*; from that day he was marked for life.

Since then, every day, all day at School, he kept his eyes on his work, his breath held tightly in his chest. He never spoke unless it was absolutely necessary. He barely moved, lest the wild drummer at the heart of his private orchestra break into a solo.

Even now, he could hear the eccentric rhythm echoing in his chest. It counted four normal pulses and then tripped out several that were completely out of time, and then returned to a regular count of four, followed by a quick triple count, and on, and on, as though the drummer in his chest were impatient with the song.

As soon as each School day ended, Jack logged out, sprang from The Shower, and let his heart loose in a playground of music. His father's vast collection of vinyl records was the largest of its kind in all seven ships of The Fleet. Jack loved nothing better than to slip the precious discs from their sleeves, and gently press the needle to their grooves. For hours on end, he would lose himself dancing and singing along to 'the classics', echoes of the world humanity had left behind: Jimi Hendrix, Pink Floyd, Billy Holiday. These legends were his friends. These musicians knew all about Jack's loneliness. They said so with their guitars and drums, their trumpets and keyboards, their tender yet mighty voices and their wise, rhyming words.

Sometimes, when Jack was feeling especially blue, he let the needle crackle at the end of the record, and sang wordless harmonies of his own: rising, falling, ribbons of sound, like birdsong.

He wondered when the day would come that he would fill these melodies with lyrics of his own. He did not know yet what he wanted to say, or who would listen when he did. But he knew he couldn't keep it in much longer.

He was a Jack-in-the-box. Every hour spent in School turned the handle, wound the spring tighter, and tighter.

Now, alone in the dark, Jack did not want to go back in to face yet another Induction Day. He wanted to stay by the window, gaze at the night, feel the oceanic swell of engines far behind him, and the eager tapping of his hungry heart.

He wanted to find his song.

He wondered if he stilled himself for long enough, he would.

He let his eyes sink deeper into the field of stars and listened.

His mind reached into the void.

His heartbeat slowed, drumsticks poised to play.

Then, for a moment, he sensed a tingle, a whiff, a whisper of melody. It rose out of the silent night like a radio signal from static, or laughter from another room. Or a memory.

Ting.

Another alert. The bell for First Period.

Jack growled and listened closer to the night. He pressed his ear to the chill glass, but the song was gone.

Ting. Ting. Ting.

At first, the high ping of the School alert rang as pleasantly as a church bell. It sounded like a summons to the higher things in life: an education in Science, History and Mathematics.

Jack ignored it.

The bell grew louder and sharper.

Tang. Tang. Tang.

Jack let it ring.

TONGTONGTONGTONG

On and on, louder and louder, the gong clanged through his family's cell. It shuddered and boomed off the windowpane. It rattled the bowls and plates on the shelves. It reached right into Jack's skull and banged upon it until he couldn't imagine a single note, other than that one invincible monotone.

Finally, gripping his head, Jack stumbled towards the only place in the cabin where he could find relief from the awful alarm.

He obeyed the call, zipped up his suit, and climbed into The Shower.

2. LUCY AND HER MOTHER WAR

Lucy opened her eyes and held her breath. In the space between dream and wakefulness something lurked, like a crouching tiger, or a circling shark. She flexed her eyelids wide, willing her retinas to open so she could see. There, in the corner, next to her door, a coiled body breathed.

'Mum?'

How long had she been there? Her shift had finished soon after Lucy's sleep period began. She could have been there all night, waiting for her daughter to wake, wondering what drill to spring upon her.

'Get up, Lucinda,' her mother intoned.

Lieutenant Commander Hannah Gemini only called her daughter Lucinda when she meant to frighten her. Lucy clenched her stomach, balled her fingers into fists.

'You've slept long enough, my girl.'

'It's Induction Day, mum,' Lucy started. 'Our birthday.'

'So?' asked the shadow in the corner. 'Will a celebration stop a meteor shower ripping through the hull? Will a date on the calendar keep the life support running?'

'No,' her daughter replied, 'but I need to be sharp for School. I want to make a good start.'

'This is your *good start*. On your feet!'

Her mother lunged across the room. Lucy slid out from under her, over the edge of the bed. Hannah flung Lucy's blanket over her like a net and tackled her daughter to the ground.

'You think marks are all you need to survive in this world?' she seethed through the fabric. 'Do you know how many people get a promotion one day, only to get kicked down an elevator shaft the next by a crewman who wanted that same job?'

Lucy writhed under the blanket, trying to shift her mother's weight from her shoulders. She reached through the folds and grabbed Hannah's wrist. It was like touching a live wire. A fatal current of fear and anger tremored under her mother's skin.

'Do you know how many of your classmates aren't their father's children, whose mothers were too weak to fight off a troll from Maintenance, or a snake from Admiralty?'

Lucy didn't answer. She moved her grip up her mother's arm to her shoulder.

'Now fight, Lucy. Fight!'

Lucy made her fingers rigid and stabbed up at her mother's throat. The woman gasped in shock and pain and fell backwards. Lucy rolled out from under her and in the same motion wrapped the blanket around her mother's neck, and twisted it.

Hannah's hands rose to her daughter's cheeks. But she did not tap out. Her fingers remained still, as though this were the only embrace she could bear. Lucy let go and her mother fell forward on all fours, coughing and spitting. Lucy stared at her. She dare not touch her or ask if she was alright. Her concern would only be mocked, and that hurt more than punches.

Gradually, Hannah gained her breath and sat back against the bed. She pulled her sweat-slick hair away from her face to reveal a smile. She pointed at her daughter. 'That's the spirit,' she said.

Ting.

The first bell. Mother and daughter both looked at the door to Lucy's Gravity Shower. Hannah rose to retrieve a fresh cadet suit from the wardrobe and handed it to her daughter. Lucy took it in silence and began to change. Silently, her mother watched her, saying nothing about the old yellow bruises on her daughter's wrists and shoulders, or the fresh red marks on the small of her back. None of these would appear on the skin of the avatar seen by Lucy's teachers and her peers. But as Lucy zipped her uniform up to her chin and turned to enter the black chamber of the Shower, Hannah caught Lucy's hand and squeezed it.

'Give em hell, Luce,' she said.

Lucy did not reply. She did not look back. She bore her tears boldly into the darkness.

3. JANGLING JACK

The Shower poured a simulated ripple of tropical breeze through the tight, dark fabric of Jack's uniform. His feet hissed in the sensation of sand. The Cap over his head showed him a beach that ran in one long circle round a lake of crystal-bright water. Around that, a lush green jungle teemed with birds and flowers, loomed over by a ring of smouldering volcanoes.

It was a beautiful sight, spectacular really, but Jack could not join in the joy felt by the other one thousand and thirty-eight freshly minted fifteen-year-olds frolicking on the beach. He could not forget where he really was; standing in a dark, narrow cubicle, separated from stone-cold space by a fragile metal shell.

He hummed to himself and tried to smile at all the avatars of his classmates. He didn't like being this way. He wished he could just go with it and enjoy himself. He wished that he could run up to someone, take their virtual hand in his and dance with them across the fine white sand. But anything he did here was just a gesture, no more real than a smoke signal, or a text message: *XOX*.

He did not know if anyone else his age felt this longing for real touch. But he knew with whom, if he could, he'd form the actual *O* made when arms entwine and the tender *X* of lips pressed together.

Lucy.

Lucy Gemini.

He looked for her amongst the laughing children, and wondered why she made him feel this way. He had never spoken to her. He hadn't even had the courage to like or comment on anything she had done in School or Sandbox.

Just one glimpse of her across the sand was all it took to remind him.

It was her eyes.

They were almond shaped and chestnut brown, just like his mother's.

Just like his.

She didn't modify her avatar and disguise her face. She didn't dress her online form in the uniform beauty her peers borrowed from ancient movie stars: the bronze skin on long strong limbs, the blonde hair and ice blue eyes that showed neither pain nor embarrassment. She stood before them *'naked'*, as she was (what they all were behind their masks): an unformed, imperfect self, halfway between childhood and maturity.

This disturbed her classmates. They couldn't express how she made them feel except to whisper she was some kind of freak. But to Jack, seeing her standing there amongst the tall, muscular, glamorous forms of her peers, she did not seem small or ugly or weak. In his eyes, she towered above them like a queen. She feared nothing and no one.

Jack, on the other hand, was always afraid.

There were so many ways, hacks great and small, the cadets used to torture and belittle one another. To *mirage* someone confused them about what they were looking at, making them run in terror from false horrors no one else could see, or wander blindly into real dangers others could. *Saturday Night Fever* caused infected avatars to break out in graceless dancing, a trick usually reserved for the middle of Mathematics. But what Jack dreaded most was *Dacking*. This hack stripped you of your chosen avatar and showed everyone what you really looked like, *naked*.

Jack imagined his pale skin, his skinny limbs, his tangle of black hair, but mostly his dreamy double-lidded eyes, exposed to the light of his classmates' derision. He had pictured it so many times, it felt like a prophecy, a certainty, not something that might happen, but something that was simply waiting, just around the corner of the present moment, to occur.

'Hey Jangles,' chuckled a familiar voice from behind him. 'Why don't you take off that heavy skin and come for a swim?'

It was Max Mercury. From their first Induction, Max had been built like a wrestler, which would have been hilarious in a five year old, if it weren't also so terrifying.

'Yeah, let's see what you're really like,' seethed Max's comrade in cruelty, Jenna Pionner. If you believed her avatar, she had passed puberty at the age of seven, and since then had used her dark eyes and figure to inflict all the pain and confusion she could.

Jack could almost feel their hacking fingers probing his defences, searching for a way to unstitch them and expose him. Thankfully, his Net-Cop father, Michael, had built for him an impenetrable firewall, a digital suit of armour. But that did not stop the fear. That was already there, under his skin.

Desperate to escape their attention, Jack reposted the latest Number 1 song from Fleet Radio to all of his classmates.

"*Here we go. Here we go. Here! We! Go!*" the computer voice enthused over a trilling adagio.

"*Ya ya you got this*

Got this, got this, ga!

Ya ya you got this

Got this, got this, ga!"

Jack rolled his eyes. Surely, he thought, this empty jingle, like the bawling child of a faulty elevator pad and an exercise video, could not have been made by a human being who had ever been moved by a song. It was more like the idea of a song, something a computer might devise to provoke a physical-emotional response in a lab rat.

And it did the trick.

All around him, the cadets started to dance, and like and comment upon one another's moves. Their dancing was as joyless as the smiles that didn't reach their eyes. Some closed them tightly, trying too hard to will some meaning from the lyrics; or they kept them too wide, too long, moving like manic marionettes between photo poses.

No one wanted to be the first to admit the music was bad. Not even Max and Jenna were above conforming to the beat, and turned away from Jack to clumsily jerk their perfect limbs in metronomic time.

Only Jack and Lucy did not dance.

He couldn't *make* his body move to that awful noise.

And she didn't need to pretend, nor resort to any tricks.

No one messed with Lucy.

Years ago, in History, she had been presenting her research on the Ancient Greek Olympics. Max Mercury hacked her speech so that every syllable she spoke came out like the sloppy buzz of farts. Once she realised what was happening, she took a javelin from her virtual exhibit and threw it straight through Max's face. The blow was so swift the safety controls missed it, and so brutal that after that no one ever dare lay a finger on her avatar again.

Or dared speak to her.

But that was about to change.

In the two weeks break between the last School term and this one, Jack had made a vow to himself to finally, after all this time, talk to the girl he loved.

He moved away from the dancers, across the sand, toward her. She stood alone at the water's edge. Her shoulders were rising and falling like she was sobbing. She held a flower in her hand. She turned its pale blue and orange blossom before her lovely lidded eyes, closed them and took a deep breath. She held that breath for a moment. All the blaring noise faded to nothing. Then she sighed, 'If only it was real.'

Jack's heart beat triple-time.

His ears rang like crashing cymbals.

Had she spoken to him?

He checked the preference settings of his avatar in the top right-hand corner of his vision. He scanned its small selfie-screen to see if he was as handsome as he thought she'd like him to be: green eyes, curly black hair, snow-white skin stretched across sharp cheek bones and toned muscles. He'd tweaked his eyes for hours, until, by degrees, they hinted but did not declare their true shape. He was sorely tempted to touch them up again, but stopped himself. There was no time. It was now or never.

But what would he say?

Everything he'd rehearsed suddenly dropped out of his mind.

Don't give her a line, he told himself. Talk to her. But what had she just said?

If only it was real.

He racked his brain for the right words to express his absolute agreement with her but in a relaxed way that wouldn't creep her out. But by the time he'd passed several drafts of the right sentence back and forth between his brain and his lips, finally decided upon, 'Yeah, totally,' and turned to perform this brilliantly witty remark, she had already moved off down the beach.

The moment was gone. A new bell was tolling.

The children stopped dancing and walked in unison toward a clearing in the jungle.

The Admiral was about to speak.

4. LUCY MAKES A RUN FOR IT

One of the few advantages of having a paranoid manic depressive for a mother (who distrusted the world so much they would do anything to protect you from it) was that they always left the Shower door unlocked. Any time Lucy wanted to leave School, she could. However, Lucy didn't want to be at home with her mother, any more than she wanted to be in School with her vain, violent classmates. So, she had worked out a convenient compromise. She kept her avatar active in the online world, but paused the live feed between the Shower's sensors and her suit. This way, she seemed to be present in class, leaned forward over her desk, with a look of concentration fixed upon her face, while her body was free to float in the darkness.

She spent a lot of time like that.

Waiting for the bell to ring and her mother to leave for her shift.

Or her father to come home from his.

More than anything, she wished she could be with him, outside.

He had been a respected doctor, a leader in his branch, but scandal had resulted in Major Chiang Zu Gemini's demotion to Maintenance. Now he spent long hours moving about in space, tethered to the hull of the ship, repairing it. It was dangerous work. So much could go wrong. But, as with his practice of medicine, he had quickly become a skilled and admired hand.

His parents never discussed what he had done, why he was being punished, but Lucy knew her father had accepted his lot, without complaint, as the natural consequence of the choice he had made, and would make again if he had to. She also knew this made her mother resent him even more than if he *had* regretted it.

Whatever *it* was.

Floating in the darkness of her Gravity Shower, the Cap off her face so she only heard and felt, but did not see the online scene, Lucy could pretend she was facing the depths of space with him, and that neither of them was alone.

Today though, Lucy wanted to conduct an experiment. She wanted to test a theory.

She was going to make a run for it.

She wiped the tears from her face.

She zipped up her uniform, bracing her bruised flesh.

The black speaker tiles powered up, humming all around her, lifting her off the floor on a swell of subatomic vibrations.

She pulled the Shower Cap down over her face.

Her eyes filled with the tropical scene.

Her suit warmed under the simulated sun.

She dug her toes into the illusion of sand, coiled her torso in a sprinter's stance, and bolted.

Within seconds she had left the mob of her classmates behind. The beach was a ring around the lake. Her feel slapped against the simulated sand. She hit her top speed. She pushed harder. The lower left side of her back, where her mother's knee had held her to the floor, ached like ice, drawing the heat from her muscles, and the will from her heart.

It's no more real than this beach, Lucy told herself. I'm what's real. I'm what's real. The thought drove her forward, faster and faster. The pain became just another thread in the curtain she was pushing against, searching for a way through. She drove her legs against the sinking sand, told herself that there was nothing really there but dense ripples of gravity, until she could not tell where her legs ended and the simulated grains began, until all she was was energy in motion.

But nothing changed.

There was no parting of the curtain to reveal a world beyond.

The beach kept rolling towards her, a digital version of the painted backdrops they used to roll past silent film actors to give the appearance of movement.

Lucy collapsed to the sand and pulled up handfuls of the gritty stuff like she might tear away the feeling of her mother's grip upon her skin. Until, exhausted, she let herself go limp and stared out across the water at the cadets playing in the shallows. She brought her hands up to her face to hide her tears, only to remember that her digital avatar would not repeat the marks of woe she wore in the shower. Her tears, like her bruises, would not show here.

Something as gentle as the wing of a butterfly kissed her eyelid. She looked at her sandy hands and found a fragile orange flower lodged between her fingers. She blinked and took it in her other hand, turning its tear shaped petals around. She stood and walked to the water's edge, eyes fixed on the delicate illusion, trying to read it, like it was a note dropped from heaven.

What really hurt, Lucy thought, was not that there was nothing beyond this false world. What she wished most was that the magic world was real, that it did not have an end, so that she could disappear into this fantasy forever. Instead, she only ever got glimpses. She was only ever rehearsing scenes from a play whose opening night would never come.

Her father felt the same. His favourite movie was Singing in the Rain. A musical. In it, the characters are singing dancing actors who are themselves making a movie musical. It's a film within a film, a reality within a reality. But no matter whether the scene is in their real world or the world they are creating, they are always singing, always dancing. They live for music.

Lucy didn't know what she was meant to live for. Who was she? she wondered. What was truly *hers*, the constant music *she* moved to, whether she was here online or in her family cabin?

She looked down again at the flower and sighed, 'If only it was real.'

She did not notice the young man standing behind her, agonising over how he would answer.

A siren howled in the distance.

At least she knows, Lucy thought. The Admiral knows what *she* lives for.

5. JACK ON THE MOUNTAIN

As far as Jack knew, none of the children had ever seen Admiral Armstrong with their own eyes. When their parents spoke of her, it was either in proud toasts at the dinner table, or whispers when their kids were in the other room.

Now she mounted the platform above the birthday boys and girls and stood there like a monument dedicated to all that was bravest and boldest in humanity. Her deep blue uniform was an ocean upon which sailed a fleet of medals. Her hair was a great grey wave breaking over the craggy features of her face: thin, grim lips, hard straight nose, a black patch over her right eye. Her good left eye, a brilliant green, stared fiercely into the heart of every child assembled.

No other presence online, not the most titanic monster or fabulous beast in any of the Sandbox games, not even the Great Red Dragon of *Dragon Quest*, could inspire awe the way she did. And though he had heard this speech every Induction Day, so many times he had learnt it by heart, Jack still hung on every word she spoke.

'Children of Earth,' she began, 'today is the first day of your sixteenth year.' She sighed and smiled. 'You are all still so young. But you know, you and I have something very important in common.' She paused. 'Not one of us here today remembers the Earth, not as it was. No one alive has felt its gravity, the warmth of its sun upon their skin.

None have felt the touch of its grasses, its breezes, its free-flowing waters.'

At her mention of these, the children's avatars were transported from the bright tropical jungle to a tranquil forest scene. Between tall red-trunked trees, a cool stream ran over glistening rocks down into a lush green valley spread out under a clear blue sky. Deer grazed along the banks. Birds sang and danced in the air. And in the forest shadows, ancient human voices gurgled and cooed in the language of the birds and the river, a sound more music than speech.

'It's not *your* fault you can't be there to feel it,' The Admiral continued, her husky Texan drawl darkening. 'It's not *your* fault it's gone.'

Beyond the trees, the human voices turned guttural. They droned and clanged like tuneless machinery. The ground quaked with the booming march of leaden feet. The sound of metal scraping upon metal chased the birds from their nests into a cloud of alarm that mingled with a thickening pall of smoke.

'The hands that destroyed it,' The Admiral spat, 'belonged to *them*!'

With a roar of engines and screeching saws, the trees on the opposite bank fell to reveal a great gang of enormous humanoid robots. Behind them, where had been rolling hills of thick forest, was now a wasteland of concrete and tar.

Their slow heavy limbs were thick with power. Within the

domed cockpits of their heads, Jack watched their pilots move their pale pudgy fingers across the controls, and glare at the world with small, mean, hungry eyes. When they weren't squeezing tubes of sweet creams into their mouths, these awful creatures stuffed their guts to bursting with dead animals. They plucked birds from the air and fried them whole. From cages on their backs they drew four-legged beasts and threw them into the ovens blazing in their chests.

The drivers' greed was only surpassed by the appetites of their machines. Across the river from the horrified children, they stopped to feed their grumbling engines. They sunk their drill fingers into the ground and sucked forth oil to grease their whining joints and ripped great handfuls of coal from the earth to fill their slack-jawed furnaces. From their mechanical behinds, black smoke farted and filled the air with a plume that darkened day to twilight. They squatted over the river and expelled their engine's waste until the water was too thick to run.

Waves of heat rose from their metal backs.

The air grew hotter.

Tornadoes stirred into life and shrieked about them like monstrous banshees crying havoc.

Jack's ancestors did not once turn around to see where the sound and the heat were coming from. And while the storms blew their clumsy metal bodies to the ground and buried them in soot, they kept turning up the air-conditioning and the volume of the shows they had projected on the inside of their windscreens.

Jack watched the bloated face of the man closest to him. As the ash rose up around the visor of his robot, and his screens used up the last flickering watt of power, he looked up angrily through the window as though to ask who had ruined his day. As the sun disappeared behind the smoke, understanding dawned upon him. A tear rolled down his flabby face and the world became one long, hot, screaming darkness.

This moment always seemed like it would go on forever.

The Earth's death-cry pierced Jack's brain and shook his heart.

But the children of *Hamelin* could not turn away. They could not simply log out and leave their Showers. This was School, not the Sandbox. They were being taught a lesson.

The howling sound went on and on until Jack thought it would drive him insane. In that sound were the cries of all the billions of people who had died in the firestorm that scorched the Earth. For what seemed like all the years their fleet had been in space, those voices chased them.

Then it stopped.

The children remained in dark silence for five more suspenseful seconds. It was always five. Jack counted them down, '5, 4, 3, 2...'

'A few escaped,' their Admiral's voice breathed through the darkness. 'The very best of humanity. They banded together. They built our fleet. They spied a glimmer of light and set off for a better world.'

Seven points of light appeared in the dark above their heads. They formed a ring of stars, the emblem of The Fleet. As she named each ship, each point of light glowed brighter, and the children of its nation touched their palm to the insignia on their chests.

'U.S.S. *Harbinger*,' she said, and those amongst the children who were from the American craft cupped their hearts and gave a cheer.

'*H.M.S. Dauntless.*'

Up went a shout from the British.

'*The Europa, The Shiva, The Heavenly Tower, The Star of Russia,* and *The Hamelin.*'

On rolled the wave of applause through the Europeans, the Indians, the Chinese, Russians and Australians, until all seven stars shone brightly.

'You here today,' The Admiral declared, 'are nearer to our goal than *any* who have *ever* lived.'

At the centre of the circle of stars appeared one brighter than them all. This was their destination, the blue Star of Uroun. It zoomed to fill Jack's eyes.

Orbiting that blue giant was a planet slightly smaller than the Earth. It was covered in a swirling, rippling rainbow of cloud. Beyond that beautiful veil, his teachers assured him, awaited oceans brimming with life and continents covered in forests and fertile soil.

No matter how many times they saw it, this vision never failed to inspire tears of joy. It was the one hope shared by every single person in The Fleet, no matter their age, nationality or occupation.

Uroun was the future.

Uroun was life.

Uroun would be home.

For a moment, Jack forgot he was not really seeing this and clapped his hands and hollered and hooted along with everyone else. It felt so good to let it out - all of the past year's fear and frustration - and turn it into joy.

'A place without walls,' Admiral Armstrong promised, 'a place without fear. But sadly, dear friends,' and the cadets' cheers died out, for they knew what she was about to say, 'this is a place that *we* will never see.'

She paused to give this solemn fact its moment.

'The distance we must travel is too vast. In our lifetimes, we will go only a small part of the way. After our generation, many more will be born. They will train, crew our ships, and pass on their knowledge. We are but a link in a chain that stretches from the old world to the new.'

She raised her fist.

'You must be strong or the chain will break. You must study hard. You must do your duty. And who knows,' she said with a wry smile, 'one day, one of you may strike the spark that shoots us in an instant,' she snapped her fingers, 'to our destination.'

She levelled those same fingers at the students. 'If not you…?'

'WHO?' the children recited.

'If not today…?' their leader prompted.

'WHEN?' the children declared as one and burst into applause.

Jack looked around him at his generation. Every mouth was cheering. Every pair of eyes were filled with hope. Even the meanest among them believed.

Just then, a wind swept though their ranks, muffling their jubilant cries. It carried upon it a fragment of song, the same he had heard at his cabin window, but stronger now. It was the rising falling sound of a lone piper. The melody thrilled up Jack's spine, up into the crown of his head.

At this same moment, Jack noticed the volcanic cliffs behind The Admiral grow taller and merge, rising higher and higher into a colossal, ice-blue mountain. The Star of Uroun shone directly above it. The piper's song wailed around its peak. Jack looked about him to see if anyone else had noticed, but no one had. They were too busy cheering. He closed his eyes and shook his head.

'The ultimate prize,' The Admiral bellowed in Jack's ear, 'is the survival of the human race.'

Jack opened his eyes and gasped. He was now standing on top of the mountain. There was nothing left between him and the Star of Uroun but air. He tottered on the icy summit.

'But first you must win the private battle!' cried The Admiral far below. 'Overcome fear!'

Was this a new twist to the Admiral's speech? Something reserved for fifteen year olds? Jack kept his balance by fixing his eyes on the star and stretching his hand out towards it. The pipe music grew louder.

'Learn all you can in School,' The Admiral roared. 'Test your skills in Sandbox. Perform great deeds that will last forever as legends told by *your* descendants, the children of *Uroun*!'

The cadets kept on clapping and cheering. Jack looked at them and saw that they too were balanced on their own mountain peaks, spread in all directions to the horizon. Suspended above every cheering child, glowing like a naked lightbulb, was their own personal Star of Uroun.

Jack felt the ground beneath him give a little and he looked down. Beneath his feet was a pile of skulls, impossibly high. The bleached bones shone bright blue under the starlight and clunked and scraped as his feet struggled for purchase.

He jerked his feet away from the hollow eyes, lost his perch and fell toward the void. A hand caught him by the forearm. He looked up from the abyss and saw that Lucy was standing with him atop the same summit. They stared agape at one another and then about them at the thousand other children leaping up and down upon their private mountains of bones.

Lucy's fingers slipped along his arm and caught again about his wrist.

'Do you hear it too, Jack?' she demanded. 'The piper's song. Do you hear it?'

Before Jack could answer, Lucy lost her grip on him and he tumbled backwards into the night. He threw his hands up, one after another, trying to catch hold of the pulsing light of *Uroun*. But from the icy air his fingers clutched only gusts of pipe song and into fathomless darkness he fell.

6. LUCY PUNCHES A HOLE IN THE WORLD

Lucy fell out of the shower and collapsed to her bedroom floor, coughing, gasping for air. She had almost drowned in that vision. That nightmare. It had summed up all of her fears, all her suspicions about life as a cadet. It was the shadow cast by The Admiral's bright vision of a long unbroken chain of lives lived in service of the dream of reaching Uroun: a mountain of skulls, heaped from the lives of children, who stood tiptoed upon their fallen peers, struggling to touch a fantasy forever beyond their reach.

Lucy looked up at the poster of The Admiral her mother had pinned to the wall over her bed. The great heroine stood there in full dress uniform, her hands upon her hips, a smile of grim determination on her lips, and a look in her one good eye that said she knew Lucy, but not as she was, as she could be if she answered the call of duty.

Was this all a lie?

Who had sent this vision? Surely, it wasn't an intentional part of the Induction Day speech. It was a hack, a pirate broadcast, but from where?

And why had Jack seen it but no one else? Why had the two of them been singled out for the message?

As if in reply to her unspoken questions, a rumour of pipe song wafted into the room. Lucy looked about her, all her senses tuning in to locate the source of the sound. It came again, rising and falling like a bird's playful morning call. She listened at the door of the gravity shower. All she could hear inside the chamber was the muffled yells of Ms Turing berating her Physics class.

Another trill of piping drew Lucy towards the wall next to her bed. She crouched on her blanket before the poster of The Admiral. Tentatively, she pressed her ear to the Fleet Commander's chest. The piping chuckled right into her, as though tickled by Lucy's touch. Lucy leapt from the bed and stared at the glossy paper. The music rose and fell patiently, letting Lucy make the connection, and fairly blared when Lucy reached out, pulled the pins from the paper and let the poster fall.

From under her pillow, Lucy drew the multitool her mother insisted she keep there 'Just in case anyone but me or your father ever come through that door.' From its heavy little fist of screwdrivers, picks and blades Lucy pulled a flathead and inserted it in the seam between the pair of metre-square plastic wall panels over her bed. The panel to her right popped out and released a sigh of stale air. Lucy pulled the cream coloured sheet away, leaned it against the wall and stood back. Where had once been a picture of her proud commander, was now a jumble of wires and pipes. She gave a brief, Ha. All this time in her tiny room, she had never thought to lift the skin and have a look.

But now what?

Pipe song briefly vibrated the exposed wires like the wave of a hand across harp strings.

Lucy came closer, pressed her fingers to the multicoloured mess of circuitry, and then, on a hunch, pushed her hand through their jumbled surface until arm was in up to the shoulder and her cheek was up against the wires. There was space in there. She pushed her other hand through and parted her arms to reveal, one metre in, a narrow cavity, like a chute, running between her deck and those above and below.

Lucy drew in a full breath and exhaled it slowly. This was the first time she had seen beyond her family cabin. This was no public passageway where she would meet other people in the flesh, but it was, technically, *outside*. And where it might lead…

She tucked the multitool into her uniform and pulled herself up through the gap, through the thick curtain of wires, and stood up into the crawlspace. She gripped the threaded circuitry like it was climbing rope, looked up into darkness and down into black. She had no torch. Nothing to guide her.

Nothing but slowly babbling notes of pipe song below, reaching up into her veins, beckoning her to descend.

Lucy wrapped her feet around a thicker thread of wire and slid down until her face was level with the gap she'd made in her bedroom wall. It was eerie, staring down a narrow tunnel of wires, glistening like tendons and veins, into the room she had spent her whole fifteen years of life. Despite the almost claustrophobic closeness of the crawlspace, it seemed smaller back there. An inch long vertical dent in the panel on the opposite wall, collateral damage from one of her mother's training sessions, a mark which Lucy had not noticed for months, from this angle caught the light and seemed to point down, and away.

She took a deep breath, closed her eyes and followed the sign.

Down into the darkness she slid, guided by her her shins crossed over the wire, and her hands passing her weight between them, like she was dolling out the cable of her life into the darkness. The circuitry was warm with activity. It sizzled with information shooting past at quantum speeds. It pulsed and sometimes seemed to heave, expanding and contracting, like Lucy was being swallowed down the gullet of a dragon. But whenever she became scared, and slowed, or paused and gripped the wires tightly, the rising falling of pipe music would return to reassure her and beckon her downward.

In the dark, she could not tell how much time had passed or how far she had gone, but soon her thoughts roamed, to what she was leaving behind, School, Sandbox, her family, and what she might be moving towards. The source of the pipe song. The sender of the warning vision.

Then she thought about Jack.

Jack Voyager.

She had been surprised to see him in her nightmare, there with her atop the mountain of skulls. But here in the darkness she realised that there was no one else in her class she could imagine sharing such a terrible view of their world.

Once, back when they were in Seven, the age partitions between their Sandbox and the seniors' had failed. Fourteen-year-old cadets strode about them like giants, belittling and bullying them at will. Max and Jenna whined and simpered, tried to cosy up to their superiors in cruelty. They repeated the awful words the seniors spat at the children. They laughed as their classmates were pushed to the ground. But that didn't protect them. It was even funnier for the fourteeners to bully these little bullies. A senior with hair as sharp as broken glass held Jenna up like a bat and called 'Roll the arm over, Rick!' to his friend. Ricked plucked Max from the ground and tossed him through the air.

That was when Jack stood up.

He broke Max's fall in a fumbling catch, and took the swing of Jenna's weight against his shoulders. All three of them fell to the Sandbox floor.

Max and Jenna scrambled to their feet first. Embarrassed, they turned on the only person who had tried to help them.

'Nice catch, Jangles!' Max cried.

'Yeah,' said Jenna, 'you ruined the game!'

'Jangles?!' Rick scoffed. 'Is this kid called *Jangles*? Let's see if he's earned the name, eh?' And he went to pick Jack up.

Jack slapped away his hand and got up. 'No!' he shouted. 'You guys get out of here! You're mean and this is wrong!'

'Oh, come on, Jangles,' Rick's friend moaned. 'None of this is real. What does it matter what we do?'

'It matters to me,' yelped Jack and struck his chest.

For a moment, no one spoke.

Then the fourteeners all fell about laughing, striking their chests and declaring in mouse-voices, 'It matters to me!' And 'I am JANGLES!'

But Jack didn't back down. And so Rick couldn't enjoy himself, so he slapped the little boy across the face. He raised his hand, ready to do it again, when the partitions restored and the seniors all disappeared. Yet their presence was still felt.

None of the children approached Jack, who lay on the ground, sobbing tearlessly. He showed the fear everyone else felt, yet no one wanted to admit. Yet Jack had also showed them all the courage they longed for but could not find, and for that they could not forgive him. Before this, Max and Jenna had bullied Jack as an amusing convenience. From then on, they hated him with passion.

Lucy's hands paused on the wires. The memory had soaked through her, like she was back there, feeling as she had that day. Going deeper felt like leaving Jack lying there all over again. But she couldn't go back for him. How would she find him? Perhaps, like her, he was making his way out now, guided as she was by the piper's song. She hoped so, and threaded the rope of wires between her hands.

Deeper down into darkness she slid, drawn by the electric touch of music.

7. JACK GOES THROUGH THE MILL

Jack tumbled away from Lucy's outstretched hand, past the mountain of skulls and down into the darkness at the bottom of the vision. He could not tell what was more terrifying, the physical feeling of an endless nothing, or the thought of the distance between him and *Uroun* getting wider every second he fell.

'Mr. Voyager, are you with us?'

He kept his eyes fixed on the distant star.

'Jack Voyager, are you awake?'

Jack recognised the voice but he was too busy falling to answer.

'Cadet Voyager! Open. Your. Eyes.'

Jack remembered who the voice belonged to and, hoping she might help him to stop falling through the cold abyss of space, he obeyed and opened his eyes.

The star of *Uroun* did not disappear. He could still see it at the centre of his vision. Now it was joined by the rest of The Milky Way. His ancestral star, *The Sun*, was a speck of light glimmering on the arm of *Orion*. A dotted line joined these two stars. A third of the way along that a small flashing triangular icon pointed towards *Uroun*. The words YOU ARE HERE hovered next to it.

Jack heard chuckling and looked about. The twenty assorted avatars of his classmates hovered either side of him. With a deep sense of dread, Jack realised his predicament.

He was in Physics class, First Period.

More precisely, he was floating within a star map that showed the route The Fleet was taking from Earth across interstellar space towards *Uroun*.

Worst of all, he had just spent he could not say how long drifting about in the simulation with his eyes closed, waving his arms and legs like he was falling, watched by his teacher and his fellow students. Their fear of Ms. Turing kept the pack of cadets from chewing Jack up with laughter, yet they couldn't conceal their hungry, toothy grins.

He searched for Lucy's gaze, to see his fear and confusion reflected in her eyes, but he could not find her.

Ms. Turing hovered in the space above his head. Her skeletal limbs were strapped so tightly within her uniform you could see the thick cords of her veins through the fabric, and her cold blue eyes glared down at Jack from beneath a thick blaze of red hair.

'If I discover, Mr. Voyager,' she seethed, 'that you have been projecting a fake avatar into my classroom whilst you muck about in Sandbox, you will have hell to pay, mister. Do you understand me?'

'Yes Miss. Sorry Miss. I was...'

'Yes?'

Jack could not think of how to explain what he had seen. 'I was just thinking about what The Admiral said.'

'Good,' she said, softening at the mention of her supreme commander. 'So should we all. But we should not let ourselves become distracted. This is Period One, Day One of your sixteenth year. You have much to learn and very little time. Don't waste it.'

'Yes Miss. Thank you, Miss.'

Ms. Turing now addressed the whole class. 'Your problem today, and every day until you either solve it or you die, is how to get from there...' She pointed down at to the pale blue dot representing Earth's Sun '...to there,' and jabbed her thumb behind at her at the rainbow-coloured icon for *Uroun*.

The students zoomed in on the triangle moving imperceptibly along the dotted line. It was composed of seven smaller triangles. They zoomed in closer still and the icons expanded into full scale representations of the seven ships of The Fleet.

The Australian students coasted in the space alongside their craft, *The Hamelin*, in its place in The Fleet's great circle between the Chinese and American ships. *The Hamelin* berthed a mere twelve thousand souls. She cruised humbly beside the massive eagle form of the *USS Harbinger* - transporting its crew of one hundred thousand- and the long spine of China's *Heavenly Tower* – whose three great turning wheels contained the last three hundred thousand of what had once been a nation of billions. Though small by comparison, *The Hamelin* was proud as an old sailing ship. Jack never tired of watching her triple-mast of solar sails, abloom with interstellar radiation, draw her sleek structure across the invisible sea.

'Now, the complication,' Turing growled. 'Every second of every day, space wants to kill you. It is entirely hostile to all of your basic needs for food, water, air and shelter. This ship, whose hull protects you, and whose farms and recycling systems sustain you, must work constantly and without fail to keep you alive.'

She gave a rare smile.

'Of course, the best way to survive is to get where we're going sooner rather than later.'

She turned her back to them to wave her hand at the armada of variously shaped vessels travelling together in circular formation.

'Each ship has its own design,' she said. 'Each ship's crew is working night and day to speed us faster to *Uroun*.'

She paused and cocked her head back over her shoulder.

'Something funny, Mr. Mercury?' she asked ominously.

With a snap of her fingers, Turing halted the simulation.

Jack turned in time to catch Max Mercury's exaggerated expression of terror, eyes closed, mouth wide open, his hands and feet pawing at the air for Jenna's amusement. At the sound of his name, he straightened to attention.

'What Miss?' Max bawled. 'Why are you always picking on *me*? You let *Jack* get away with anything.'

'Jack is not in danger of failing,' their teacher barked and turned around completely to face him. 'Perhaps this year, Max, you will finally make some use of our time together. Or do you intend to follow your father into a career in Maintenance?'

Max's beefed up avatar slumped. He folded his massive biceps over one another and tried to tuck his movie star face between them, but Turing wasn't finished with him.

'The human brain is the most extraordinary thing in the universe, boy, capable of incredible leaps of logic and imagination. What have you done with *yours*? Hmmm?'

Max said nothing. She cast her rage across the rest of the class.

'You children are the inheritors of thousands of years of human knowledge. Fields of study that once took Earth's best minds decades of schooling to learn – physics, chemistry, engineering - you must master by your eighteenth year.' Her head snapped back to her right. 'What have *you* learned, Mercury?'

She prowled back and forth before the cadets. 'Our Fleet has been in space for nearly two centuries. At our current speed, it will be *eight hundred and sixty-five more years* until we reach *Uroun*! Do you *want* to be just another *"link in the chain"*?'

'NO, MA'AM!' the cadets hollered in unison.

'Don't you *want* to see *Uroun*?'

'YES, MA'AM!'

'Well then,' she continued in mock surprise, 'you're going to need to do something miraculous, aren't you?'

'YES, MA'AM!'

'How fast will you need to travel?'

'Faster than light!"

'*How* fast?'

'FASTER THAN LIGHT!'

'That's right,' their teacher growled, and she lunged right up to Max's cowering figure. 'I want to get there too, Mercury. So keep out of the way of those who want to use this,' she pointed her boney finger at Jack's head, 'to get there,' and with her other hand she grabbed Max's chin, lifting his gaze level with the distant star pulsing within the circle of ships.

Max shook his face free and nodded, slowly, shame and anger burning in his eyes.

Satisfied, Turing floated back to her position above the line of cadets and began to outline the semester's course: Interstellar Navigation.

'Our units of study will cover: 1. Black Holes, 2. Worm Holes, 3. Multi-Dimensional Gravity Tides…'

As more and more of her words fired into Jack's brain, his mind turned inwards, away from thoughts of the future, and back towards the vision he had been shown. Had it really happened or had he just fainted and dreamed it?

Careful not to show Turing that he wasn't paying attention, Jack opened up a new screen within his vision, his personal video stream, in which all of his online experience was recorded. He scrolled back to find the Admiral's speech. He fast-forwarded through the end of the world and came to her conclusion. There was no mountain. No piper song. Only the Admiral's rousing final words and the roar of the students' applause. But there was something wrong with the image. It didn't look like he remembered it. He paused the video and stared at it for longer than was good for a student pretending to be paying attention in class. Then it hit him. The angle from which he viewed the Admiral was wrong, but only slightly. It was as though he was seeing the video stream of the cadet standing just to his right.

He felt a cold sweat break out under his uniform.

He felt the fabric clutch and cloy his flesh with clammy fingers.

'Voyager!' Turing spat.

'Yes, ma'am,' Jack barked automatically.

'You've been staring at the homework instructions like they're written in hieroglyphs. Do you understand them?'

'Yes, ma'am. Thank you, Ms Turing.'

'Very well, then. Get yourself to Fukuyama's class. You don't want to keep The Minotaur waiting.'

8. MONSTERS INSIDE AND OUT

Jack heard the bellow of a hungry beast. Stone walls rose about him, flickering in dim torchlight.

Jack's History teacher, Mr. Fukuyama, appeared beside him in the long white robe he preferred to his fleet uniform. His silver top knot and long white beard completed the ancient movie image of a Kung Fu master. Jack sometimes wondered if the actual teacher, at home in his Shower, really looked like this, or if he was perhaps some nervous young man who put on this image to inspire respect. For all Jack knew, Mr. Fukuyama might not even be a flesh and blood person, but a program made just for School. After all, he started every lesson in exactly the same way, just like the boot up intro sequence of a single player Sandbox game.

After emerging from the shadows, he appeared to each of the students individually, like a wise old master with his pupil, and led them round dark turns and down steep stairs, deep into the past. All the while, the heavy hoof steps and snorting of a beast, half-man, half-bull echoed after them along the dark stone passageways of the labyrinth. The Minotaur smelled the children's innocence. It tasted their fear.

'Consider this,' Fukuyama grumbled. 'Why do we travel for hundreds of years across the vast reaches of space to found a *new* world if we have not understood why we destroyed the *last* one? Hmm?'

Jack was not expected to answer.

'Ms. Turing, is right. The human mind is a wonder. But it also contains monsters. Between the brightly lit halls of imagination and intelligence there are dark places: dead ends, dungeons, ancient bloodstained rooms haunted by pride and envy and fear.'

The monster at the heart of the labyrinth roared again. The sound was as sad as it was savage. Fukuyama put a hand on the cadet's shoulder and promised, 'Together, Jack, we will find these demons and face them. Down here, we will revisit and relive the worst moments from Earth's history, when your ancestors' ignorance tore their world apart.'

The next turn brought them upon the ancestral crime scene he wanted to show them that day.

In the previous year, he had taught them about Earth's 'Age of Discovery'. Under Fukuyama's watchful eye, the students' avatars had assumed the forms of natives, explorers and invaders. They had learned what it felt like to be Australian aborigines, losing their land to gun-toting British colonists. Then they had swapped roles, and in the name of the English Queen had lied and murdered and stolen and thrilled at the prosperous nation they were building.

Down into the past, back up towards the future. Whenever Jack emerged from History, he was grateful to live in the present, far from Earth's dark days, and he felt all the more impatient to reach the future on *Uroun*. Yet sometimes, after class, in the real world of his cabin, memories of the simulation echoed. They made him feel like his bedroom was just one small chamber in a vast vertical maze, that all the horrors of the past were stored in *The Hamelin's* lower decks, and just outside his door stalked an ancient and unnamable evil.

'In this, your sixteenth year,' Fukuyama now intoned, 'you will experience the World Wars of the 20th Century.'

Jack reached the bottom of the spiral staircase and walked down a corridor lined with doors. Each opened onto a horror more terrible than the one before:

Blood-soaked trenches.

Blasted battlefields.

Bombed out cities.

He wanted to look away, but he couldn't. His vision was hijacked by the Shower Cap over his head. Facts and figures scrolled before Jack's eyes, listing the numbers of the dead and the various machines and methods by which they were murdered. He could not comprehend the sheer scale of the destruction. But he knew he would have time to understand it.

He had a whole new year of death and misery in Fukuyama's dungeon to look forward to.

But this first day of School was not yet done with him.

He had still to face the third and final period of the day, Mathematics with Ms. Eleanor P. Cruikshank.

She did not dress her classroom up as Turing and Fukuyama did. The floor was white. The ceiling was white. The walls were white. So too were the desks and chairs.

Upon entry to this bland prison cell, the students' avatars were automatically stripped of their painstakingly crafted personal modifications. They sat, hour after hour, behind the same white desks in the same blank and genderless avatars. Their faces were replaced by a selection of only three basic emojis: frowning, smiling and listening. Their voices were stripped of character and came out in a whining electronic drone. They were only ever allowed to use these empty voices to address the teacher. The barest whisper could be muted instantly by a click of her fingers.

'To help you focus,' the ever polite, yet utterly cold Cruikshank assured them.

The only way to tell who was who was the student ID tags floating above their heads. These constantly displayed their current grade point average, coloured green to indicate success, down through shades of yellow and orange and finally to red to 'encourage' cadets who were falling behind.

Jack felt his Shower's simulation of a cold hard metal chair cramp and chill his bottom and knew from the dark orange glow flashing over his workspace that his meagre score from the previous year had carried over into Year 16.

'Welcome back, Mr Voyager,' a voice behind him purred like a cat about to dine. 'It seems that we have quite a lot of work to do this year, don't we?'

'Yes Ms Cruikshank,' he muttered and glanced at the deep red light that hung over Lucy's empty chair. She was always on the wrong side of the teachers, but Jack believed that if anyone could get him out of this prison, faster than the speed of light, it was her. But for now, he was trapped, and the doors of his Gravity Shower would not open until the lesson ended, he fainted, or the Net-Cops decreed a state of emergency.

Jack closed his eyes against the equations squiggling into view, like a nest of electronic worms crawling up from his screen to eat into his brain, and prayed to his father to push the big red button.

'Come on, Dad,' he whispered. 'Can't you see I'm in pain? I'm dying. Let me out of here.'

'ALERT! ALERT! ALERT!'

Jack opened his eyes.

'Dad?' he breathed, though he couldn't believe his father had heard his prayer.

The classroom was flashing red. The anonymous avatars looked up from their desks to the screen at the head of the class.

'ALERT! ALERT! ALERT!' it read in time to the dry yet urgent voice that spoke the words. 'THIS IS A FLEET-WIDE ALERT. ALL CADETS EXIT YOUR SHOWERS AND REMAIN IN YOUR CABINS. CODE GAMMA. ALL HANDS, CODE GAMMA!'

Code Gamma meant two things:

One. Space debris such as micro-asteroids, anything solid enough to damage the hull, was approaching the ship. At the speed *The Hamelin* was travelling, rocks the size of rice grains could slice through whole decks, depressurising them as they burst through flesh and muscle and bone.

Two. The blast shields designed to protect them from such danger were not working.

One by one, the blank avatars of each cadet winked out of view as they logged out and left their showers, followed by Cruikshank.

Jack waited. To his right, Hank Apollo 6 was staring into space.

'Hank!' Jack called, 'LOG OUT!' But Cruikshank had muted the students' avatars and Hank could not see Jack's waving arms.

Jack dragged himself up out of his seat. The avatar's movements were leaden. In his shower, Jack strained against the thickly vibrating air. He struggled across the floor and reached out his hand to turn Hank to face him. The boy's sightless eyes kept straight ahead and with mounting dread Jack realised he wasn't there. Hank had left his avatar on a loop in Maths class to go play in Sandbox.

'ALERT! ALERT! ALERT! CODE GAMMA! PROXIMITY WARNING!'

Jack gripped Hank's shoulders and called into his ear, 'Come on, mate. You've got to get out of there.'

But the boy could not hear him. His head was in a cloud of

entertainment. He would never know why he died, or even that he had. The asteroid, no bigger than a coin, split his cabin window and entered through the back wall of his gravity shower at head height. One second, Hank was navigating Level 6 of *Speed Racer*, the next he was no more.

In the virtual classroom, the shoulders of Jack's classmate flickered and vanished.

He then experienced the utterly confusing sensation of looking at the virtual world while being yanked about in the actual. While Jack was still logged in, his father had used his security override to enter Jack's gravity shower and pull his son from the dark chamber. He snatched the shower cap from Jack's head. Real world light splashed across Jack's vision. His father screamed, 'GET DOWN!'

They fell together to his bedroom floor. The air flashed red and rang with alarm, 'ALERT! ALERT! ALERT!'

'Stay low,' Jack's dad seethed. They crawled commando-style into the family room. Jack's mother was crouched next to the entryway to their cabin.

'Quickly, into the lock,' she called.

She waited for them to scramble into the anteroom before she slid through and slammed the lock button. The heavy metal door slammed shut. All three of them embraced, breathing into each other's shoulders, and waited for the storm to pass. Every family cabin had such a room, separating their living quarters from the corridor beyond. It was composed of some of the strongest materials on the ship and, after the blast shields, was their best defence against space-debris.

Over the sound of their panting and the alarm, they could hear screaming through the floor.

'*Hank*,' Jack said, gripping his father's uniform.

In reply, his father put his hands on his son's and nodded solemnly and said, 'Deck 6 was hit.'

The deck just below theirs.

The family held onto each other and tried not to listen.

Suddenly, as though a sniper was in their cabin, taking pot shots at the anteroom, the inner door began to ping with tiny strikes that caused small bubbles of metal to pop at them from shin height up to their necks. The Voyagers jumped and pressed together against the outer door.

Michael's wide blue eyes fell to the exit button. Xinjuan's almond browns searched his and trembled. One more strike on a spot that had been weakened and they would be sucked instantly against the hole. Their skin would stop the gap for a moment, but after an excruciating second, their blood and insides would rush out, leaving a pile of bones on the welcome mat of their family home.

Jack watched his father raise his keycard to the lock and held his breath. His hand hovered beneath it. Jack's eyes willed him to raise it a little further.

Another ping rang and another bubble appeared in the door behind them.

'Damn protocol,' Michael seethed and lifted the key into place.

The lock did not open. A small red message appeared on the lock panel, *Unauthorised Exit.*

He pressed it again.

Unauthorised Exit.

Whilst Michael and Xinjuan were permitted access to every part of the ship, Jack, like every other adolescent, was confined to his family cabin. This rule was so important, it seemed the ship would rather all three of them died than break it.

More debris struck the door. The metal rang like a dinner bell, summoning the dark jaws of space to feast upon the family. Michael slapped the card repeatedly against the console. 'Come on!' he yelled.

And then, the bullets stopped.

The alarm went silent.

Jack, Xinjuan and Michael waited in breathless terror.

An electric chime sounded and the damaged inner door to the cabin slid open.

'CODE GAMMA HAS ENDED. CODE GAMMA HAS ENDED. BLAST SHIELDS OPERATIONAL.'

The family fell into their cabin, shocked to be alive and surprised that so little had changed within. The cluster of bubbles in the inner door had corresponding holes in the cabin window. This was entirely blacked out by the now functional blast shield. All the items that had been sucked at them had now fallen to the floor. Cracked records. Burst books. Kitchen utensils. But the cabin was otherwise intact.

'Right,' his mother sighed, ran her hands through her hair and tied it up in a single plait, 'who's hungry?'

9. LUCY THROUGH THE LOOKING GLASS

Lucy heard the distant whine of the alarm.

She felt as much as heard the roar and shriek of ripping metal below.

Then her narrow tunnel became a vacuum, pulling her down with the force of a thousand cold, furious fingers.

To stop herself from falling, she buried her hands and feet into the dense vines of wires around her and then pulled them back in towards her body, hugging the sizzling crackling cables. She held on against the banshee wail of wind crying in her ears, screaming through her bones, until its fury seemed spent, and she was again alone in pitch black silence.

As though frighted away by the screaming wind, the playful beckoning piper was silent. Yet Lucy couldn't rest. She had no choice. She had come too far and was too tired to scale the height she had laboured so hard to descend. She had to go on.

Within a few metres, Lucy's feet felt the sharp shredded edges of the wires. Using only her hands, she lowered herself down to the limit of her lifeline and dangled her feet into nothingness, searching with her toes for something to stand on. Chancing her ability to pull herself back up with her right hand, she released the grip of her left and sank a few centimetres more.

There!

A soft yet firm surface kissed her pointing big toe. Carefully, she released her grip on the wire and lowered both feet onto the invisible plane. A bed? She crouched there and waited for her eyes to adjust to this new darkness, wider than the tunnel she'd been passing down. The faint glow of a single console button cast the barest ripple of light across the space. It was a bedroom. The mirror image of her own.

For one insanely practical moment, Lucy was struck by the pattern with which all the cabins were laid out. The kitchens of adjoining cabins were either side of the same wall. So too the bedrooms. It was efficient. All same types of pipes and wiring were in the same crawlspace. Lucy had been climbing down though the cavities which separated rows and rows of identical children's quarters.

Yet there was one crucial difference between this room and hers, a jagged hole where the Gravity Shower should be. Whatever claw had ripped through that had reached right into the room and torn a gash through the ceiling and the wall.

She stepped down carefully from the bed and looked into the darker chamber of the busted shower. She was afraid of what she would find. She reached down into the black well, imagining the feeling of severed limbs wrapped in the fabric of a cadet's uniform. But it was empty. She sighed with relief and then was struck by the thought that the cadet must have been evacuated, by one or both of their parents, and that they might right now be huddled together in the front door lock space of their cabin. Lucy didn't know whether she wanted to rush to meet them or run back to her secret tunnel in the wall.

She drew her hand back and her fingers brushed an unfamiliar shape. It was not smooth or angled, like every object she encountered in her world. It was uneven, in some places jagged, in others pocked with little holes, utterly alien, like something brought up from the bottom of the ocean. She gasped. An asteroid! She slid her fingers around it til they found a grip and yanked once, twice, a third time, when it gave with a little shriek from the Shower's acoustic tile.

She held it up in the faint light and tried to see it. But there was nothing there. Her fingers felt its surface, but the rock blended into the darkness around it, refused to catch the little pulse of light from the console. It was like holding a ghost.

She wondered what it must be made of. In the furnace of what star was it formed, from elements not found in Earth's tiny corner of the galaxy? When that star exploded and seeded space, how long did the gravity of those elements take to draw together, spinning, tumbling, in a chaos of matter, until they formed larger bodies of rock, which maybe became planets, which came close to forming a solar system. What doom befell that fledgling world, to explode it and send forth into the night pieces as large as moons, and as tiny the shards, like this one she held now? How long had it been traveling through space, no aim, all momentum, to end up lodged in the tiles of some human kid's

Shower?

She put it in her pocket. It was on a new trajectory now.

Lucy stepped through the broken cubicle into the living area beyond. She could tell immediately that most of the destruction had ripped through here. There was no outer window. Indeed, the entire outer wall was gone, torn right down to the seams where it met the floor, the ceiling, and the port and stern walls. In its place was a blast shield. Its diagonal bands of yellow against black glowed faintly in the gloom. Nothing personal was left in the space. Cupboard doors hung open on empty shelves. Everything that might have told who had lived here had been sucked out into the vacuum of space.

Lucy shuddered. She knew she couldn't stay here. But where could she go?   The piper was silent.

The song had led her to the crawl space, but the thought of going back into that deeper, tighter darkness made her want to scream. Besides, she thought, wasn't it peaceful here? Wasn't this what she had been craving, room beyond her own? For a moment she imagined keeping this tomb of another family's abandoned life as her own secret hideaway, a refuge she might visit.

As she contemplated this sad and desperate notion, a circular panel, the size of a basketball, opened in the top right hand corner of the blast shield. Like a snake from its hole, a long black arm emerged. At its protruding end was a barrel that turned silently in the darkness. When the shaft was two metres into the room, it paused, tasting the air.

With a faint sigh, the barrel split open. Five steel talons unfurled from its fist and flexed in the shadows. Lucy heard the movement before she saw it. She crouched down and drew the multitool from her pocket, easing it out from under the asteroid.

The stone tipped out and fell to the floor with a clatter.

Instantly, the claw in the shadows swivelled the points of its talons towards her. From its palm, a beam of white light emerged, shot directly into Lucy's eyes.

She spun on her heals and dashed for the wreck of the Shower. The claw swooped down and grabbed her left ankle. As its long snake body pulled her up, she caught hold of the crumbled edges of acoustic tile. For a moment, she was horizontal, one leg kicking, one leg caught, her arms stretched out towards the bedroom, as though she were trying with all her might to escape from this nightmare and get back into bed.

The crumbled edge gave way in her hands. She toppled forward and dangled upside down in the air above the lounge room carpet. Lucy flailed about. She kicked at the talons with her free foot. She tried to raise herself up to grab at the metal fingers which held her fast. Yet they were immovable.

While she struggled, the outline of a new portal, drawn in red light, appeared in the blast shield. It was an elongated diamond, flat at the bottom and the top, like an upright coffin. When the outline was complete, the red light turned green. Then came the sound of a low metal clunk, like a great lock turning, and from the green shape emerged a metal box, one metre deep. Now the resemblance to a standing coffin was unmistakable.

Lucy stopped fighting the serpent's grip and stared, wondering for one wild moment if her ship was in fact the secret crypt of some vampire.

The coffin lid opened and out of it stepped the hulking form a spacesuit. Its surface, coming from the frozen void of space, steamed in the relative heat of the family cabin. The person, for it could have been a woman or a man under all that rubber, metal and polycarbon, stomped towards Lucy and stopped right before her. Its wide inscrutable visor came level with her upside down dangling face and her downpour of straight black hair.

'Luce!' the voice of the space suit rumbled from deep within its helmet. 'Your mum is going to kill us.'

10. JACK VOYAGER 1, GUITAR HERO

That night, to celebrate Induction Day, Jack's parents threw him a party. There were, of course, no other guests. Jack's friends, even if he had any, would not have been allowed to leave their cabins to visit him. The family might have all gone together to an online Sandbox restaurant, but Michael and Xinjuan knew how crowds made their son feel. Instead, they had planned an 'evening in', full of the things that Jack liked best to do.

Music was spilling warmly from Michael's record player. It was a relic from Earth that was still in fine working order, thanks to his father's meticulous care and attention, and his father's before him and his before him, all the way back to the original Voyager 1 who had first packed it on board and cherished it above all his other earthly belongings.

After the emergency, as soon as Michael was sure everyone was safe, he had rushed over to inspect the ancient device. He ran his hands across the plastic lid, gently lifted it, and kissed the turntable. Next he gathered up the sleeves and discs of the records that had been sucked out of their particular positions on the shelf, where they were divided into genres - Rock, Blues, Funk, Jazz, Electronic - and alphabetised by artist. Jazz had fared the worst. Jack didn't mind that so much, but his father had stared for a long time at the black shards of the last vinyl copy of John Coltrane's *A Love Supreme*.

It might have seemed strange to their shipmates that the Voyagers preferred the hissing, crackling sound of their small library of vinyl records, when every song ever recorded was available in perfect condition at the push of a button. But the Voyagers felt they had a mission to preserve something of Earth, something real, a seed that their descendants would one day plant in Uroun. Each record was physically connected to the singers and musicians who had created the music. The vibration of each note had passed from their lips and instruments and been pressed into the vinyl disc, like a sculptor carving an image out of stone. The Voyagers felt, perhaps superstitiously, that it was not merely a copy of the music, but an echo of the musicians themselves, that traveled with them through the stars.

Once the surviving records were back in place, Michael took his son's favourite from the shelf, slipped it from its sheath, and deftly lowered the needle arm into the opening groove. He then turned and winked.

'Jimi Hendrix,' he said, 'for my own little *Voodoo Child*.'

As the legendary blues man's guitar purred and meowed, Jack picked nuggets of space rock out of the cabin door and his parents prepared his favourite meal: algae-pasta in flavor-enhancers #235, #197 and the rare and precious #56.

Michael and Xinjuan hummed along as they moved around each other in the tiny kitchen space, stirring the ribbons in the pot, arranging the plates, and keying the timer and temperature into the oven in time to the music.

They were a strange and lovely couple. His father was long-limbed and freckled. His red beard and curly hair made him look like a cross between a pirate and a clown. His mother could not have been more different. Her limbs were slender and pale as porcelain. Her hair was long, straight and black as jet. Yet when they moved together, they were as one, as though their bodies spoke the same secret language.

At the end of their dance, they mock-staggered together with the heaving plate of spaghetti and set it down before Jack with a sigh and a cheer.

'That lot should last you until next Induction Day,' his father quipped and gave Jack's ribs a tickle.

'You'll need your strength,' Xinjuan beamed and rolled her lovely almond eyes. 'I remember how hard it was to get through sixteen.'

'Thanks Mum. Thanks Dad. This is great,' Jack said. But he barely tasted the simulated tomato, garlic and cheese. He simply chewed it up along with the steaming white seaweed and algal extract dyed and shaped to look like meatballs. Normally Jack would dive into the red mess of strings and goop and only come up for air to wipe the sauce from his face and declare his love for bygone Italy. Tonight though, he simply stared at the mountain of pasta and chewed. His mind was caught in another mess.

After the emergency sirens had ceased, Jack's thoughts turned from relief to frustration. He had been so close to leaving the cabin. He could not shake the feeling that if he had he would have found Lucy.

The thought recalled mountains of skulls. Children tip-toed upon them, grasping at their own *Uroun*, never to reach it.

And the sound of a pipe. The tune haunted him even more than the vision. He felt it echoing in his bones. Like it was lurking in the shadows of his skull. Or it had awoken something that was already waiting there?

Lucy had been there. She had heard the piper and seen the mountain. Could he talk to her? Should he message her now? What should he say? Say nothing. Play cool. It could just be a glitch. Or a prank hack, though he wouldn't credit any of the bullies he knew with the imagination to come up with such a poetic vision.

The more he thought about it, the more panicked and miserable he felt.

'Penny for your thoughts?' his mother asked, pushing a tuft of Jack's long black fringe out the way of his fork.

He wanted to tell his parents. But he knew they would only worry. His Mum would hold him close like she did when he'd woken from nightmares as a boy. His Dad would not let him back into the Shower until he'd dismantled and triple-tested all its systems, located the problem and deleted it.

Meanwhile, how would he reach Lucy?

Jack swallowed the food in his mouth and lied, 'I'm just worried about the Big Game tonight.'

'Ah-ha!' his father cried happily and slapped the table. Xinjuan sighed and slumped in her seat. Jack could see that she wished there was something more personal she could discuss with her boy than the ups and downs of Red versus Blue. He was sorry to disappoint her, but his father was immediately in his element and Jack didn't have to say another word.

'I know, mate. It's a big one. Blue's had a rough run of it lately, but don't you worry, Jacky-boy. I reckon Red'll go off the boil tonight and then we'll pounce. How do you want to watch it? Cricket? Soccer? Aussie Rules? All three? How bout we start with Cricket, flick over to Soccer, see the wickets done again as goals, and then, if it's a close finish, watch the final minutes as footy?'

'Sounds good, Dad,' Jack enthused, but inwardly he didn't care how they viewed the game. If Blue lost, he'd feel like it was his fault. If they won, he'd know it had nothing to do with him.

Because of the limited space onboard the ships of The Fleet, sporting matches could only be contested online. Intra-fleet games were also limited by the fact that different countries and their crews excelled at vastly different sports. The Americans, Russians and Chinese didn't play cricket, and that was the only sport the Indians ever wanted to play. Soccer was played worldwide, but the thought of playing the same sport for centuries put off even the most diehard fans of the old 'world game'.

It was the brilliant idea of the second captain of the Chinese ship that a grand competition be arranged. It would not be country versus country, but in the new spirit of humanity, there would be only two teams, Red and Blue. Anyone could choose to support either, but once selected, each crewman was bound to that team for life. Thenceforward, every activity in which they participated in Sandbox would win their team points. If you were a Red and in your own spare time set a new record on *Speed Racer*, your bonus points would contribute to Team Red's overall score.

Each Friday, the scores made during the week by crewmen from throughout The Fleet were tallied. That night, everyone could view the results visualised as a match between Red and Blue in any sport they liked.

According to Jack's father, Red vs Blue was one of the most complex programs in the whole of The Fleet's online operations. According to The Admiral, it was essential for fleet morale. Jack was always receiving pop-ups from her, reminding him to play. 'Don't forget, Cadet Voyager 1, your personal development counts towards the development of The Fleet.'

But Jack did not play, so Jack did not contribute. And Jack always felt like apologising to his father when their Blues went down to the Reds. Worse still, on the rare occasions when Blue won and his father grabbed him in his arms and yanked him to his feet for a jubilant victory dance, he felt embarrassed. So it was with a familiar feeling of dread that he sat down with his father on the couch before the window screen to watch Blue play Red in a 50-over game of cricket.

Many of the same crewmen as last week had scored enough points for each team to have their avatars featured as players. The opening bowler for the Reds was Rick Mercury, father of Max Mercury, Jack's chief tormentor in Sandbox and School.

'How's a grown man and father find the time to rack up so many points each week that he gets to open the bowling?' his father wondered aloud. 'I mean, he must just finish work and go straight to Sandbox.'

'I don't think his son minds,' mused Jack. Max was always bragging about his father's exploits in the virtual arena. No one ever had the courage to remind Max that his father wasn't actually bowling the cricket ball or striking goals off his own boot. It was the computer showing him doing that as a reward for playing hour upon hour of *Candy Crush*. But that would not sway Max from his opinion that he was the son of The Fleet's greatest champion and all his classmates should treat him with the same fear his father's simulated opponents were made to show. So it was not without some personal anxiety that Jack watched Rick Mercury steam in off the long run to deliver a savage bouncer at the Blue team captain's throat.

After a few overs, it became clear that it would be Red's night again. Blue lost wicket after wicket to Mercury's men. Flicking over to soccer, Red was up 3-1, and in Rugby 32-11. They even had a look at the tennis, where Max's dad was walloping some Blue player they hadn't seen before by two sets to love.

Eventually, with a sigh, Jack's dad flicked off the screen.

'Not our night, kiddo,' he said with a pat on Jack's head.

'Oh no, did we lose?' Xinjuan muttered from the kitchen table without looking up from her book of poetry. 'What a tragedy. How will you men ever recover?'

'I have an idea,' Michael exclaimed. 'Presents!'

'Finally,' his mother sighed and put down her book.

Instantly, all the feelings of confusion and anxiety that had been weighing Jack's spirits lifted. As Xinjuan joined them on the couch, Michael pulled two boxes out from under the seats.

'Happy 15th, Jack,' his father declared.

'Happy 15th, darling,' chimed his mother.

Jack went immediately for the larger of the two boxes. Inside he found something that made his heart sink: a Blues cap.

'Put in on,' his mother chirped. 'Let's have a look at you. Oh yes, that's very handsome.'

'Now open the other,' his father encouraged gently. As Jack did so, his father explained, 'I know you don't spend much time in Sandbox. But I think your mother and I have found a way that you can play *and* win points *without* needing to deal with all the annoying so-and-sos online.'

Jack opened the box and revealed his prize. It was a small computer drive with a simple port. He held it up to examine it.

'That, my friend, is an extremely rare bit of data,' Michael said.

'Go on,' said his mother with a giggle, 'plug it in.'

Confused, Jack stood up and pressed the drive into the port at the edge of the window. After a moment of buffering, the opening titles of the drive's solitary program appeared on the glass. As the introductory music and graphics played, it dawned on Jack that this was perhaps the greatest moment of his life, for he was standing not five inches away from the legendary game, *Guitar Hero*.

It was a low-res program briefly in fashion during Earth's early 21st century. Players used a physical controller in the shape of a guitar to manipulate a very basic avatar to play classic rock n' roll songs in front of a virtual audience of screaming fans. Points were scored for hitting all the right notes on the guitar buttons in time with the song.

There were no physical musical instruments in The Fleet except, it was rumoured, in a private museum somewhere on *The Dauntless*. Jack's dad had promised years ago to try and find a way for the family to do more than play air guitar along with Hendrix. Tonight, he had finally delivered.

'You wouldn't believe how hard your father worked to find this,' purred Xinjuan. 'Tell him, Mike.'

'Well,' Michael began, suddenly bashful, 'once I found out there was a collector of vintage console games on *The Star of Russia*, I had to find what he'd want to trade and what that person wanted for that and blah blah-blah blah *blah*. What I'm really happy about is what my mates in Programming were able to do with it. Notice anything weird?'

Jack looked at the screen. On the game stage stood his avatar, a skinny punkrocker with a blue Mohawk, dark sunglasses and studded bracelets, holding a flame red guitar. At his feet roared a vast auditorium full of virtual fans. In the top right corner was a song list to scroll through. But where was the…

'Controller,' Jack yelped. 'There's no controller. Does that mean?'

His dad smiled, 'It sure does. Give it a go.'

Jack raised his arms and the avatar on screen lifted the guitar over its head. The window's built in infrared was scanning Jack's every move through the motion-capture nodes woven, fingertip to toe, into the fabric of his uniform. Every stitch of intelligent thread, from the seven-star insignia on his chest, to the seams round his soles, shimmered briefly an electric blue.

'It's programmed to respond to your suit only,' chimed Xinjuan.

'And,' his father stated proudly, 'every point you score will be recorded as a point for Team Blue.'

Jack's hands dropped and his avatar strummed its guitar into a beastly electric snarl that set the game fans cheering.

'See,' smiled his father, 'you're a natural.'

'Well, come on Jack,' Xinjuan tittered. 'Play us something.'

Jack scrolled through the options in the menu. All his heroes were there: Hendrix, Led Zeppelin, The Smashing Pumpkins, AC/DC.

Jack's eyes lit up. '*Thunderstruck*!' he read.

He selected the song and put his hands and fingers before him just like he'd seen guitarists in old movies do. As the backing music rose, a bass drum beat slowly and ominously over a guitar's wicked trilling. His parents nodded their heads and shook the fists in the air to the beat, chanting, 'Thunder!'

Jack smiled and focused on the screen. A window displayed the sequence of notes he would have to hit on his virtual controller once his instrument, the lead guitar, kicked in. They were all represented by coloured balls that scrolled down the screen to the line that showed now was the instant they should be played.

Together, the family watched the first line of notes approach. His parents counted Jack in, '1, 2. 1-2-3-4...'

The sound that emerged from the screen was not the song they knew.

It could not even be called music.

At Jack's command, the punk on screen hacked at his guitar, making it scream and wail in agony. The awful noise shook their tiny cabin. Xinjuan and Michael dove to catch the books and bowls shaken from their shelves. But Jack kept his head down and struck fiercely at the air. The virtual audience blocked their ears and booed. Jack ignored them and pounded on until the final note's coloured ball disappeared from the screen and his virtual bandmates laid down their instruments, shaking their heads.

In the silence that followed, Jack stood with his back to his parents, staring down at his hands. His narrow shoulders heaved with each breath. The ship's hull groaned.

Xinjuan looked at her husband, who shrugged helplessly.

'Well,' she said, and rose out of her seat to stand beside her boy and put an uncertain hand on her his quivering shoulder, 'you sure have your own…style.'

Jack raised his head, and the curtains of his messy black locks parted to reveal that he was not upset or disappointed. He was grinning and panting with exhilaration.

He wanted to thank them, but he couldn't speak.

Music that no one but Jack could hear trembled in his fingers.

Mike and Xinjuan saw it in his eyes and smiled.

Suddenly, this was no longer Day One of Year Sixteen.

This was the day that Jack took his first step into a dream.

To become a musician, and live in song.

11. LUCY LOOKS OVER THE EDGE

Lucy stepped out of the coffin-shaped access hatch, onto the long smooth hull of *The HMAS Hamelin*. The space suit was bunched up around her elbows and ankles but in the vacuum of space she was weightless, held to the metal panels by the magnets in her boots and the guy rope her father used to draw her back towards the stern of the ship.

She gripped the cable with both hands and looked around her.

All the simulations of School could not prepare her for the terrible emptiness she suddenly felt. In Physics, the other ships of The Fleet were always shown close by, in tight circular formation. Now she could see that the truth was they were travelling at a distance so great that Lucy could only see their blinking navigation lights. The ships themselves were not lit up, as they were in the sims, except for patches where crews like hers were at work. Mostly they were but shadows in the night, above, below, to port and starboard. A ghost fleet.

Yet there was a beauty here which School could not simulate. The ships moved between the stars of a single arm of the spiral Milky Way Galaxy. Because their Fleet traveled parallel with the spiral plane, these billions of stars appeared like a thick ring all around them, describing a horizon in space. It was like a great tsunami of light was crashing in on them from every direction, out of the deep.

She looked up along the hull, past the rows of portals, each looking in on an identical family cabin, towards the upper deck where she could just make out the outer edges of the three broad solar sails which propelled *The Hamelin* across the ocean of night. Looking back, she could also see other crewmen in spacesuits, working with hand held welding torches and operating robotic arms like the one that her father had been piloting when he found her in the wreck of the cabin. The damage to *Hamelin* was confined to only three decks out of twelve, and was now covered in yellow and black striped blast shields. The swathe of colour looked to Lucy like a the ship was slowly being dressed up as a bee. But she banished the thought from her mind, remembering that for every one of those panels, a life had probably been lost. Had she known any of them? Was one of them Jack?

"Eyes front, Lucy!" her father barked at her over the intercom. "You need to look like you're meant to be out here, not a tourist." And he waved collegially to a nearby crewman, who only nodded in return.

Lucy waved too and he nodded to her, only pausing for a moment, but long enough to waken her up to the reality that she and her father were presently embarked on breaking one of the most fundamental taboos of life in The Fleet: no child was to leave their cabin until Graduation, at the close of their eighteenth year. Lucy breathed a sigh of relief that her helmet's visor was a one-way mirror and her face was hidden from the other crewmen. She did not want to even imagine the look of confusion on the nearby stranger's face, wondering who this little worker was, whose spacesuit hung on them like uncooked dough. Her only consolation was the thought that no one could imagine a cadet getting out of their room, let alone onto the hull of the ship.

Gradually, her father guided her down the long starboard length of *Hamelin* to the immense, dark and silent cavity of the primary engine. This was far away from the damage and no other crewmen were about. This massive circular enclosure was now entirely obsolete. This engine had been used to propel *The Hamelin* up to its cruising speed, building in velocity until they reached the edge of Earth's solar system, at which point, lasers stationed on Earth shot a steady beam of light at The Fleet, a broad beam which ignited their solar sails and pushed them out into the emptiness beyond the Sun's farthest planetoids in the Kuiper Belt, out where the Sun began to look like only a brighter star amongst the billions of The Milky Way. Since that moment, the primary engine had been cold. The only light which now emanated from the stern of the ships was a ring of exhaust ports around the main engine, which channeled the only energy the solar sails now gathered, the fainter but far more constant light of stars.

"I like it here," Chiang Zu said as he sat down and dangled his legs over the round edge. "I can think."

His daughter said nothing.

"Look back there," the man said, and pointed out towards the seam of stars in the distance behind them. "Do you see it?"

"Earth?" Lucy ventured.

He chuckled, mirthlessly. "I don't know. Maybe. The lasers

don't reach us anymore. There are no more messages. No more news from home. For all we know the storms have wiped the last people from the face of the planet. Maybe we're still living, somewhere, hiding underground. But what's for sure is that whatever they've got back there either isn't strong enough to be felt out here. We're on our own. All we've got is each other. For better or for worse."

Was he talking about her mum? Was he trying to let her know he understood why she had escaped? And was he also explaining why she had no choice but to return?

"I can't go back there, Dad," she whispered over the intercom.

He sighed and pulled her close to him. It may have only been her imagination, but she felt him communicate his warmth to her through the dense fabric of their suits. It made the course material feel softer, more secure, like bedtime years ago, before things had changed.

"She wasn't always like this, Luce," he said eventually. "She was proud, brilliant, just like you."

"What happened?" Lucy breathed.

For a moment her father was silent. Then the words spilled forth like a tide he had been holding back for years. He said, "I learned something I didn't want to, about what we do here, how we survive. I couldn't accept it. For her own reasons, your mother decided that she had to accept it, but to do that she had to change. She saw that our world has a terrible cruelty at its heart. And she took that into her, made it a part of her, and she wants to teach it to you. Because she loves you.

Because she wants to protect you. So that when you learn the truth it won't break you, like it did her."

Lucy held her breath. She felt the awful truth suspended in the air between them and dare not ask what he meant, for fear her father would spook and end this close yet oh so terrifying moment between them.

Then, from the distance, up towards the bow where the other Maintenance crewmen were working under the blast shields, a low siren droned and an artificial voice intoned, "Repair Crew 6, meal time. Repair Crew 6, meal time. Leave the outer hull and return to barracks. Leave the outer hull and return to barracks."

"Should we go?" Lucy asked.

Chiang Zu only shook his head.

"They're only being polite," he said. "So no one has to be out here and risk seeing this." And her father pointed downwards at the space below the lip of the engine ring over which their legs dangled.

At first, Lucy did not understand what she was seeing. It was like the ship had started shedding snowflakes, white crosses spinning from under the ship and out into its wake, flowers cast upon the ocean. Then with mounting horror she realised that these cartwheeling forms were human. And alive. Ten? Fifteen? Twenty souls jettisoned into space and certain death.

Lucy grabbed her father and dragged him to his feet. She was desperate. She did not know what to do. She wanted to scream in his face to do something. She wanted to leap off the edge and catch them. She wanted to cry. But all she could manage was to whisper, "Why?"

"Because they're old," her father replied grimly, grimacing at the taste of the bitter pill he'd had to swallow years ago, now fresh on his daughter's tongue.

"Your mother is military. She found it easier to accept. Necessary losses. Sacrifice of the few for the many. But I'm a doctor, Lucy. I made an oath, to do no harm. Once I knew, once I was promoted to a position in which such things were discussed as openly and practically as work rosters…" He paused to let his voice return to even. "I was given the task of evaluating older crew members, assessing whether their contributions to the ship were worth more or less than the cost of keeping them alive on board. Like they were only parts of a machine. Not people."

"And they accept that," Lucy gasped, "when they're told they have to go."

"Most do. It's made pretty clear to them that they're a liability. That they are risking The Fleet's chances of making it to *Uroun*. They accept it."

"Links in a chain," Lucy muttered.

"Exactly," said Chiang Zu. "But not everyone feels that way."

"And what happens to them?"

"The military."

"Mum?" Lucy whispered.

Her father nodded. "Sometimes."

Lucy couldn't speak. She stared out into the void, trying to see them.

For a moment she thought she saw a glimmer of golden lights, like meteorites streaking through an atmosphere.

But then they was gone.

Was this what makes it bearable? she wondered. That they disappear? Don't their children remember them? Their crew mates? She looked up at her father. He smiled.

"I've still got years to go, Luce," he said. "I'm still useful. But I don't plan to wait around until someone like me is forced to stamp my form red."

"But what can you do?" she asked him. "Mutiny?"

"No," her father retorted with a chuckle.

And then he began to whistle.

Lucy's lips dropped open. It was the shimmering tune she had heard played on a pipe in her vision of the mountain of skulls. The electric rivulet of song she had followed through the wall and down into the wreckage.

"Are *you* the piper?" Lucy gasped. "Is that *your* song?"

Her father smiled sadly shook his head. "I once heard a whole chorus sing it. Just before they…" He pointed at the space directly below where they'd seen the bodies fall. "Ever since then, I don't know if it's just the memory of that moment, or whether its' calling to *me* now, but whenever I'm out here, I hear it, coming from back *there*."

Chiang Zu raised his hand to point directly backwards, into the starry centre of their wake.

"*Earth*?" asked Lucy, hope kindling in her breast.

"No. Closer. Just out of sight. Just out of hearing." Chiang's eyes scanned the invisible horizon. "Sometimes I feels like it's got its hand on my heart, and it's pulling me back there. Sometimes I feel like I could just…"

He flicked his fingers out into space, like he was tossing a ball into the abyss.

"Then one day, the song was so strong, like a tide rolling through me, I tried singing it for myself."

Lucy couldn't help herself. She groaned. Her father rolled his eyes. "I know," he said. "You and your mother gave strict orders."

"I don't know what's worse than tone-deaf, Dad, but you're it."

"I know. I know," he chuckled, and then grew still. He looked deeply into Lucy's eyes. "But this song is different."

Keeping his eyes fixed on hers, Chiang Zu began to hum. The piper's tune brimmed on his lips, softly, simply, but truly.

And then he did the unthinkable.

He unfastened the latches of his helmet.

'Dad! NO!' Lucy reached for her father, scrambling to pull the protective dome back down over his head.

He stilled her hands and hummed even more loudly the strange tune.

His smiling face did not freeze. It glowed. A glimmering haze of sparks puffed about his lips, filling his helmet.

Lucy slowly let go her father's hands.

The hardware floated free of Chiang Zu's face.

He was singing now, in full voice, and from his lips flowed, like water from a deep underground spring, a wash of golden light, shimmering warm and animate against the deathly frozen night.

DAY 33

12. JACK'S MAGIC THEATRE

'Ladies and gentlemen, friends from every civilisation in The Milky Way, welcome to *The Magic Theatre!*'

The crowd roared. Arms, tendrils, wings and appendages with no earthly classification, waved and clapped and wriggled in the air beneath a night sky strewn with alien constellations.

'We have a special treat for you tonight. All the way from Earth, a young man who has mastered the songs of Earth's ancient maestros. He's a rock n' roll refugee. He's a living legend. Will you please welcome him onto the stage, Cadet number 5-6-7-8, Jack, John, Voyager Onnnnnnnnnnnnnne!'

As Jack strutted out to the microphone centre stage, the drummer and the bass guitarist struck up a dark and funky rhythm. His guitar, the rings in his nose and ears, and the studs in his black leather braces, sparkled under the spotlight.

'Thank you. Thank you. It's a real pleasure to be here,' Jack declared over the music's driving groove. 'We've been on tour for weeks now. We've played to every life form in the galaxy – from *The Great Hall of Tholus* on *Atabraxia* to *The Love Shack* on *Beta 3* – but we always long to come home to *The Magic.*'

On cue, the digital audience whistled and cheered.

'This first song is going out to creatures everywhere, suffering under the tyranny of kings, dictators, parents and…' Jack breathed the last word angrily into the microphone, 'teachers.'

At the mention of teachers, his digital audience responded with happy boos and merrily shouted curses. Jack had populated the crowd with aliens and celebrities from Earth's past, but also with versions of his classmates. His tormentors, Jenna and Max, looked up at him with the same mixture of admiration and excitement as Dwayne 'The Rock' Johnson and Charlie Chaplin.

And in the front row, was the guest of honour, Lucy.

He had hardly seen her in class, these past weeks. And when she was there, their teachers kept them so busy that he'd still had no chance to talk with her. Every night his finger hovered over the send button for countless drafts of messages, asking if she was ok, if she wanted to talk about anything. He even once wrote a long message about the vision he thought they'd shared, but it all looked so crazy written out on a screen. And because the only other thing he felt he really needed to tell her was how she made him feel, he decided it was wiser not to send any message at all.

Instead, each night, he performed for an image of her, here in his *Magic Theatre*.

'This one's going out to my friend, Lucy, who never backs down from a fight. It's a protest song from my home world. It's called *Five… to One.*'

The organist lay down rich chords of sound that swelled up

under the rest of the groove. With a nod of his Mohawk to the animated instrumentalists at his back, Jack began to sing, letting his voice relax into an imitation of the husky howl of *The Doors'* legendary front-man, Jim Morrison.

The coloured balls that indicated what notes Jack should play at this part of the song began falling before his eyes. He didn't even need to watch them. He had been gifted the program three weeks ago and since then he had practiced until late every night. He knew exactly what to do. As his actual fingers danced across his virtual guitar, the balls exploded before his eyes, and in the top right-hand corner of his gaze, his score went up in thousands.

This was not the only way to win at Guitar Hero. Jack's updated version awarded extra points for stagecraft. As he sang the second verse, Jack stalked up and down the stage, winking at the crowd, pointing to Lucy like he was singing just to her, kicking his legs out just like he'd seen all his heroes do in the concerts recorded long ago before the Earth exhausted its wealth of joy.

Jack rocked his head back, raised his guitar high in the air, and plucked from its simulated strings a shower of notes that poured down upon him and rolled like a wave over everyone in the auditorium. The crowd swooned at the genius of his solo. Rising on the tide of their moans of pleasure, Jack's score swelled up past his previous best. Fireworks erupted overhead in the electric sky, spelling 'JACK' against the star-pricked dark.

The crowd began chanting the player's name, just as they were programmed to do whenever a new high score was won.

'Jack? Jack!' a voice closer than the front row called.

For a few more bars of his extended guitar solo he ignored it. Then it was joined by a knocking sound.

'Jack? Jack, mate.'

With a sigh, Jack paused the game and pulled the Shower Cap from his head. His father's muffled voice came clearer through the door.

'Jack, you've gotta come see.'

Jack slid back the door of his shower and poked his sweaty face out. Michael, dressed in his austere black and white Net Cop uniform, was practically jumping on the spot like a Year 5 Cadet.

'Sorry to interrupt, mate,' his father beamed, 'but you wouldn't believe what's happening in Red Vs Blue.'

Jack raised his right eyebrow, incredulous that anyone, even his dad, would get that excited about a game.

'Aren't you on duty, Dad?'

Michael realised he wasn't making himself understood and took a breath.

'Yes. And I wouldn't skip out if it weren't important, would I? You'll want to come and see this. Just…' he wagged his fingers, 'come on.'

Doubtfully, Jack slipped the rest of his body out of the Shower and followed his father into the living room. There, on the window screen, he saw exactly what had made his dad so excited.

As though in some kind of funhouse mirror, Jack's sweating face was presently looking back at him from under the visor of a Blue cricket helmet. His avatar was facing down the pitch towards Rick Mercury, steaming in at a gallop to hurl the ball at the rookie player.

Michael gripped his son's arm.

'You've made it, Jack. You've scored enough points on Guitar Hero to get onto Red Vs bloody Blue.'

Jack looked up at the scores. Sure enough, his private successes on the musical program had been recorded by Sandbox and translated into selection for the Blue team. On top of that, he had scored twenty-three valuable runs for his team. This was the last over of the match. He only needed to hit a single run to win the game for Blue.

Mercury delivered a thunderbolt that reared up off the pitch towards his chin. Jack's avatar swung blindly. The ball ricocheted off his chin guard, thudded into his chest and rolled down his arm. Looking for the ball, Jack's proxy turned to his left. The motion spilled the rolling ball from his forearm onto the stumps and dislodged the bail. Wicket lost. No run. Red victory.

'OH NO!' his father bawled and swept Jack up into a bear hug. 'So close! Don't worry. You gave 'em a run for their money, mate. Chin up. You'll get 'em next time.'

'I'm fine, dad. Really,' Jack said, and his eyes turned back towards his room.

'Well, do you want to watch the replay with me?' Michael asked, raising a couple of glasses of carbonated #328 he had handy. 'Or as soccer? A close game's a close game and you played really well.'

'Dad,' Jack sighed, looking for the words. He pointed at the screen and shook his head. 'It's not me.'

Michael stilled, lowered his eyes for a moment, and nodded. The ice tinkled in the glasses. 'I know, bud. It's just a sim.' He looked up at his son. 'But you earned this. These past weeks, you've mastered that game of yours and all your effort's being rewarded. Cheers.' He held the glass out for Jack to take. Jack accepted it and they clinked glasses and drank.

In the silence that followed, Michael grew more serious. The dad went out of his voice, leaving only the man. 'This life, Jack…' He searched for the words. 'It's not easy. For anyone, least of all you kids.'

He trailed off, staring into his drink.

Jack shifted his weight from foot to foot.

Michael seemed to find the words he was looking for amongst the bubbles in his glass. 'It's just that life out there is hard.'

He pointed his glass at the entryway where, Jack noticed a new door had replaced the asteroid scarred barricade he and his parents had hidden behind. When had they replaced that, he wondered.

'It's hard,' his father continued, 'and if you're going to survive, you need to fit in. So, this is important.' He pointed at the screen. 'What happens in School and Sandbox sets you up for life.'

'Thanks dad,' Jack mumbled, though he sensed his father was warning him as much as praising him, and the boy did not care what happened on the field of Red vs Blue. An altogether different arena was calling to him.

'Do you mind?' he asked.

Michael's mouth opened to speak. He looked at the drinks in their hands. Then he looked again at the purposeful expression on his son's face, the energy rippling through his limbs, and smiled. 'Yeah, of course,' he said. 'The show must go on, eh? What are you playing?'

'*Five to One.*'

'Nice,' his father said and affected his own Jim Morrison impression, '*Gonna make it yeah we're taking over…*'

Together, they called out like wolves howling to the moon, '*COME ON!*'

Jack slipped out of the room, leaving Michael to drink both drinks and watch the replay on his own.

Back on stage, Jack played out the rest of the song, but even though he played like a virtuoso, and the audience cheered him on like a rockstar, the feeling had gone out of him. Seeing himself replicated in Red Vs Blue had reminded Jack that, for all the modifications he had made to it, Guitar Hero was still just another simulation. Sure, he was performing all the moves that made the music play. He was singing the songs that made the crowd roar and the scores soar. But they weren't his songs.

The crowd began stomping its feet and hooves and claws and tentacles. They were impatient to hear the next classic hit. Jack raised his hand to them and leaned in close to the microphone.

'I hear you,' he assured the program. 'I really do, but tonight I'd like to try something new.'

He turned around to his backing band, who each bobbed on the spot, instruments at the ready to mime playing whichever preinstalled song he selected.

Jack grinned nervously and invited them to, 'Follow along, if you can.'

He lifted his guitar and looked down at it as though the notes he sought were written there. They weren't, so he closed his eyes and listened. The stamping feet resounded even louder in the stadium. He concentrated harder, listening deeper into the noise, past the crunch, past the grind, down in amongst the echoes.

He held his breath.

In that moment of stillness, he imagined himself by the window of his family cabin, crouched in the morning dark. That was where he had sat for years, listening to his father's records. That was where the dream of becoming a musician had taken hold of him. Now, to escape the chanting mob, he saw himself back there, and looked out through the glass. A vision ghosted amongst the distant stars, of a mountain. It rose towards Jack, reaching to him through the star-shot night. Jack could hear an icy wind whistling around its peak. Like an iceberg, the mountain drifted closer, looming larger upon the starlit sea. And as it filled his vision, the first notes of a melody emerged from the whistling wind.

In the theatre, Jack splayed his fingers across the neck of his instrument and struck the opening notes of the mountain song.

The audience went silent. The band stilled, fingers and lips poised upon their instruments, waiting to recognise the tune.

His eyes still closed and fixed upon his vision of the mountain, Jack slowly spelled the notes he heard playing about its icy summit. It was a sad refrain. It rose and fell like an ancient Celtic tune, or a blues riff from the old Deep South. It was the song the pipe had played in his vision of the mountain of skulls. Jack had almost forgotten it. In the thrill of mastering his instrument and the thought that Lucy might one day hear him and be drawn to him by his playing, he had barely even thought of that waking nightmare. He had only once or twice found himself humming the tune, felt it rise up out of his bones like it was always echoing there, and then, reminded only of music, he had dashed back into the shower to practice his growing repertoire of classic rock songs.

Now he felt the piper's song rising within him again.

It flowed out of his skull like cold spring water from mountain rock, thrilled down along his arms, his hands, his fingers, and into his guitar.

And the audience did not like it. No, not one bit.

They whistled. They hissed.

Jack played on, letting the babbling stream of music rush through him.

'STOP THE SHOW! STOP THE SHOW!' they chanted and hurled digital rotten tomatoes that splattered across his avatar.

The Gravity Shower faithfully reproduced the feeling of the slimy fruit pulp trickling down his neck and into his shirt. The cold wet oozing woke Jack from his vision. He looked out at the heaving sea of angry faces.

He understood their fury. This was what they were programmed to do when a player went so far off the melody of a song that it became unrecognisable. It was written into the code of the musicians to shake their heads and cast away their drumsticks and guitar picks in disgust at any player who didn't play along. Jack didn't mind. He'd learned all of their antics the first week he'd started playing. Their boos had helped motivate him to hone his skills.

Now he closed his eyes against them and returned to his vision. But the mountain was gone. In its place, The Admiral's face now loomed, blotting out the stars with her glare. His imaginary *Hamelin* made straight for the black cavern of her open mouth. From its abyss poured forth the hollering and jeering of the crowd, chanting, 'STOP

THE SHOW! STOP THE SHOW!'

Jack opened his eyes and lifted his fingers from the guitar. All trace of the song was gone. All he could hear was the audience's programmed fury.

'Jack? Jack.'

It was his father's voice again. But angry.

A quick glance up at the left-hand corner of his viewscreen told Jack why. Flashing there was his mathematics teacher's fat, feline face. Next to it, the title of her message read 'Test Scores.'

Jack dropped his hands, slumped his shoulders and looked up. In the black sky over his private stadium, fireworks had written the words, 'STOP LOSER, STOP PLAYING! STOP, RIGHT NOW!'

Through the fire and the smoke, Jack caught a glimpse of the outline of a mountain. Its frozen peaks were silent, yet glistened blue under the unblinking light of a single star.

13. LUCY SNEAKS A PEAK

Lucy and her father stood outside the Voyagers' cabin door.

The helmet of Lucy's Maintenance uniform, which had now been fitted with power boots and taken in at the arms so that she looked taller and more plausibly adult, still tended to lean to one side on her narrow shoulders. In this disguise she had first made her way home with Chiang Zu, not via her secret tunnel, but in the full view of adults, straight through the service corridors. Most crewmen, it seemed, wore their helmets inside.

'Working diagnostics?' Lucy had asked her dad.

'Watching shows,' he'd told her. 'Just don't bump into anyone and no one will notice you're a little short for a storm trooper.'

Lucy had groaned at her father's ancient Star Wars reference, but she'd obeyed nevertheless and kept close to Chiang, plodding along on the other side of him to the crewmen they passed. It wasn't until they'd reached their cabin and Lucy stumbled inside, removed the heavy helmet and brought her adrenalised breathing under control, that she'd reflected on how preposterous and unlikely her journey through the ship had been. She had been schooled to believe in the absolute focus and diligence of her superiors. But they had seemed like zombies, shuffling about the corridors, barely aware of their surroundings. They seemed to Lucy little better than their ancestors, those childish, pudgy pilots of oil-guzzling robots.

Now, after weeks of skipping School to sneak about with her father, she had become used to it. There was the odd clear-eyed crewman striding about purposefully, watchfully. But her father took care of all the talking and the modifications he had made to her uniform had transformed the appearance of a deflated doll into an adult crewman, albeit one on the short side. She had even perfected the distracted shuffle of someone watching sitcoms or Red Vs Blue on the inside of their visor. She was never given a second look.

Tonight, she had the added camouflage of a large auto-trolley carrying a new entryway door. Destination - the Voyager 1 residence.

On either side of the Voyager's outer door were the faint outlines of graffiti which had ben recently cleaned away, leaving a white imprint of the original dark letters that made the message seem harsher, more damning, like a scar. MURDERER! It screamed on the left, and to the right, RAT CATCHER.

This wasn't the only graffiti Lucy had seen. Down other corridors she'd seen ironic messages, mocking The Admiral's pep talks, telling the crew to KEEP UP THE GOOD WORK, RATS! and WORK YOUR WAY DOWN THE DRAIN! These were cleaned away by Maintenance as soon as they appeared, but her father told her that this was a joke because most of the words were written by crewmen *in* Maintenance. The most creative piece she'd seen was around her own front door. Her mother, like Jack's father, was a Net-Cop, in charge of surveilling online traffic, and occasionally, supervising the 'retirement' of elder crew members: '*Rats down the drain*'.

To celebrate her unacknowledged distinction as the only female crew member who took part in 'retiring' her crew-mates, around the Gemini's front door was drawn the massive maw of a dog, (a female, according to the word scrawled angrily above its ears) its teeth pointed inwards, savage eyes staring down on every passerby. Every week it was cleaned away. Every week it was retouched with different coloured ink, by a different hand.

The Voyagers got off lightly. The message outside their door didn't look like it had been written for some time.

As he lifted his Maintenance skeleton key to the lock, her father told her to, 'Remember why we're here, Luce. I know he's your friend, but we're not here on a visit. We need data. Evidence. Anything that can tell us about…'

He twirled his fingers from his mouth in a spiral back towards the stern and the mystery that waited in the dark behind The Fleet. Back there, they hoped, was the source of the piper's song, and its miraculous ability to turn the cold vacuum of space into warm, breathable atmosphere. If anyone knew anything about what was going on out there, it would be the man whose job it was to keep tabs on Fleet communications. They dare not ask Hannah Gemini, Chiang's wife, Lucy's mother. They dare not admit what they planned to do with that information once they had it. But secretly they each held the same candle of thought. Escape. Exile. Floating free down the golden river of song to a better life.

The door opened. The inner entryway door, their official reason to be there, was pocked with bubbles of metal where the asteroids had struck. Chiang Zu steered the auto-trolley through the open hatch and, while he loosened the rivets around the door frame, its robotic arm extended from the trolley base to steady the broken door panel with its claw.

Lucy stepped in after them and got to work. Turning away from the kitchenette, she faced two identical doors. One led to the senior Voyagers' bedroom. The other one led to Jack's, where now he would no doubt be in his Gravity Shower, playing in the Sandbox, along with all their fellow cadets. To think she was only two metres away from his physical self, when all her life she had only ever known him as a digital projection, made her forget for a moment why she was there.

Rather than enter through his parents' door, wherein she expected Michael was most likely to keep any sensitive material, she looked back into the Voyagers' shared living space. The first thing which caught her eye was the bookshelf. The Geminis had one, but it didn't have any books on its shelves. The Voyagers' was crammed solid with them, every inch, but for one small nook in which there was a picture frame. Lucy picked it up and drew it up close to her face. It was a photograph of mother, father and son. Lucy smiled. There you are, she thought to herself, touched and amazed to see her classmate's face for the same time, and to recognise her own mix of Asian and European features. Like her, Jack's parents were Chinese and Anglo, but in the opposite order to hers. She looked deeper, past the obvious, and saw in the eyes which peaked out from behind his long black fringes, something else she recognised - vulnerability, intelligence and grace - and something she had forgotten to feel for a very long time - joy. The source of that joy certainly wasn't his online life. It was the smiling faces either side of him. A sob leaped up into Lucy's throat, where she held it. Jack, she realised, felt loved.

'Lucy,' her father seethed, 'get on with it.'

Lucy passed her fingers over the spines of the books. Most of them were poetry. One shelf was all biographies, and all of those the lives of musicians. Then her eyes fell down to the left upon the two long low rows of records. She kneeled before them, not understanding what she was seeing. She slipped one from its plastic sheath and turned the black vinyl disc in her fingers. She saw the turntable on the shelf above, connected in her mind the hole in the record with the spindle at the centre of the same-sized rubber plate, and united them. At a guess, she lifted the arm to the right of the plate and the record began to turn. She brought her face right down to where her fingers and the needle met with the spinning vinyl, a third of the way in from the edge, in the middle of a song. Music filled the air, a swooning, mournful woman wailing for the moon.

In three steps her father crossed the room, lifted the needle from the record, and pushed Lucy back towards the finished repair. That very second, the door opened and there stood Lieutenant Commander Michael Voyager 1, humming happily to himself, a bottle of carbonated #328 in his hand.

Over Lucy's shoulder, he saw Chiang Zu first.

'Chiang?' said the Net Cop. 'What are you…?'

'Your door, Mike,' said the Maintenance man. 'It's fixed.'

Lucy pulled down her visor and slouched, as she had practiced, into the disaffected air of someone who was bored with life and wanted nothing other than to be back home in front of their video screen.

Michael only glanced at her. He was more interested in the record sleeve and turntable needle in each of his old classmate's hands.

Chiang lowered his eyes. 'Sorry mate,' he said. 'I couldn't resist.'

Michael sighed. 'Don't worry about it. How's your little girl? How's Lucy? I see she's been out of School a bit.'

Lucy was surprised how familiar the two of them were. It made sense that they should know each other, but to seem so intimate.

'Yeah, poor thing can't seem to shake a bug. But she's good, thanks. And Jack?'

'Great!' Michael said a little more loudly than he meant to. 'The little trooper's on Red Vs Blue, right now! I've skipped work to watch it with him. Do you want to…?' He held up the bottle of soft drink.

'No,' Chiang Zu replied, a little quicker than he meant to, 'thanks. House calls to make.' He pointed at the auto-trolley and its load.

'Yeah, right,' Michael said with a grimace, not seeming sure how to respond to his demoted peer's bitter joke. 'Okay, then.'

'Yeah, cheers mate,' said Chiang, putting down the record and needle and moving past Michael to the door.

His superior offered his hand. Chiang Zu took it and for a moment the two men were truly equals. Both fathers. Both with their shares of hope and regret.

'Okay,' said Michael.

'Yup,' said Chiang, and he led the masked and silent Lucy out the door.

All the way home, Lucy wanted to ask her father about what she had just seen. They returned the auto-trolley and its payload to Maintenance, where the metal would be smelted and repurposed for use elsewhere on the ship. Then, when they reached their family cabin and paused before the (now) blood red face of their front door dog, she finally said it, 'Were you and Jack's dad friends?'

Chiang Zu stared at his daughter for a long time. 'He was my best friend, Luce,' he told her. 'And he was the man who arrested me when I broadcast my protest against 'retirement'.'

'He betrayed you?'

'I don't know if he had any choice, but yeah, it was him who came for me. I'd like to think he petitioned on my behalf. There are worse fates than Maintenance.'

Lucy lifted her visor and waited.

Her father sighed and stated grimly, 'Do you think it's only the elderly who go down the drain? They're not the only ones The Fleet no longer finds useful.'

Lucy's mouth fell open.

'Come on,' her father said. 'I'll explain later. Let's just get inside. Your mother will be home soon.'

He pressed his key to the door. The dog's jaws parted, and there, on its tongue, waited Lieutenant Commander Hannah Gemini.

'Welcome home, Luce, *darling*,' she spoke, smiling at them through clenched teeth. 'How was *your* day?'

14. A PIPER AT JACK'S WINDOW

'Thirty-six percent.'

'I know.'

'Thirty-six percent?'

'Yes.'

'Thirty. Six. Percent!'

'Michael, honey, I can read. Jack got thirty-six percent on his latest mathematics test. I agree, it's concerning.'

'Concerning?' Jack's father snorted. 'The build-up of plaque on my teeth is concerning. The shortage of flavour #28 is concerning. A Voyager getting thirty-six on a *maths* test is *catastrophic.*'

Finally, Jack's parents turned to face their son.

'Shall we watch your teacher's message again?' Michael asked with mock eagerness. 'Shall we remind ourselves what great deeds our son has worked to bring the Voyager name to this *peak* of glory?'

'Mike, no,' Xinjuan sighed. 'He understands. Don't you, Jack?'

Jack nodded mutely.

'I'd like to check again,' Michael seethed. 'Let's go the replay, mate.'

This would be the fourth time the message was played. The first was when Jack was still in the shower. The second was when his father pulled him out to 'answer for himself', and now again that his mother was home to see it.

Ms Cruikshank's bespectacled face filled the window screen behind his father, and opened its lips into a version of a smile that looked like she was about to eat him. Jack had not been able to shake the impression, imprinted upon him when he first met this teacher in Year 5, that his teacher's wrinkles resembled whiskers. She had the demeanour of a cat too. She slinked silently about her classroom, cosying up next to students as they worked. And though she never yowled or spat, her words clawed deeply.

For this message, she had taken time to compose her words into sharp little daggers that pinned Jack like a mouse to the floor.

'Mr. and Mrs. Voyager, I like your son,' she began. 'I see great things in him.'

'Really now?' his father marvelled sarcastically.

'The Fleet is always in need of strong backs to help shift the wheels that drive our ships forward.'

Michael paused her there. 'She's talking about *Maintenance*. You realise that, right?'

The message resumed, 'In such a role, he would be free to sing and tap upon the engine parts as he worked. No doubt, he might find other musically inclined colleagues with whom to share his,' she coughed slightly, 'talent.'

'I can't watch anymore,' his father grumbled and the screen went blank.

'Singing, Jack?' his mother asked. 'Tapping out songs? In *Cruikshank's* class? Darling, what were you thinking?'

Jack wondered how best to explain to her that by the time third period came around each day he was exhausted. He practiced Guitar Hero long into the night and woke each day longing for at least another hour of rest. He was able to muddle through his first two classes, in which he had some skill, but when he sat down in Cruikshank's stark white room to find the value of x, all he could see upon his desk was an endless stream of scrolling coloured balls.

'I can do better,' he replied at last.

'What's that, Jack?' his father asked.

'I can do better,' Jack insisted, more firmly. 'I know what I need to do.'

He rose slowly from the couch and went to his room.

'This isn't over, mister,' Michael called after him.

Jack returned to the lounge room, crossed to his mother, placed a small black data drive in her hand and said, 'I'm sorry I disappointed you.'

He went to the kitchen and began his nightly chore of setting the table. Xinjuan held the drive up for her husband to see. At the sight of it, Michael dropped his head. It was labelled 'Guitar Hero'.

Silently, Jack's parents moved together into the kitchen and surrounded their son in an embrace.

'We'll hold onto it for you, mate,' his father's deep voice rumbled gently into Jack's back. His beard tickled Jack's neck. 'Until after the next test, OK?'

Jack nodded and his parents held him closer.

'We're all under so much pressure, dear,' Xinjuan whispered, her forehead resting on her son's shoulder. 'I know it's hard, but it's so much simpler, how things are for you now. Try to enjoy what freedom you have.'

Jack felt her head turn towards the door of their cabin as she said, 'There's so little of it waiting for you out there.'

Later that night, the family was curled up on the couch, a tangle of legs and synthetic popcorn before the window screen. Their favourite show was on, *Stars of Uroun*. Each storyline was edited to suit its audience. Families on the *The Shiva* saw it in Hindi and the setting of the sitcom was an Indian colony of *Uroun* called *New New Delhi*. The version Australians and New Zealanders saw was set in a sleepy seaside town on a beautiful beach in a pristine bay, just like the ones their ancestors used to fish and surf in, before the fish all drowned in acid and ocean waves swept their cities away.

The town was called *Hamelin*.

It was a safe place. A cold and endless void did not press against its walls. The air was warm and rich with oxygen. There was no constant sense of desperate longing for a home no one had seen. Everyone had already arrived and was exactly where they wanted to be. Between the forest and the sea, they had all the room they needed to feel free.

In that night's episode, the two main characters, Bram and his neighbour Monica, had discovered seeds from Earth amongst their parents' belongings and planted one in the yard. The seed sprouted from the alien soil into a monster. Jack and his parents laughed along with the soundtrack audience as Bram's Grandpa Ted whacked away at the hungry plant's grasping tendrils with his broom.

Then something odd happened.

From every corner of the yard, rats started to appear.

Michael and Xinjuan stopped laughing. They watched with great seriousness as the rats gnawed at the giant plant and upon the handle of Ted's wooden broom. They listened intently as the soundtrack of laughter was drowned out by squeaking and the gnashing of tiny teeth.

The camera cut to all the regular scenes in town. The Hamelin Café was infested with rodents. They climbed over the cakes and under the feet of the panicking patrons. They poured out of the desks in the Hamelin Schoolhouse. The Mayor of Hamelin, speechifying in her hall, could not sound her gabble on her mighty desk of *Uroun* oak for all the rats crawling upon it.

'Our town's going to ruin!' she cried. 'If we don't stop this rising tide of cheese-eaters, I'll have no town to rule, the policeman no streets to patrol, and the farmers no grain to feed us. Won't somebody, anybody, save us?'

'I've got your remedy,' came a high and happy voice, and the camera panned from the sweating Mayor of Hamelin's face far off to the entrance of her great hall. Silhouetted in the doorway stood a tall thin figure. His face was in shadow but from his shoulders hung a cloak with stripes of every colour. Rainbow tights hugged his legs snugly. An odd little cap with a feather in its side sat upon his head and on his feet he sported pointed leather boots.

In the stranger's hands he carried a slender wooden pipe.

On either side of their son, Jack's parents stiffened at the sight of this piper.

They turned and searched one another's eyes.

'Stranger,' the mayor called out, 'if you can rid us of this infestation, I will give you whatever you want. Ask *any* price. We will pay it.'

The camera zoomed in on The Piper's smirking lips as he pronounced, 'Very well, your mayorship. In exchange for removing every last unwanted creature from your town, you must promise that on her thirteenth birthday, you give me your first-born child. She shall from that day forth be my apprentice.'

The mayor was flabbergasted. While she contemplated The Piper's offer and counted the rising tide of rats at her feet, Jack's father tried changing channels with the remote. His mother turned to Jack and said, 'Well, that's enough of that nonsense, eh? That show's really gone downhill, don't you think? What else is on, Mike?'

But every station Jack's father tried carried the same broadcast.

The Mayor turned back from consulting with the panicking elders of Hamelin. On her face she wore a grim, determined expression. For the first time Jack noticed how much like The Admiral this actress looked.

'Well?' asked The Piper, his fingers hovering over the seven holes of his slender reed. 'Shall I play and save your town? Or would you prefer to let all of Hamelin's food be eaten, its air grow pestilent and filthy, and its every path and chamber sink under the swelling tide of jostling tooth and claw?'

The mayor smiled thinly and said, 'You have your deal, piper. On her thirteenth birthday, my daughter shall become your apprentice.'

With a smile and a wink to the camera, The Piper raised the reed to his lips and blew.

The sweetest melody Jack had ever heard came flooding into the room. It was the song from his vision, the one he had let thrill down his fingers and into his guitar. But this was not Jack's interpretation of the tune. It was the original and pure stream of pipe song that beckoned and teased and buoyed the listener on its shimmering icy waters.

His father leapt up and banged upon the screen, trying in vain to change the channel or turn it off, anything to stop the sound.

Rats gathered at The Piper's feet and with a flourish he sprang from the Great Hall's steps and led the rising tide of tails down the channel of Main Street. Wherever he passed, from every house, streams of rats emerged, their little whiskered snouts raised up to sniff the delicious melody dancing over their heads.

'Time for bed, I think, Jack,' his mother said in a tone she had not used with him for years. She wiped the popcorn from his lap and not too gently smoothed the hair over his head. 'Pop off and brush your teeth.'

But Jack was transfixed.

The rats were now a flood surging at The Piper's skipping heels. He led them all the way down to the beach and danced a jig as the rats poured over the railings and across the snow-white sand into the water.

'Jack!' his father snapped. 'Do as you're told!'

That broke the trance and Jack stood up from the couch and sidled into the bathroom, watching the last rat tail disappear into the waves. The Piper, satisfied the job was done, ceased blowing and tucked his instrument under his rainbow cloak. Jack quickly brushed his teeth and wished his parents goodnight from the doorway to his room. He knew that if he pretended to be tucked away, he could listen on in secret to the program that refused to be turned off no matter how his parents fussed with the controls.

Over their bickering, he caught the next chapter of the story.

Thirteen years had passed and The Piper had returned to claim his prize. The Mayor stood guard before her house, refusing The Piper entry, forbidding her daughter to leave.

'Why do you refuse to pay my fee?' The Piper asked. 'Did we not agree that I would save the whole town in exchange for one single life?'

'Take gold, take grain, take glory,' pleaded The Mayor. 'But I cannot give you this.'

To the townspeople The Piper asked, 'Do you all stand by your leader in refusing my request?'

'We do,' their voices chorused. 'And we beg that you take something else in its place.'

'So be it,' rejoined the musician with a jolly and sinister laugh. 'If one will not come forth to learn my craft, *all* shall be instructed!'

With that, he began to play. This time the tune was even sweeter. It reached into Jack's heart, took hold of it, and sent shocks of mountain-cold electricity shooting through his veins.

He could barely stop himself from flinging open his door and running at the window screen to be closer to that glorious song.

Breathless, he opened his door just a little wider.

On the window screen, The Piper's playing summoned the children of Hamelin from their homes. Their voices rose to meet the song in a chorus of singing, whistles and laughter. They lifted their arms above their heads and clapped their hands to the rhythm. Their legs spun them up on the tips of their toes and lifted them up from the cobble street.

'Stop thief,' roared The Mayor. 'You shall not take our children!'

The Piper ignored her and all of Hamelin's whirling innocents flocked to him. Yet the Mayor's will was strong and her townsfolk loyal and though they were all gripped with fear for their children, they quickly gained their wits and set to work to break The Piper's enchantment.

From their kitchens they fetched pots and pans and metal spoons and from their shops they purchased gifts of brightly coloured toys and dresses. They banged the kitchenware together and yelled at the tops of their voices to drown out the spellbinding tune. They waved the dolls, games and costumes about to catch their children's eyes. As soon as the sway of The Piper's song faltered, and their kids' prancing feet touched the ground, their parents grabbed them, bore them back into their houses and locked them inside their rooms.

The Piper continued to caper and sound his sweet song down Main Street. Yet one by one, each new player in his band was stolen back by their parents' clever, desperate hands.

All, save for two.

One was a blind girl. Without her sight to distract her, she heard the Piper's call more intensely than all of her peers. She swam upon the stream of music. Her spellbound motions moved her up and down and around the arms of her crying parents. They could not catch her with promises of pretty clothing. She was blind to their glamorous snares.

The other was a boy with one lame foot. He saw the toys bought for him by his parents, and reached for them, but his feet would not obey. He fell in step with the rhythm of the music, and whenever his parents leapt to catch him, his irregular feet sent him the other way.

Led by The Piper, the boy and the girl danced all the way out of town. Their parents received no help. The other parents of Hamelin were too busy keeping shut the doors to the rooms of their own wayward children.

For miles The Piper bopped and bounced and the pair of children did not weary. On into the night they dipped and swung, through the forest and up the side of the mountain, until Hamelin was a small ember of light far below. At long last they reached the end of the path. It led right to the face of a tall dark crag looming high in the mountainside. Above the peak a single star shone and pulsed in time to the music.

The sight of the mountain and its starry crown made Jack shiver. He remembered the vision he had seen on Induction Day, when he and Lucy had stood together on a summit of skulls, one of thousands their fellow cadets tip-toed upon, all trying to reach their own private image of *Uroun*.

However, in the story unfolding on the window screen, The Piper did not lead the two children up to the peak of the mountain. He raised his pipe and sounded one clear note, like a siren in the night. The great cliff split and two mighty doors opened inward. The high stone portal was washed from within by a golden, glittering luminescence. From deep inside the heart of the mountain, a roaring echo promised an ocean's worth of the music that flowed through The Piper's slender reed.

The Piper stepped to the threshold. The light from within cast his face in shadow, but Jack felt his eyes upon him. He gave one last wave, spun upon his pointed shoes and stepped nimbly through the door.

Yet it did not close. Not yet.

The boy looked over his shoulder at the town below and shivered against the cold wind blowing off the mountain. He was so high, so far away from all he knew, he began to weep. The girl heard the boy crying and felt for his hand. He looked at her. She was so strong, so sure, it calmed him.

She gave his hand a squeeze. He squeezed back. They both turned away from the town, took a deep breath and stepped across the threshold.

As soon as they were through, the great stone doors in the mountain closed.

From far below came the sound of the people of Hamelin. The industrious villagers were banging their pots and pans, working their looms to sew new dresses, carving and hammering new toys and games.

On the floor before the window, Jack's parents knelt silently with their heads in their hands. They remained that way while the show's credits rolled and even past the point when the next show came on. They were that way still when Jack closed his door and went to bed.

15. LUCY, MUM AND DAD HAVE A NICE LITTLE CHAT

'I thought I'd surprise you. Thought we could eat dinner together for once. But I see you two made other plans, without me.' Lucy and her father were still too shocked to speak. 'So is this what you've been doing, instead of going to School?' She didn't wait for Lucy to reply. 'Pretty convenient to have an *ex*-doctor for a dad to write your sick notes.'

At this, Chiang stepped forward, his hands palm-out in a plea for calm.

'Hannah…'

'Mum…'

'No,' the woman whispered. It was enough to silence father and daughter at once. 'No more of your lies. Ok? I'm going to speak. I'm going to speak some truths. And *you*,' she pointed at both of them, 'are going to sit down and *listen.*'

Lucy and Chiang Zu sat down at the dinner table. Satisfied that they weren't moving, Hannah sat down too. This was indeed the first time they had all been together for some time. Weeks? wondered Lucy. Months? She looked across the stainless steel tabletop at her parents and could not help thinking of the picture on Jack's shelf - his mother and father smiling either side of him. She imagined for a minute that she was sitting down to dinner with Michael and Xinjuan, happy, secure, on the right side of life. Then she remembered, the right side of life was awful, cruel, horrifying. Her father knew it. Her mother knew it. Surely Jack's parents did too. How did they keep it together? How were they able to keep on loving each other?

'I've come to a decision,' her mother began, clearly struggling to keep control of her rage. 'It's not unheard of. And I think, *for now*, it's best.'

'No,' her fathered intoned.

'What?' Lucy yelped.

Hannah turned away from her husband towards Lucy, 'A separation. Your father will live elsewhere for a while.'

'No!' Lucy wailed.

'There are empty rooms available…'

'And why is that?' Chiang countered.

'YOU KNOW GOD DAMNED WELL WHY!' Hannah snapped and slammed her fists down on the table. 'And now she knows too!'

She was breathing heavily. Lucy and her father waited, in awe of her emotion and the truth she was speaking. The words fell loose from her lips. 'How selfish are you, Chi? You're not content to throw your own life away. You have to risk any chance our little girl has to make a life of her own?'

'She was about to find out herself,' Chiang started. 'She'd run away, Hannah. From you.'

'What?' Hannah growled. 'How dare you, you pathetic little man. I am her *mother*.'

'You're her bully,' he said, and let the word sit there on the table between them. Quietly, he added, 'And the only good thing I can say about that is that you're *all* she's afraid of. She can take anything The Fleet can throw at her. She just can't take you.'

'Lucy? Honey?' Her mother turned to her and grabbed her hand across the table. 'You're not scared of me, are you? Sweetie? I know I'm hard, but I have to be, to help you, to get ready for the world. I wasn't ready. I was only half cooked when I graduated.' She tried to laugh. 'I only wanted to believe in the good things. Honour. Duty. Optimism. I, I didn't want to see, and when I finally did, I...'

'No,' Lucy said.

'What honey?' pined her mother, reaching further across the table to touch her daughter's hair and smooth it down. 'No what?'

'I'm not afraid of you,' Lucy said.

Hannah's hands stilled. Her face froze.

'I look at you,' said Lucy, 'and I feel nothing.'

Except pity, she thought. And shame.

Later, when the Gemini's window screen came on, seemingly of its own accord, and the Pied Piper of Hamelin played, none of them was watching. They each moved as though through a dream. Chiang Zu put together some things into a duffle bag. Lucy made her mother and her a meal. Hannah sat staring across the table at where her daughter had sat with the same blank expression, like something had been turned off inside of her.

As he left, her father turned to Lucy and said, 'Are you sure you want to stay?'

Lucy nodded and said, 'She needs me.'

'And when it's time?'

'I'll be ready,' she said. 'Until then, I'll keep up appearances in School.'

Chiang nodded, turned away, and then turned back and crossed the room to Hannah. He kneeled down beside her and took her hand. On the screen behind them the Piper claimed his payment and The Mayor refused, and the song of beckoning began.

'He's calling all of us, Hannah,' her husband said. 'You know that, don't you?'

She did not reply and Chiang Zu left.

Lucy and her mother ate in silence, their minds turned inward, away from the fable on the screen, chewing away at each word that they had spoken, and all that they had left to say.

DAY 57

16. THE SECRET LANGUAGE

For the next two weeks, Jack did not play.

He studied.

Instead of bursting brightly coloured balls with perfectly executed strums and picks of his guitar's strings, he crunched numbers, factorised, inverted, found the common denominator, all in search of that elusive x. In his proud parents' eyes, Jack was working so hard to prepare for his upcoming test, because it would determine whether he passed or failed Term 1 Mathematics. Yet in Jack's heart he toiled to win back his instrument and answer The Piper's call.

He knew he'd caught a glimpse of something he was not supposed to see. That strange episode of *Stars of Uroun* had revealed some terrible secret to him. The expulsion of the rats from Hamelin, The Mayor's betrayal, The Piper's revenge – all played through his dreams. He barely slept for thinking of the children of Hamelin and the lame boy's fate. Yet he rose early each day to stare at his sums, and worked deep into each night to complete them.

Come the day of the test, Jack was wound so tightly that he felt certain he would snap at the first sight of Cruikshank's feline sneer.

Come the bell for Period Three, Jack had convinced himself he was doomed to a career in Maintenance, where the only music was the constant hammering of the ship's pistons and gears.

He waited for the sight of Fukuyama's sorrowful features to fade into Cruikshank's twisted grin. In his dread, he could already feel the simulated fluorescent lighting of her dismal examination chamber sucking his soul out through his eyes. He waited for the long rows of cold hard metal chairs and tables to materialise.

But none of these things appeared.

Instead, as the final bell faded to silence, Jack and his classmates found themselves adrift amongst a simulation of deep space. There were no ships, just the horizon of stars spread out around them by the arms of The Milky Way.

The children cast worried looks at one another. Tingles of fear crept up their spines. Quiet moments of uncertainty were rare in School. At every moment of every lesson the cadets knew what was expected of them. This was not right. This was not part of the program.

'Oh *god*,' moaned Jenna Pioneer, trying too hard to sound bored and scornful, 'it's a bloody emergency.'

'Another stupid drill,' Max complained.

'Maybe something's wrong,' Lucy whispered. A smile ghosted about her lips. 'Maybe School is broken.'

Lucy had recovered from whatever illness had been causing her absences, but since returning she had not once spoken in class.

Now, at the sound of her voice and its grim pronouncement, her classmates fell silent.

What if she was right?

A distant sound peaked the students' attention. It was faint but definitely there: an eerie, rising-falling tone, like laughter in an empty hall. It faded to nothing and the classmates all looked about, scanning the simulated stars for signs of the strange sound's origin.

Then it was there again, an alien, bird-like warbling, rising up from beneath their floating feet. In unison, they looked down and saw a glint of something metal deep in the starry distance. As the sound grew louder, the shape grew larger, until they could begin to discern its shape.

Jack inhaled sharply. He knew the outline of that radar dish, and those antennae sticking out at all angles. And with that he realised what the music was. That unearthly female voice, trilling up and down a roller coaster of notes, was an aria from Mozart's opera, *The Magic Flute*. He had heard it many times before. It was on a playlist that had been passed down from generation to generation of Voyagers. It was *their* playlist. The original was recorded on a golden record, attached to the side of a fragile craft, no bigger than a washing machine, hurtling alone through interstellar space: *The Voyager 1*.

Launched more than a century before their planet died, *The Voyager 1* deep space probe bore greetings from the leaders of Earth and an open invitation to any intelligent life to come visit. Most importantly to Jack, its antique record disc bore music: folk songs, symphonies, ceremonial chants, even rock n' roll and blues.

But what was it doing in Mrs Cruikshank's Mathematics class?

A disembodied voice began to murmur in Jack's ear.

'Are we alone in the universe?' it wondered aloud.

The other cadets heard it too and stilled to listen to the lilting words, born to them on waves of *Magic Flute*.

'Will anyone out there hear our song?' the spectre continued in tones half-serious, half-mocking. 'And if one day it reaches alien ears… will they dig it?'

The voice of the opera singer climbed higher and higher.

'I believe they will,' said the stranger. 'Vibrations move our hearts, no matter what they're made of.'

The invisible singer reached a note so high and loud and clear, it felt like an angel calling. In that instant, the *Voyager 1* probe shot up through the students' ranks, like an express train thundering through a station, sending the students spinning away in all directions.

For a moment, the universe whirled before Jack's eyes.

The next, he and his classmates were standing shoulder to shoulder in a vast field of golden flowers that waved about their waists. And at the centre of their circle smiled the source of the teasing, musical voice.

The man was tall and thin and dressed in a jet-black suit. His hair was wild and silvery-grey and floated about his face as though it were underwater. The only colour in his avatar was in the bright, swirling rainbow-coloured tie he wore loosely round his unbuttoned collar, and his eyes. They were a piercing green and wrinkled at the edges, as though he were constantly about to sneeze, or laugh, or break into song.

'Hi!' he exclaimed and twirled around so that the arc of his waving right arm rose and set before every child in the circle. 'My name is Mr Pfeif.'

He paused and in the silence beamed at them.

'Where's Ms Cruikshank, Sir?' ventured Evan Apollo.

'Ms Cruikshank,' Pfeif began slowly, and gave a long, deep nod of his head that made his hair wave like seaweed, 'has come down with a virus. *Okayyyy?* So, I'll be teaching you Maths until she's feeling better. *Yeahhhh?*'

Pfeif and his high hair went still and waited as though Evan might challenge this idea. The boy nodded and the lanky teacher's avatar went liquid again. 'Great!' he said and clapped his hands in one loud smack. 'So, what shall we do this afternoon?'

The children were perplexed. No teacher had ever asked them that before. And none of them dared to mention the test that was scheduled that day. Eventually, Breanna Hubble asked timidly, 'Don't you know, sir?'

'Me?' Mr Pfeif chuckled, 'Oh, I tend to just pop up and see what happens.'

'Oh,' Breanna sighed. 'Well, perhaps we should start by wishing you a good afternoon?'

'If you like, young lady,' Pfeif replied, bowing with playful gallantry.

Breanna began to intone the familiar phrase, and the students' voices fell in line. 'Gooood-aaaaaf-terrrrrr-noooooooooon-mis-terrrrrrr-fiiiiiiiiiiiiiiiif,' they droned.

Pfeif's face drained of colour. He shot his hands up over his ears.

'Good lord,' he gasped. 'What a noise!'

He looked about at the students, tapping his nose with his finger. 'It seems we have a lot of work to do.' Running his fingers through the waving silver tendrils of his hair, he exhaled heavily and called, 'Right! I want everyone to take a step back.'

After a moment's hesitation, the students complied.

'Now put your arms out and keep stepping back until you have enough space around you so that you can only just touch the fingertips of the kid either side of you.'

The children gave one another sheepish grins and reached out their hands until their circle in the field was wide enough for their teacher's purpose. Satisfied, Mr Pfeif approached Breanna Hubble and said, 'Breanna?'

'Yes, sir?' she replied, a little frightened.

'Breanna, you are an A.'

'Thank you, sir, but I…' Breanna blushed, 'I haven't done any work yet.'

'No silly,' the teacher chuckled, 'you're the musical note, A. Like this,' and the teacher sang in the same note, 'Baaaa, this-is-an-aaaaaaaa. Can-youuuu-dooo-iiiit-Breeee-aaaaa-naaaaa?'

Very earnestly, Breanna opened her mouth and lifted her voice around until it matched the note her teacher was singing. The teacher stopped his voice to listen.

'Very good,' he said. 'Can you remember that? Excellent. Keep doing it in your head. Try not to get distracted by everyone else. Just keep making that AAAAAAAAh sound in your head. OK?'

Breanna nodded and closed her eyes to listen to the note she had been given. Pfeif stepped to the next student. In this way, he went around the whole circle, assigning Jack's classmates notes of different pitch. Finally, he reached Jack.

'Mr Voyager,' the teacher said with a wry smile. 'Quite an auspicious name.'

'Th-thank you, sir,' Jack stammered.

'Now, what note are you, young man?'

Pfeif bent down and peered deeply into Jack's eyes. Then he closed his eyes and inclined his head, as though he were listening to something playing deep inside of him. After a moment, he nodded and stood up straight.

'Hmmmm,' he intoned. 'You sir, are a G. G sounds like this...'

But Jack had already opened his mouth to form the sound.

The teacher didn't say anything. He simply smiled and turned to face the rest of the class. Once satisfied that all were still and ready, he raised his arms and said, 'OK guys and girls, on the count of three, I want you all to sing your note.'

The eyes of every child were fixed upon his fingers.

'Alright? One, two, three…'

He let his hands fall gracefully and from the assembled group of children rose a complex harmony of sounds that wrapped them all in its vibration, thrilling through their bones, swelling their hearts with wonder at the great beauty their small voices made together.

At the centre of the circle, their teacher raised his arms and began to spin on the spot. He smiled at the children of Hamelin, encouraging them to do the same. Shyly at first, they began to turn. Like the gears of some disused engine, they gradually shifted their feet and arms, gaining momentum, until the whole class was whirling in the sound.

From opposite sides of the circle, Lucy and Jack's eyes locked briefly and Jack's senses focussed on the harmony that she and he alone were making. It was a warm sound, like hands pressed together. He guessed she sensed it too because she smiled faintly and looked away. Yet the smile remained.

As kids ran out of breath, they gulped in fresh lungfuls of air and rejoined the chorus. Some laughed as they did so. Others experimented with higher or lower notes and how that affected the larger sound they were all making.

After a few minutes, Mr Pfeif raised his conductor's hands again, signalling that he was about to end the music. At the lowering of his hands, the children rounded out their notes into silence, and brought their spinning bodies to rest.

All, that is, except Max and Jenna. Arms wide, they kept spinning on the spot like a pair of tops. Their mouths remained open, emitting a tone that did not vary because they did not stop to breathe. Their eyes were still and expressionless. It was clear to all that they had snuck out of class and left these digital dummies in their place. Pfeif gave the students a wink and clicked his fingers. Instantly, the activity Max and Jenna were actually involved in became clear. Their true avatars hovered above the ground, crouched forward with their arms in front of them, manipulating invisible steering wheels.

'Can you believe that creep?' Jenny screeched over the engine noise only she could hear.

'I know, right?!' Max yelled over his own car's roar. 'It's Maths class, not *music*.'

'Quite right,' Mr Pfeif chuckled and the startled truants realised they had been exposed. Their vision returned to the meadow. Their feet returned to the ground and they lowered their heads, waiting for the teacher to rain insults and punishments down upon them. Instead, the man with the floating hair and tie of shifting colours simply nodded his head.

'You've seen right through me, Max,' he said. 'I'm supposed to be training mathematicians, not musicians.'

Max and Jenna kept their heads down. Cheerfully, Pfeif bent his body over so that his eyes were level with theirs and continued in a bright, conversational tone, 'But you know, the two have a lot in common. They're both breeds of magician.'

Max and Jenna looked up. Pfeif's face followed and he leaned in as though sharing a secret, 'They're both about using the hidden relationships between things to transform them. Change a number in an equation, the answer is different. Change one note in a melody, you've got a different song.'

'Yeah, whatever,' Jenna spat under her breath. 'Save us the lecture, Sir. What's our punishment?'

'Punishment?' Mr Pfeif seemed genuinely confused. 'Why would I want to punish you? You two are both clearly geniuses.'

Some of the students sniggered. They assumed that the teacher was being sarcastic. But he persisted, 'Music and maths are just two ways to transform things. You two practice a different, but no less powerful sorcery.'

Max and Jenna stared at him blankly.

'Coding!' their teacher declared. 'You two are programmers, aren't you? Sure, you're a little naughty, but to hack the School interface like you just did takes an extraordinary amount of talent, and guts.'

Max and Jenna shifted uncomfortably on their feet. They were unaccustomed to praise.

'It's pretty simple, really,' Max muttered.

'Really?' Pfeif said, clapping his hands with delight. 'You must show us. Please?'

Max looked at Jenna. She shrugged her shoulders. He stood a little straighter and said, 'You promise I won't get into trouble?'

'Mr Mercury,' the teacher intoned, with a bow and a flourish of his hand that invited Max to come to the centre of the circle, 'the stage is yours.'

Max stepped forward cautiously. He looked around him at the students he had spent most of his adolescent life either teasing or intimidating. They stared back, bemused. They were used to class stopping while teachers told Max off. This was a novel disruption, to see him take over the teaching of the lesson.

He took a deep breath and began.

'Well,' he said, and scooped his arms out through the air before him.

This gesture revealed floating lines of code, illuminated in red and blue. He pointed to the blue lines and said, 'The basic code that our avatars are based on is pretty straightforward.' Then he pointed out the red lines interspersed throughout the blue. 'The trick is getting past the locks, all these firewalls set by School.'

'Shall we get rid of them then?' suggested Mr Pfeif.

Max sighed and replied, 'Sure, but you can't just click your...'

Mr Pfeif clicked his fingers and the red lines of code

disappeared. Max was astonished.

'Proceed, Mr Mercury,' the teacher said cheerfully. 'We have only an hour left in the period.'

'Yes, sir,' Max said and rubbed his hands together.

For the remaining hour Max and Jenna were their instructors. They showed their classmates how to rewrite the code of their avatars so they could appear however they pleased. At first, the children chose merely to morph into the forms of their favourite Earth stars of olden times. The boys puffed themselves up into the great action heroes: Stallone, Schwarzeneggar, 'The Rock' and Van Damme. The girls stretched and pursed themselves into the screen sirens Garbo, Jolie, Beyonce.

'Imitation is the beginning of creativity,' Mr Pfeif agreed. 'Copy what attracts you. Be guided by your passions and tastes.

Then some students turned their avatars into grotesque parodies of their idols. They inflated their heads and stretched their toothy smiles beyond the borders of their faces. They stretched their dancing legs and loped about like weird dream versions of the stars.

'That's it!' their teacher encouraged. 'Make fun of your idols! Test the limits. Find out what's beyond them. That's what's truly you.'

When the students bored of playing with these familiar forms, the 'sorcerers' Max and Jenna opened up for them a secret store of possibilities locked in an old zoological program the children remembered dimly from the earliest years of School. They copied and pasted the various qualities of each animal they desired. Evan Apollo walked about squawking birdsong from the falcon head upon his human shoulders. Others kept their faces, and prowled about on the legs of lions, wolves and bears. The combinations kept shifting into more and more fabulous creatures until it seemed to Jack their class had brought to life all the ancient gods and monsters of mythology. Finally, they transformed themselves entirely into animal form and pounced and loped and soared about the playground Pfeif had made for them.

He stood amongst them without comment. As his pupils wheeled and gambolled about him, Pfeif simply whistled - the contented, knowing, mischievous eye of a storm of singing fur and feather.

Only Lucy did not change herself. She sat off to one side, on her own, and peeled back layers of blue and red code from the air in front of her. Deeper and deeper she dipped her hands into the fabric of the online realm as though digging for a way out.

In the form of a dragonfly, Jack hovered behind her and peered over her shoulder into the tunnel she was making. There was no light at the end of it, only darkness.

She cocked her left ear and leaned in.

Jack held his breath. He knew what she was listening for.

In the shower, he pursed his lips to whistle the piper's tune, but all that emerged from his insect avatar was a feeble buzzing.

Without looking up, she swatted him away.

Jack flew off, cursing his stupidity and swore he wouldn't play to her until he had it down perfect, and on an instrument worthy of the song.

When the final bell of the school day tolled, the students were surprised to find that, for the first time since they were infants, its peal did not quicken their pulse. It was not the sound of freedom because they did not want to escape. They did not want this School day to end. As they all turned back into their usual avatars, Jack saw the same look of disappointment reflected in each of his classmates' eyes.

They had all decided long ago that their teachers were not actual people. They were the teeth of the machine through which they were doomed to pass each day, biting and grinding away any part of them that did not fit the shapes The Fleet required them to take: careers in Medicine, Engineering, Farming, Communications or Maintenance. The jobs they would work until the day they died. Because his mother was a Farmer and his father in Communications, Jack knew that he would eventually be chewed into either of those vocations. He knew full well that these were respected positions, and that he was in competition with his classmates for entry into their ranks. He knew that his every action in class, his every remark, even down to how long he took to answer a question, was monitored, recorded and assessed. Yet this new teacher, this *maths* teacher, was encouraging him to play, to experiment and explore possibilities that *he* chose for *himself*.

So it was with a sense of inescapable dread that Jack and his classmates bid farewell to the mysterious Mr Pfeif. Surely, they thought, the indomitable Prudence Cruikshank would not be ill for two days in a row. Surely tomorrow they would all go back under the teeth of her wheel. But for now, they had enjoyed a taste of liberty. They had learned something of the way the universe was made and glimpsed who they might be beyond the dark enfolding fabric of their uniforms.

17. LUCY'S SURPRISE VISITOR

Lucy did not have time to reflect upon the wonderful and mysterious Mr Pfeif. As soon as she stepped out of the shower, all her thoughts were erased by the delicious aroma of familiar cooking.

That was her first surprise. Since her father had left, her mother had intentionally chosen night shifts, out of sync with Lucy's School schedule, so that she could be home to ensure Lucy was locked in her shower for all three periods of every day. Then, at the final bell, when Lucy emerged from her room, the lieutenant commander would say a curt goodbye, and leave their family cabin.

The second surprise was when her mother greeted her warmly and said, 'Set three places, Luce. Your dad will be here soon.'

She offered no further explanation.

Lucy laid out the plates and cutlery and a few minutes later a knock came at the inner door. Hannah laughed and opened it.

'Ever the gentleman, Chi,' she said and Chiang Zu walked into the room. Seeming wary and self-conscious in his wife's presence, he gave Lucy only a brief hug and sat down. Lucy lowered herself into her seat and looked at him, remembering the last time they had sat down at the table together, and wondering if for him too this felt like a dream.

'How have you been, Hannah?' her husband asked, the verbal equivalent of pinching himself, or pinching her to see if this sudden and unexpected friendliness was real.

'Ha!' his wife replied. 'I will get to how I'm doing in just a minute. First, I need to strain these noodles and get comfortable.

A minute later, she brought the dinner over and placed it with a flourish on the table.

'Cha Kwai Teow,' she announced. 'Still your favourite?'

Father and daughter nodded in unison.

'Great,' Hannah cheered and almost jumped into her seat. 'Well, don't stare at it. Dig in!'

Lucy and her father took turns heaping the spiced noodles onto their plates.

Then Hannah gave herself a helping. Aware of the lieutenant commander smiling expectantly at both of them, father and daughter began to eat. Soon their caution gave way to the pleasure of the meal. They each slurped down the noodles and guzzled water.

'Hungry?' Hannah asked, and they each gave a little laugh. 'That's the way. Have some more,' she said and took their plates to serve them more.

They barely spoke except to groan with pleasure and praise the meal.

Hannah did not touch her food. She simply sat and smiled.

When her daughter and her husband's plates were empty and the serving dish was clean, they all leaned back with a satisfied sigh.

'Thank you, hon,' Chiang Zu said, like it was years ago.

'Thanks, mum,' said Lucy.

Hannah smiled at them so intently, her eyes crinkled up so tightly, she seemed like she would burst. *'Babe,'* she whispered to herself. 'That's nice.'

Silence returned to the table, and with it the dis-ease they had felt when they'd first sat down to eat.

'So,' Hannah started, 'don't you want to know why I'm so happy?'

'Because we're together,' Lucy offered, hopefully.

Her mother reached over and touched her cheek and then closed her eyes, laughing, or was it crying. 'That's right, sweetie. We're together. But for how much longer? Hmm?'

'Hannah…'

'Shut up, Chi!' his wife snapped. 'Just be quiet. Just shut your mouth. You two said quite a bit to me last time. I've been thinking about what you said. Now *I'm* going to tell *you* what I think.'

Lucy wanted to speak. She wanted to apologise. She wanted to say that she'd been thinking too and she regretted what she'd said. She loved her mother as much as ever. She was just sad, and frightened. And she wanted her mother to know that she would try to understand how she felt and why she worked her so hard. But her mouth wouldn't do what she wanted it to. Her lips felt numb. So did her arms. Now her legs. She looked up at her father and he was struggling to get up. His face was wrong, like a ship leaning over into the sea.

'Sit down, darling,' his wife crooned and pulled him back into his seat. 'I want to tell you some good news. There's a way to make everything better. And it's all thanks to The Admiral. Ma'am?'

On the wall-wide window screen, the face of their supreme commander appeared. She gazed down at the Geminis with her one good eye, and seemed to see them all, right down into their hearts, and care for them. For a moment, Lucy felt absolute trust and a deep desire to be told what the Admiral thought was best for her, for her father, for her family.

'Thank you, Lieutenant Commander,' the Admiral cooed at Hannah. 'You're so very brave to come to me, and wise. I was never a mother, and I can only imagine how hard this decision was. But it was the best course of action. Well done.'

Thank you, her subordinate mouthed at the screen.

'Now, Seaman Gemini,' the Admiral addressed Chiang Zu. 'You have been quite the trouble maker. In light of your superb acumen and competence, and your value to your family, we have made many allowances for your disruptive and frankly treasonous behaviour. Too many allowances. You will be placed in protective custody until a court martial can be arranged to decide what appropriate action should be taken against you.'

Chiang Zu didn't answer. Like his daughter, his eyes were alert, but his body was paralysed.

Lucy looked at the half-eaten plates of food before her and her father, and the full plate before her mother. She tried to scream at her, 'How could you!' But her lips would not move.

Now the Admiral turned from her father to her. 'As for you, Lucinda. What strength you have. What courage. Your mother is so, so proud. And so am I. I am confident, that with the right guidance, you will make a formidable commander, perhaps, one day, even Admiral.'

Lucy slunk down in her chair, struggling to raise her head, to say anything to let the Admiral know that she would rather die.

While the Admiral droned on about her potential and her future in The Fleet, her mother rearranged the couch so that it lay length wise, pointed towards the window. She hefted Lucy onto the cushions and propped her head up so that it faced up into the Admiral's eye.

The eye began to expand, filling the screen. Inside of it spun a vortex of red and blue spirals. Lucy felt herself drawn into the centre. A droning sound filled her ears like warm water, drowning every thought.

'That's it, sweetheart,' her mother soothed. 'Soon you'll forget all the terrible things you've seen. Soon you'll forget, the things I've done. You'll only remember the good things. And you'll love me.'

18. MAKING A MONSTER

Jack stood outside his Gravity Shower and felt the small black data drive weigh heavily in his hand.

He shouldn't have it.

He hadn't earned it.

He hadn't even sat Cruikshank's exam, but when Jack got home that night, his parents had been waiting to congratulate him. As soon as Period Three had finished, an alert had appeared in their inboxes, informing them that Jack had achieved a perfect score.

'Darling, it's so amazing!'

'All that hard work, mate. It's paid off.'

'We're so proud of you.'

'Keep this up, and you'll be Admiral!'

'Let's not get too far ahead of ourselves, Mike. But Jack, this does show that you can do anything, be anything, if you simply focus.'

'But that doesn't mean you can't have any fun. Here you go mate.' His father was beaming as he passed his son the Guitar Hero cartridge. 'Go make some noise.'

Jack hadn't argued and his parents had taken his silence for humility and been doubly proud of him for it. Now Jack wondered how soon it would be until the mistake was discovered and his lie revealed.

That is, if it *was* a mistake.

He put the Shower Cap over the crown of his head, slid back the door and stepped into the cubicle. He shut it behind him and in the darkness tried to steady the sound his breath made echoing off the tiles.

Jack leaned his forehead against the wall's warm hum, until the sound of his breath evened out. He knew he was taking a risk. His father was a Net Cop. Any second Jack could be caught out in his lie. But he had to hear his whole band play. He had to hear out loud the music that haunted him. Besides, Jack reasoned, how would Jimi Hendrix or Bob Dylan or Björk, or any of the legends his parents idolised have become who they were without breaking a few rules along the way?

He pulled the Shower Cap down from his crown over his head to cover his face and neck and groped for the dial on the wall that turned on the stream of sonic information. He felt the familiar tingle move from the soles of his feet, up through his legs into his torso and out along his arms. The Gravity Shower filled to its brim with a pool of echoes. Jack felt the currents and eddies of that humming water wrap around and buoy him in an eerie embrace. His head buzzed. His ears filled with a high singing tone. His eyes soaked in the golden light of boot up.

Jack was greeted to the stage by a hostile audience. The program had saved his most recent game so, as he appeared under the spotlight, the stadium-full of aliens booed and yelled at him to 'Get off!' and 'You stink!' Worse than that, the musicians would not even acknowledge him. They picked up their instruments and left the stage.

Jack was prepared for this. Just as Max and Jenna had demonstrated, he motioned his hands through the air in front of him. The program's code appeared in the air before him. After some rummaging, Jack found the subroutines that controlled the audience and switched all the setting preferences to 'Off'. As he did, all the humanoid and nonhumanoid species with whom he had populated his audience —from the wooly Wookies to his classmates and the gangly green Martians — disappeared.

The Magic Theatre went silent. Jack sighed.

He pondered the artificial sky. It was too pretty, shot through with ribbons of coloured stardust. He patched in the live feed from the window of his family's living room and pressed enter. Instantly, the sky above the stadium filled with the actual view of the stars passing Jack's quarters on *The Hamelin*. Suddenly, it felt like the whole arena was his own private spaceship making its way through the heavens towards *Uroun*.

Satisfied with the view, Jack set about his work. He lifted his guitar and carefully sounded out the Piper's melody. This time he did not have to concentrate past howls of complaint. He could listen more closely. He was amazed how such a simple melody could carry so much feeling. It flowed like a mountain stream whose course carried the listener, as well as the player, up and down, down and up, through shadowy hollows and flashes of sunlit air. At times it would quieten to a trickle, and then the next moment burst forth into a molten glacial river. Its source felt so distant in the lofty peaks where it had taken hold of his imagination. And its destination felt to Jack's strumming fingers to be as wide and endless as an ocean horizon.

As he played, Jack lost all track of time, but at some point he began to sense the presence of another instrument: a drum. It stopped and tripped, stopped and tripped, like the irregular rhythm of his heart. He tried tapping the beat out but his punk avatar's sneakers made only a soft squeaking sound upon the stage.

He opened another window and tinkered with a different set of code. In response, from the wings of the stage stepped forth the drummer who moments before had flipped Jack off. Now he held his sticks up eagerly. But Jack didn't need the character to play. He needed its skills and sound. He opened up the drummer's code and copied all the sections he needed. He then opened up his own avatar and copied the drummer's subroutines to the parts of him that controlled his own avatar's feet. Once the patch was complete, Jack tapped the stage a couple of times with the toes of his right sneaker. Tsssst-tssst, a snare drum sounded in reply. Now he stomped his heal and a solid bass drum sound boomed back at him.

For the next hour Jack tried to coordinate playing the melody on his guitar whilst stepping out the drumbeat with his feet. It was like picking a combination lock. At first the sounds tumbled randomly. But once he got the different parts of his body to move as they needed to, making the right sound at just the right time, the next part of the song unlocked.

He heard an organ. Its soulful chords swelled up through the drums and the guitar, binding them, deepening the tones of the song and broadening its flow.

Jack summoned the keyboardist from backstage and performed the same operation on him as he had on the drummer. Yet when he opened his own avatar to paste the code that he had copied, Jack realised he did not know which part of his digital body to assign the controls. It couldn't be his hands, for how could his fingers operate a guitar and a keyboard at the same time?

He looked at his feet. They weren't playing a drum kit, yet they made the right sounds. He looked at his guitar. He looked at his fingers. Then it struck him. Why did he need to hold an instrument at all?

Jack was the player. His *avatar* was the instrument!

Jack whistled and all of the musicians stored in Guitar Hero — trombonists, cellists, flautists and fiddlers, saxophonists, bassists and backing singers — crowded round him on the stage. Jack unpacked them all and helped himself to their music.

Once he had their sounds and skills within his data banks, he tried taking a single step to the right, to see what sound this made. He nearly retched. The smashing crashing cacophony that came was like a half-chewed orchestra spewed from the belly of a tone deaf beast. Every instrument was out of sync and out of key. He had to find a way to make them work together in concert.

He went very still.

He felt the potential for music humming in every inch of his digital body.

He thought of James Brown, whose dance steps were inseparable from his music, whose thrusting, kicking moves worked like a conductor's baton, telling each section of his mighty funk orchestra what he wanted them to play.

There was no escaping it.

A thrill of horror mixed with glee quickened Jack's pulse until the words shivered out of him, 'I have to dance.'

All through the night, Jack twisted and jumped and shimmied and shook his way into his musical skin. From simple steps, involving just his feet or his head or his hands, he built up a repertoire of moves that combined different instruments at the same time. He pointed his right foot and shot out his right arm and a piano cord of G would strike in harmony with the strain of a violin. He threw his head back and struck the air before him with both fists and a crash of horns would ignite the air.

He thought of all the different ways that his classmates had moved while they were animals in Pfeif's zoo. The swooping and flapping and subtle arrangements of feathers in the wings of birds. The swooshing tails and long leaping limbs of predatory cats. The intricate relationship of snakes' undulating scales and muscles. He added these animal qualities to his human avatar.

Wide wings grew from his shoulders. To their feathered spans he shifted the instruments of the string section.

His legs he made able to pounce and tumble his body through the air, to raise the volume and stretch the sounds the rest of him was playing.

His arms he made as twistable and articulate as an anaconda's tail.

He needed all of these qualities. He needed to become more than the boy his parents and his classmates knew him to be. Only a fabulous beast, a monster sprung from his mind, dare take Lucy by the hand and dance with her up The Piper's mountain.

DAY 64

19. LUCY IS HAPPIER THAN SHE'S EVER BEEN!

'Daddy!'

Lucinda's cry spilled out of her dream into the darkness of her room.

She sat up, wiped the tears from her eyes and wondered, where was he? Where was Dad?

Then she remembered. She had dreamt he was walking on a tightrope to the next ship, a black point hundreds of miles away. He was calling back over his shoulder, asking her to follow. But when Lucy stepped out onto the wire, it unravelled, and he fell.

'Dad,' she said again, with the faintest hope that she might summon him back from the dark.

A spear of light moved across the room towards here, growing, broadening as her bedroom door opened wider. When the tip reached her, her mother stepped into the frame. She paused there for a moment, a silent silhouette. Then, Lucy sniffed, and Hannah swept into the room, cooing, 'Oh darling. Oh Lucy. It's alright. It's ok. Did you have a bad dream?'

Lucy nodded into her mother's shoulder, snuggling into the little cushion of soft flesh between her bones and knotted muscles. Her mother's embrace was desperate, and crushed Lucy's neck, but it was also unwavering and so Lucy did not complain.

'Tell me again,' she whimpered. 'Tell me where he went.'

Hannah sighed and nodded. Lucy climbed into her mother's lap.

'Ooooh, my big girl,' her mother groaned happily. 'Alright, now. You remember how important your father was. He was the most respected doctor on *The Hamelin*. Medical officers from throughout The Fleet would ask him to advise them how best to treat their patients.'

'Then, one day,' Lucy prompted.

'One day, there was a fire on board *The Harbinger*. The Americans were in trouble. Hundreds of decks were at risk, thousands of people. The Hamelin went to assist and your father was one of the first to volunteer to cross over on the cables. It was him and three other medical officers, along with a brigade of firemen. They donned their space suits and exited the airlock, hooked onto the strong cables which spanned the one hundred and twenty metres from our ship to theirs.'

'The hull of The Harbinger was glowing red,' Lucy recited. 'They knew they were headed towards great danger. But their American brothers and sisters needed them. And then…And then…'

'Tragedy,' her mother intoned. 'An explosion ripped apart *The Harbinger*'s hull, right at the point to which *The Hamelin*'s cables were anchored. Your father…' Lucy squeezed her mother tighter, '…he could have pulled himself back to safety. But he stayed on the end of that line, to help his mates. He saved one of them. One hand on the cable, he reached the other out, caught him, and pulled him right back from the void. He climbed back up the line to safety. He went for a second man and, he must have been panicking. He grabbed onto your father, knocked your father's grip from the cable. They both fell away.'

Mother and daughter held onto each other. Each was the other's raft on the deep currents rolling through the silent night.

'He was a hero, Lucy,' her mother breathed. 'And he loved you, so much. He would be so proud to see the young woman you have become.'

'Thanks, Mum,' Lucy sighed. 'I love you.'

'I love you too, sweetie!' Hannah did not hide her tears. Lucy let hers slip and they stayed like that together until the bell for First Period rang.

Her mother helped her dry her face and smoothed her hair.

They went into the living area where Hannah prepared breakfast for them both. The ate in comfortable silence at the kitchen table. When their meal was finished, Lucy cleared the plates away and sat back down at the table. Her mother took her hand and they resumed their silence.

The hours allocated to First and Second Periods past.

Mother and daughter breathed, waited.

Lucy had not been to back to School for a week. She'd been sick, her mum had told her, and she'd needed to sleep. That was all

Lucy could remember doing. But she had not rested. Her week of night had been full of dreams. But now, her mum said, she was ready 'To start fresh.' Lucy was sure her mum was right. She trusted her, almost as much as she trusted The Admiral.

When the time for Period Three arrived, Lucy stood and went to her room. Her mother followed. Her last words before Lucy stepped into the shower were, 'Make your father proud, honey.'

Lucy nodded, said, 'I will, Mum. Thanks.' Then she waved and closed the door.

In the dark, she pulled down her menu of avatar settings and checked that she was dressed as her best self. Long blonde hair, just like her mother's. Eyes big, round and blue. And a smile she had borrowed from The Admiral: wry, confident, and full of optimistic purpose.

Emboldened by this mask, Lucy pushed aside her exhaustion and focussed instead upon her mission. After all, she thought with a sigh, it's what her dad, the hero, would do.

20. JACK'S DEBUT

The soldiers trudged along in single file. The deep trenches through which they trod were knee high with a sludge of mud and blood. They gripped their rifles and gritted their teeth, and vowed to one another to make it past the barbed wire and the swarms of bullets, all the way across No Man's Land to the enemy.

All except Jack.

He was bobbing up and down, whistling a tune.

His dance made little waves in the scummy water.

'Cool it, Voyager,' seethed Breanna in his ear. 'You'll give us all away.'

Jack smiled at her and lowered his volume.

'Soldiers, at your ready!' declared Fukuyama down the line of trenches. Standing upon the 'firing step', the teacher's head just above the other troops and just below the top of the trench. He was dressed in the olive-green uniform of a British Captain from World War One. In his left hand, he held the whistle that would signal the soldiers to climb up out of their protective bunkers and onto the battlefield. In his right he held a pistol, to be used on anyone who disobeyed his command.

After what seemed like an eternity of waiting, three sharp trills from Captain Fukuyama's whistle pierced the grey morning air. The students gave a roar and rose up out of the ground.

Instantly, their cheers were greeted by with the staccato rapping of machine gun fire.

Half of Jack's class fell within the first minute. The other half scrambled across the churned and blasted earth. They dashed to the left and the right. They performed forward rolls and came up into crouched position to fire. They practiced all of the battle moves they had learned in their favourite Sandbox games. Some held their guns like street crims from *Gangstar's Paradise*.

But not Jack.

Across the nightmare terrain of No Man's Land, he danced.

A shimmy to the left. A step to the right. A spin on the spot and then strutting onward like he was in music video for a song only he could hear.

Jack wasn't afraid of death.

In fact, he was looking forward to it.

When they died in Fukuyama's simulations, students were instantly transported to the Meditation Room. There the students sat alone in a featureless cell, lit by a solitary candle, and contemplated why their character had died. What cause did they believe in? What regrets might they have had about killing and being killed in the name of that belief?

Most students despised this period of forced reflection. They wanted to get back onto the battlefield so they could practice their martial arts moves. When they died, they did not sit still and contemplate the meaning of their death. They rehearsed the possible defensive actions they could have made to survive.

When they grew bored of that, they simply sulked.

To Jack though, this little room was heaven. He was no warrior and rarely survived for long in Fukuyama's simulations. But he knew how to feel the pain of the fallen. Jack had received excellent marks for the empathy he had felt for King Montezuma the day a Spanish sword pierced his Aztec heart. His tears, Fukuyama told him, had been 'the most genuine in the class: A+.'

But today, as the bullets of a German machine gun ripped through his French uniform, Jack did not look forward to pondering the tragedy of man's inhumanity to man. After his corpse struck the earth, he awoke in the quiet Meditation Room, sat up into cross-legged position, sighed heavily and began collecting his thoughts in preparation for the afternoon's performance.

He tried not to panic, yet dark thoughts kept rising up to abuse him. What had he been thinking? Perform? For Lucy? In front of everyone in his class, including Max Mercury, the kid who had made it his life's mission to humiliate Jack at every opportunity? He was about to commit social suicide.

He and Lucy had not spoken since Induction Day, when they had stood together atop a mountain of skulls and stared in horror at all the light bulb stars dangling over their classmates' heads like toys over so many kittens. In that vision, she had held his hand and looked right into his eyes and called his name. Since then, he had sometimes caught her sneaking a look at him in class. At first glance, her eyes would seem clear and wide, as though she were trying to see through the illusion of Jack's avatar, past the tall, muscular hunk he still thought she would prefer him to be, to the boy within. But as soon as she saw him looking back, her eyes would narrow and she'd look away.

He had not seen her for a few days now. She had fallen ill, Fukuyama said. But she would be back for this afternoon's Mathematics class. 'She is very keen to catch up on what she has missed.'

Jack had nearly laughed at the thought of Lucy looking forward to sitting down under the dark orange cloud that hung over her desk. But he was too excited to think on it more deeply.

Today would be the day.

She would see him now. She must.

He looked at the candle in front of him on the floor of the Meditation Room. He practiced what Fukuyama had taught him. He focused his eyes upon the flickering flame. He did not try to stop the light from moving. Stilling his thoughts calmed and straightened the glowing blade.

With each intake of breath, a thought arose.

With each exhalation, it passed.

Gradually, the flame burned the noise away.

What remained was the weeks of practice, the fabulous beast he had created, and the song burning in its belly.

Before he had another moment to lose his nerve, the bell for Third Period sounded.

Jack hovered in simulated space amongst his classmates, awaiting the approach of the Voyager probe that would signal class had begun. As always, they heard it before they saw it.

Today, it was a blues song, Blind Willie Johnson's haunting 'Dark Was the Night.' His deep voice moaned. His solitary guitar dipped and rose like a wolf call in the dark.

It made Jack glad. Someone else in the night understood. Pfeif had come into his life at the exact time Jack needed him.

Unbeknownst to the parents of *Hamelin*, Ms. Cruikshank's illness continued to ail her and for the past week Mr. Pfeif had kept 'popping up' during Period Three to instruct their children on the mysterious interconnectedness of matter, music and mathematics.

Together, they had toured the history of music - through the great cathedrals and opera houses, the amphitheatres and music halls, the stadium venues and prehistoric caves - all the sacred places where humanity had raised its voice to the heavens to shout, 'HERE WE ARE!'

Not one student in Jack's class questioned this blessed state of affairs. No one dared mention it to their parents. There was a silent agreement that they would not chance losing this great streak of fun they were enjoying. Yet each of them knew that sooner or later the music would end.

Out of deep space, the emergency teacher now whispered in the students' ears, 'OK, guys, who's ready to play?' and transported them to Carnegie Hall.

The temple of music rose up around them. Circles of ornate gold radiated over the polished cherry-tree panels of the stage. Rows of plush red seats rose to the auditorium ceiling. This was Pfeif's favourite classroom, a simulation of the acoustical palace where all Earth's greats had made their names, from the finest classical artists to the legends of rock, soul and funk.

Jack's classmates did not share their teacher's reverence for the venue. They fell about the aisles giving one another their excuses and reasons why they weren't ready and their work would be the worst. Yet each of them secretly hoped Pfeif would like theirs best.

Pfief watched them all from his seat upon the stage. A slight smile curled the edges of his mouth and his eyes. His long frame reclined far back in his chair. The heals of his pointed boots stacked on top of one another on a small desk, and he twiddled absent-mindedly the restless, swirling fabric of the rainbow-coloured tie between his fingers.

In the air behind their emergency teacher, floated words in large glowing type: DUE TODAY: CODE ASSIGNMENT: DESIGN A

CODE AND USE IT TO ENCRYPT AND TRANSMIT A MESSAGE.

Jack slumped into his seat. Behind the handsome façade of his avatar, the doubts he had burned away in the mediation room roared back into his mind, crashing and smashing away at his conficence.

So he didn't notice Max's hack creep into his code.

He didn't know that the worst of his fears was about to come true.

Max was furious with him for being the face of the Blue player who this week had blocked his father Rick Mercury's every shot on goal and more than once caught him out behind the wickets. Jack did not suspect that Max had been planning his revenge, that the changes Jack had been making to his code had left gaps in his father's firewall, and the virus Max had sent was fully loaded.

Jack raised his hand.

'Jack Voyager?' Pfief called.

Max and his coconspirator, Jenna Pioneer, were impatient to feed on their classmate's shame. They shifted onto the edge of their seats in the row behind Jack, like beautiful birds of prey on a high cliff ledge.

Jack walked down the aisle, looking about for Lucy. Where was she?

'What have you got for us today, Jacky-boy?' asked Mr. Pfief as climbed down from the stage and settled his lanky frame into a seat in the front row.

Jack climbed up and moved meekly to centre stage and said, 'Well, um, sir. I've invented an instrument.'

'Really now?' his teacher cooed, and smoothed the rainbow fabric of his tie against his shirt. 'What does it do?'

'Um, well it responds to movement. It's linked in with the Gravity Shower.' He shuffled his feet and looked down. He couldn't communicate all the complex computations and rehearsals that had gone into his creation. 'Ergh...'

'That's alright, sir,' Pfief said and offered, 'Music's not to be *spoken* about. It's to be *experienced*. So, play. Let's *feel* what your instrument does.'

Jack nodded and pressed The Fleet insignia on his chest. A blue halo emerged from the embroidered band of stars until its shimmer surrounded his whole avatar. It was a touch of theatricality he'd borrowed from an old Jackson 5 video his mother loved, *Can You Feel It?*

The stage lights went down and only the faces in the front row were visible, illuminated by Jack's blue shimmer.

Then, from the back of the theatre, golden light flooded from a doorway through which entered an angel in the shape of a girl. Everyone turned to watch her move down the aisle to land amongst them. Her hair was not simply blonde, it was gold, and glowed as though lit from a fire within. Every inch of her shone. Like an impressionist painting, every one felt they saw her their own way, and loved her for it instantly, deeply, secretly. But who was she?

The only person who seemed unmoved was Mr Pfeif, who narrowed his eyes at her and said to everyone's astonishment, 'Ms Gemini, I'm glad to see you're feeling…better.'

'Thank you, Mr Pfeif,' came Lucy's voice from within the angelic features. 'I'm sorry for interrupting, Jack.' And she sat down.

'Thas, that's alright,… Lucy,' Jack stammered.

'Nice upgrade, Luce,' Evan Apollo called out from the darkness.

Lucy's avatar smiled and politely dimmed its natural brilliance to let the stage lights shine brightest.

Jack faltered. He didn't understand. Where had Lucy gone. It was her voice, but not her… soul.

'Go Jangles!' Max called, relishing the tension.

His classmates shushed him. They were savouring a different feeling: curiosity. After all these years, the boy who had not spoken since he'd shouted down the older kids, so long ago in Year Seven, and who never came to the Sandbox to hang out or play, was going to break his awkward silence.

They set their Shower Caps to *RECORD*.

Jack could feel his classmates scrutinising him. It was very different to the simulated attention of his audience in Guitar Hero. It was like there was energy coming off them and into him. It was thrilling as much as it was frightening. But he didn't rush. He took a moment to set himself in his opening position - arms straight by his sides and his head down – and breathed.

'This is a song I once heard in a dream.' He looked at Lucy. 'Now I hear it everywhere. It's called *The Piper at the Gate.*'

He began to tap his left foot in time with the unique rhythm of his heart.

Tum, tum, tum, ta-ta tum tum.

Tum, tum, tum, ta-tutter.

Tum, tum, tum, ta-ta tum tum.

Tum, tum, tum, ta-tutter.

Within a couple of bars, the other students began to tap in time. The beat surprised them but then returned to a familiar pulse. It stirred a memory in them, an echo from deep within, of a stranger's footsteps dancing near.

Then he lifted his right arm.

The motion produced a swell of organ sound that made the children's eyes widen and the breath grip in their chests.

A doorway had opened in their hearts and the stranger stepped through it.

They stomped their feet and clapped their hands and shimmied in their seats.

Jack's nerves relaxed. With his left foot, he kept the beat going, and with his right now described a wide circle on the floor. The move produced the snarling sound of an electric guitar. In harmony with the organ, the guitar deepened and broadened the sound.

This was the stranger's deep bow of introduction.

In their Showers, the hairs stood up on the children's necks. They sensed the arrival of something mighty. The stranger was finally about to speak.

Max Mercury squirmed in the darkness of his Shower. He sensed the power in the music. He was terrified of what the stranger would say. He knew it would call upon the best and most vulnerable part of him, and once he heard it, everything would change. Therefore, what Max did next was as much to avoid hearing any more of Jack's achingly beautiful music, as it was to see Jack suffer.

With a desperate little grin, Max activated the hack.

And so it was, in the moment Jack shared his most secret self - wings sprouting from his shoulders, scales shimmering like jewels along his arms - the very moment he opened his mouth to sing his vision into being; in that moment, the bully's virus *dacked* him.

In an instant, everyone had forgotten the wondrous music pouring from the boy on stage. This was no awesome blues-rock beast who bestrode the cherry-tree boards. Instead, a little boy danced about *naked*, his real face revealed.

He was not six-foot three, with thick black curls, Hollywood features and biceps bursting at the seams of his uniform. He was five-foot two, with dark ruffled hair. The fabric of his fleet-issue onesie clung to knobbly joints, skinny legs and pale, slender arms. And he wasn't white. The fact that he was too ashamed to be seen as he was (though he shared that shame with everybody else) made him ridiculous.

Jack performed another turn before he heard it.

A rush of breath. A swell of whispers. Then a tide of laughter that rose to the ceiling in an uproar of hooting, shrieking catcalls and whistles.

His limbs froze and up into his almond-shaped eyes swept an expression of terror and pain.

He looked past the stage lights into the darkness where Lucy softly glowed.

Her expression had not changed from when she had entered. She was still smiling, completely unaffected by Jacks' humiliation. Jack tore the cap from his head but the pitch black shower cubicle still echoed with his classmates' laughter. He banged upon the door. On stage, his avatar stood there, beating its fists against the air. The cadets' laughter redoubled.

Pfeif clicked his fingers and Jack disappeared from the theatre. Yet even though no one heard it, the hall still rang with the mighty tremor of his song.

21. LUCY REMEMBERS

'Cadet Gemini, report.'

Though Period Three had ended, Lucy was still suspended in the darkness of her Gravity Shower, while her avatar stood in a simulation of The Admrial's quarters. But Lucy could not take in her surroundings. Her mind was confused. A black thunderhead of words and images rolled through her mind. Echoes of The Admiral's voice. Her mother's. The story she'd been told about her father's death.

'Cadet Gemini?' The Admiral's voice firmed from behind her desk. 'Lucinda.'

'If I may, ma'am?' It was Lucy's mother.

She appeared in a pop up box to the right of The Admiral's desk. She was speaking into the window screen of her cabin and it was an added confusion for Lucy to see her lounge room superimposed on the scene of The Admiral's office. 'Lucy,' her mother said gently. 'Honey, can you hear me? You're with The Admiral. She needs to talk to you.'

Suddenly, Lucy's head snapped up to attention, a bright smile on her face, but her eyes were red. 'I'm sorry, Mum, Admiral,' she barked cheerfully, like she was on parade, 'but I can't seem to stop crying. Very sorry!'

In Lucy's mind, Jack's face, his actual face, the one Max's hack had exposed, rose out of the cloud.

Behind his face, appeared her father's.

'That's alright, cadet,' the Admiral purred. 'Are you able to report?'

'Yes, ma'am!' Lucy chirped.

'Excellent, Lucy,' drawled the Admiral. 'We are so anxious to know what has been happening in Mathematics. Ms Cruikshank is very keen to pick up where Mr Pfeif left off, but for the life of us we can't see into his classroom.'

Lucy went quiet for a moment. The clouds in her mind rolled back, and she heard music. It came like a flash of light. Or electricity. The militant energy drained from her smile. Her gaze turned inward and she spoke in a whisper that rose from the memory within.

'There is a theatre,' she said. 'And on the stage is a boy.' She smiled to herself. 'He is frightened, but he is brave, determined to show us…' She faltered.

'Show us what?' asked her mother.

'A secret. A song.' Then Lucy gasped, like she was lifting her head up out of cold water.

'What is it, darling?' Hannah worried, and took a step closer to the screen.

Lucy blinked, looked at her mother, through her, at the widening gap between the clouds in her mind.

'Music!' she breathed. 'You should have heard it, Mum. You'd hear yourself in it. Your pain. Your anger. And deeper, deeper down, in your heart, where you still hope.'

Her mother recoiled like she had been slapped. Then she resumed her professional mask, shifted her attention to the Admiral and asked, 'Is that enough, ma'am?'

'Almost, Lieutenant Commander,' the Admiral replied and rose her impressive physique from behind her desk, prowled around it and stooped it to look into the young cadet's eyes. 'Lucy, you're doing very well. We're all very proud of you. Your father would be very proud of you. Do you remember him, Lucy?'

The clouds closed around her again.

Lucy nodded.

'He died for his fellow crewmen. You know that, don't you?'

'Links in a chain,' Lucy intoned.

'That's right, cadet. And if the chain is broken?'

Lucy lifted her arms before her and took hold of each of her forearms with the opposite hand. 'We heal the breach and carry on.'

'Thank you. You're doing so very well,' said the Supreme Commander of The Fleet. 'Tell me now about Mr Pfeif. What's he like? Did he say or do anything that dear old Ms Cruikshank wouldn't? Anything out of the ordinary?'

'Yes,' said Lucy, seeming to find her cheer again. 'He told us not to laugh at Jack. Because one day he could be the most powerful person in The Fleet. And on that day, he would set everyone free.'

'He said that to the class?' The Admiral seethed.

'Yes, and then he took me aside and he said, "Lucy, please tell the Mayor I said Hi. And remind her that she still owes me an apprentice."'

The Admiral sat back onto the edge of her desk, and turned away, her impressive features now shrunken, grim thoughtful.

Hannah reached out to the screen and asked, 'Is that all he said?'

Lucy smiled the competent, crisp and confident smile she'd copied from her supreme commander.

'That's it, Mum,' she said brightly. 'Geez, I sure am hungry. What's for dinner?'

Her mother looked at her superior with pleading eyes.

The Admiral did not turn back to them to say, 'That will be all, cadet. Thank you, Lieutenant Commander. You are dismissed.'

'Thank you, ma'am,' the Net Cop barked and saluted.

Lucy took her cue, stood to attention and smiling broadly, saluted.

The Admiral's simulated office disappeared, but in the darkness that remained, Lucy's mother was still framed in the same pop up window. After a moment still at attention, Lieutenant Commander Gemini relaxed with a sigh.

'Well done, darling,' she said. 'Now log out and we'll have some dinner. Phew! What a day! You won a lot of points with Fleet Command today, young lady. This is the beginning of big things for you.'

And with that she blinked out of view.

In the dark cell of her gravity shower, Lucy held her smiling salute a moment longer, then screamed.

22. JACK IN THE SANDBOX

'WARNING! WARNING!' blared the ship's computer.

The screen flashed red. The ship dove into a rolling evasive manoeuvre. From craters in the asteroid bearing down on Jack's ship, grinning green space trolls emerged and rained fireballs at his tail.

'WARNING, CADET! WARNING!'

For a moment, Jack remembered the parents of *Hamelin*, banging their pots and pans.

A bomb struck his wing and Jack's craft spun off course. The trolls danced and wagged their hairy tails.

Jack didn't notice. The slow spirals his broken ship described were blissful. He wondered if this free-fall feeling was what the children of Hamelin knew as they danced in the wake of The Piper's song.

A monstrous asteroid loomed up into view. The gang of trolls who populated it dashed back into their holes, their ratty tails slipping out of view like noodles sucked from a fork.

With a terrible crunch, Jack crashed.

DO YOU WANT TO PLAY AGAIN?

He didn't. He wanted to find more of that feeling of flying and falling, but without the alarms and scores against his name.

He logged out of *Jet Racer* and wandered aimlessly along the

Sandbox boulevard.

This was where he had found himself after he left Mr Pfeif's class. He'd wanted to escape the Shower and dash straight under the covers of his bed. But his teacher had apparently thought it would be better to let him loose in Sandbox without anyone else around.

It was so strange to be there on his own. Usually the cafes were overflowing with cadets his age from throughout The Fleet. All along the promenade they'd be showing off their avatar's latest upgrades - flexing imaginary muscles or braiding and teasing impossibly textured hair.

They were competing too, just like in *Jet Racer*, but between markers that were harder to see. In this endless obstacle course, you kept your shields strong and tried to avoid being hit. Shield up over your true self, speak as much as you could and say as little as possible. If you had no clear position, the bombs of your enemies could never find you. All the children were afraid of the same thing. There were so few of them out there in space, they were terrified of being different, rejected, alone. So they hid.

It was within the rules of School and Sandbox to make small alterations to your avatar. Jack's father and his colleagues in Communications were in charge of monitoring extreme enhancements of height, shape, speed and strength. Even in the more fantastical gameworlds, where players were encouraged to construct their own characters, strict guidelines governed what the kids could and could not make their avatars resemble.

It was the children who, though unofficially, had outlawed going 'naked'.

Jack felt a sudden wave of shame roll through him. It washed away all memory of his performance, and the joy he'd felt it bringing his classmates. In its wake, all he could think about was the jagged rocks of their laughter, and the wreck this had made of all his hopes.

Especially Lucy's.

This was the feeling he'd been trying to avoid by playing games. But it wouldn't leave him alone, so he tried to think about how his life might possibly get better, now that everything was ruined.

He thought about dropping out of School and going straight into Maintenance. He thought about asking his dad to stage his death. Then they'd create an entirely new online profile and pass him off as a transfer from another ship.

Mostly, Jack wondered whether, even if he survived School, would the strict limits of self-expression placed on him from above by Fleet Command and by his peers from below, still trap him when he was an adult.

He knew that at that very moment, all around him on the street, older children and adults were chatting and moving about in Sandbox. He could not see them because the year levels were partitioned from one another. Jack knew better than most why these walls were in place. They were designed to prevent bullying incidents, just like the assault

Jack and his classmates experienced when the protective barriers came down all those years ago in Seven. They were also meant to shield younger minds from knowledge of adult things before they were ready. But Jack suddenly felt bored with being so coddled. He wished he could slice the air and step through into adulthood. He was sure that if he could join the older kids he would feel more at home with them than with the fools his age. He might make something beautiful with his appearance.

He might even appear as he was.

A distant roar broke his reverie. The Great Red Dragon was stalking the skies of *Dragon Quest*. Jack scrolled swiftly down the boulevard to the high gates of Quest and stood trembling on the doorstep. Inside waited the most dangerous and challenging of all the game-worlds. There the safety controls were set to minimum. There, in the form of wizards, elves, dwarves, orcs and giants, the children of The Fleet formed little bands or grand alliances and hunted one another for sport.

Yet Jack's every memory of Quest was of being hunted. He had died so many times in there, he had no points, no powers, no spells, no protection, no chance of ever gaining a rank, and least of all, no hope of winning any friends or favour. The Admiral's newsfeed told him daily, 'The alliances you make in Dragon Quest are bonds you make for life.'

This made Jack all the more certain that he'd always be alone.

The aim of the game was simple: kill the Red Dragon. It had been attempted many times but no one had ever succeeded. There had been many plans, some cunning, some suicidal. Once, a group of elves managed to sneak into the Red Dragon's lair. They soon learned that She never sleeps. Another time, years ago, one extremely popular boy had assembled almost all his year level into a proud army of giants and orcs. He had stood at their head, a wise wizard general, and was swallowed up by The Red Dragon's maw within an hour of gameplay.

And what was the fate of all who fell to The Dragon?

Submission.

Those who felt the lick of Her flames were instantly made Her servant. White elves became black. Giants became ogres. Wizards became Summoners of the Dead.

Many didn't mind this. Max and Jenna were particularly proud of their black armour and poison-tipped arrows and they'd sharpened their smooth white elfin teeth into dank green fangs that dripped with spite and venom. They rarely left The Dead Forrest at the foot of The Dragon's Mountain. Beneath those gnarled branches they lay in wait for any new heroes willing to risk it all for glory.

Jack sat down upon the cold stone steps of Quest and pondered. They wouldn't be there now. There was still an hour left of Mathematics. This might be his only chance. It would just be him and The Dragon. His heart froze. What would he face Her as? An elf with default arrow strength? A beginner giant with strength but no speed?

A wizard with no spell but fire - the last thing that could hurt a dragon? With what weapon and by what plan could he deliver a fatal blow to that indomitable serpent?

The game sensed his presence. 'Jack Voyager 1,' growled and hisssed the The Great Red Dragon from just beyond he doorway, 'dare you enter and fasssce me? Will you take up armssss and challenge my infernal power, rissssking all for glory?'

Jack shivered and stepped off the stair onto the street. He sighed and decided he would stop trying to distract himself. Instead, he would log out and go home to the terrible shame, and the unquenchable yearning, raging through his soul.

As he reached up to tap the console in the top right corner of his vision, he noticed he had a message waiting.

It was from Mr. Pfeif.

It read, 'Hey Jack, I thought you might be bored so I've attached a ticket to an old game I think you'll like. It's a place where you can develop your music making skills, somewhere the audience is always full of fans. Enjoy. Mr P.'

Jack tapped the attached link. Across the road from the gates of *Dragon Quest*, between the facades of *Zombieland* and *Gangster's Paradise*, an alleyway appeared. It bore no sign. Between the screams and thumping hip hop, the alleyway was silent.

Jack moved slowly down the narrow brick lane. The sky above grew dark. The sounds of the Sandbox arcades retreated into silence.

He rounded several corners and began to suspect that Mr. Pfief had made a mistake and the link to his 'old game' was no longer live. Just as he was about to turn around, the faint sound of a guitar drifted to him, echoing off the bricks, inviting him deeper into the maze.

Finally, he came to the end of the lane and found a simple, unmarked door. There was no handle so he knocked. A little hatchway opened up to reveal brown eyes framed by a rectangle of maroon skin.

'What do you want?' the American beyond the door demanded.

'I, I don't know,' said Jack.

'Only a fool would come here not knowing what he wants,' the gatekeeper crooned. 'Who sent you?'

'Pfeif. Mr Pfeif,' Jack muttered.

The hatch slid closed. Scrapes and clicks shuddered down the handle side of the door.

Golden light spread across Jack's face.

Music beckoned to him from the depths.

23. OPEN MIC

Beyond the doorway, his Gravity Shower told him, it was hot and smokey. Jack looked through the haze and saw something he'd not seen before in Sandbox, only in the movies his parents watched after they thought he'd gone to sleep.

A nightclub.

Its dark wooden stage was enfolded by high blue velvet curtains. Before that spread a dance floor fringed by small round tables lit by little lamps. Around them sat the strangest people Jack had ever seen. They were every shape and colour never worn in the avatars of School or Sandbox: Africans, Asians, South Americans, bodies without any enhancement except for beautiful suits and dresses.

And Jack knew them all.

At the table nearest to him, Aretha Franklin was talking with John Coltrane. At the next, Taylor Swift was laughing with Nina Simone and PJ Harvey.

It was like Jack had died and gone to music heaven.

Everywhere he looked, his heroes, his guardian angels, held hands or leaned in close to one another in conspiratorial intimacy. And then, the archangel in Jack's private religion, took to the stage. Tassels swung from his sleeves. A broad brimmed purple hat, crowned with a peacock feather, sat at an angle across his brow, revealing only the cheeky smile Jack had stared at on the sleeves of his father's records and pondered the meaning of for years. There, under the spotlight, stood the master guitarist, Jimi Hendrix.

'Are you real?' he asked the man, 'or are you all programmed?'

'Oh, we're real alright,' the man replied, and did not smile. He examined Jack from head to foot. He was right to be suspicious. Jack could be anyone behind the broadened shoulders and lifted cheekbones of his avatar.

But why worry, thought Jack. What did they have to hide? Music wasn't illegal.

'That's Jimi Hendrix,' Jack whispered, pointing at the stage.

The man considered Jack for a moment longer then shrugged, 'He wishes he was. That crazy Russian loves the blues.'

Jack listened more closely to the legends around him. John Coltrane, the saxophonist from North Carolina, was chatting away in a thick Scottish accent. Nearby, from the face of Alabama's godfather of soul, James Brown, emerged the high lilting voice of a Japanese woman.

This wasn't heaven, it was a costume ball.

Then, the man on stage dressed in a Hendrix avatar, somewhere in his Gravity Shower on board the *Star of Russia*, lifted his virtual guitar and began to play the opening bars of *Hey Joe*. Jack held his breath. This was no recording. He wasn't simply playing air guitar. This guy could really play.

'I've got to bring Lucy here,' he breathed.

'What's that?' the man asked him.

'I said I can't wait to bring my friend Lucy here. Of course, she's not really my friend. I haven't ever really even spoken to her, but…'

The doorman picked Jack up by the shoulders. His fingernails dug into Jack like claws. 'Listen, kid. You can*not* tell *anyone* about this place. *Ever.* Do you understand me? None of us are meant to be here. This place isn't even supposed to exist.'

'But, Mr Pfeif…' Jack began.

The man cut him off, 'Who? You don't know him and you don't know me. The real question is, who are *you*?'

'Miles, dear,' an Indian voice called from the face of a Madonna, 'You're on next.'

The man, who a startled Jack now recognised as Miles Davis, smiled at her, nodded and dropped Jack down onto the leather seat of the booth behind him. 'Don't move,' he snarled and crossed the floor to the side of the stage.

The Russian Jimi Hendrix finished his song with a wailing barrage of guitar sound that rained down on the applauding crowd.

'*Spasiba*,' he muttered humbly into the microphone and strutted from the stage.

Miles stepped up into the spotlight. 'Good to see so many old faces here,' he purred into the microphone. 'We may never meet in the flesh, but we're always together in spirit.'

The silhouetted heads at his feet bobbed in solemn agreement.

A golden trumpet materialised in his hand.

'I'm Miles Sinclair, and this is a song I call *Exiles.*'

He pressed the brass to his lips and everyone in the room, including Jack, took the same long breath.

Slowly at first, with delicate kisses, Miles coaxed deep tones from his instrument. They fell like warm honey drops on cold glass. Each touched a different nerve in Jack, as though it were his heart the man was playing, not the trumpet. He felt the sadness of being alone, separated by a deep distance from the people he loved. But that distance was bridged, note by note, with a proud longing that reached out through the darkness.

It called to everyone in the room. To them and from them to whoever they were missing. Friends. Lovers. Family. To Earth, the home they never knew. To *Uroun*, the home they would never see.

The music was inspired by the legendary Miles Davis, but Sinclair wasn't pressing a basic set of buttons to reproduce the sounds of a Miles Davis song. He was blowing and spitting, grinding his lips against a virtual reproduction of an actual trumpet. This was not just karaoke. It was real musicianship.

Jack wished he could share this moment with his father. Was he watching now from his control room in Communications? Was he even aware that this place existed? He pushed the thought aside and let himself be carried away by the trumpeter's wild, sad sorcery.

When Miles finished playing, the room burst into applause. Jack leapt to his feet hollering, 'Yeah! Alright! Thank you!'

Sinclair stepped down from the stage into the arms of the crowd. He had touched them all and they wanted to touch him in return. One man was so moved, he put down his trombone, picked the trumpeter up in his meaty arms and bellowed, 'By Allah, you play better than the angel Gabreel!'

Together, the American trumpeter and the Pakistani trombonist crossed the floor to where Jack sat, agog, unable to utter any of the dozens of compliments and exclamations jostling in his mouth to be said.

As the players sat, Miles introduced his friend, 'Inzimam Riaz.'

Riaz, Sinclair, these were not the names of space missions. Jack wondered where in The Fleet these people were from. The survivors of Earth had all taken names that represented their hope for the future; the names of previous missions undertaken to space. But Jack had already met two people here in The Club who went by the old names. Was it a fashion? Or a dress code? Jack didn't dare ask. Instead he blurted, 'That was amazing! It was like Davis's Kind of Blue, but different, kinda like Coltrane too.'

'You know something of music?' the trombonist asked warily.

'My dad's got all the great jazz artists, on vinyl.'

'Your father has a record player,' Riaz asked, impressed but still cautious. He turned to Miles. 'Must be a very important man.'

'He's in Communications,' Jack enthused and then immediately regretted it.

The men stiffened and looked at one another. Jack was sorry he'd said anything.

'What sector, Jack?' Miles asked.

After a pause, the boy replied. 'Net Surveillance.'

'He's a net cop?' Riaz seethed.

The men looked at each other again, even more alarmed.

'You say Pfeif sent him here?' Riaz demanded from Miles.

'That's what *he* said,' said Miles.

'How do you *know* Pfeif sent him?'

'I don't.'

'What? Damn it, Miles. Is he even a boy?' He pointed at Jack's avatar and boomed, 'He could be anyone behind that disguise!'

The chatter in the nightclub abruptly ceased and all turned to stare at him.

'That's just wonderful,' the Pakistani growled. 'What are we supposed to do now? He's seen everyone, everything. We have to close down, relocate, *again*!'

'Just hang on, Riaz,' Miles soothed. 'We don't know that. I think he's just a kid. You know Pfeif is always looking for new players.'

From the next table, a songstress dressed in the form of Nina Simone called out, 'There's only one way to find out.'

Miles let out a sigh, nodded and turned to Jack. 'You gotta play, kid,' he said with a smile.

Jack sank deeper into his chair. 'What?' he asked.

'You,' Riaz growled and pointed his fat finger at the stage, 'up there. Show us what you've got. You must have some talent, *if* Pfeif really sent you.'

Miles leant down and purred in Jack's ear, 'Come on, Jack. It's Open Mic Night. Everybody plays.'

24. JACK OUT OF STEP AND INTO MYSTERY

Jack mounted the stage. He felt a hundred eyes scanning him from the shadows beyond the dance floor's circle of light. It was just like in Pfeif's simulation of Carnegie Hall, except this time he was standing before a room full of musical maestros. They could do far worse to Jack than *dack* him. They could expose his very soul.

'Ahhhhh,' he mumbled into the mic. 'Hi, I'm Jack. It's sure great being here, hearing you play. Um, I've got an instrument you might not have heard before. I used it to write this song. The words may seem kinda weird.'

He paused and thought about the person they were written for, and wished she could be there to hear them. Then he remembered how her golden mask had laughed as loudly as the others when he'd been exposed.

He put the thought aside, and went on, 'But then, I've been seeing some pretty weird things lately.'

'That's alright, sweetheart,' an English woman called out from the darkness beyond the spotlight. 'We know all about weird in here.'

Jack smiled briefly, took a breath and pressed the emblem over his heart. From his fingertips to his toes, a blue halo enveloped the dark fabric of his uniform.

'Someone get this boy some sequins n' glitter,' a woman muttered up the back and a titter rippled through the audience. '*The Jackson 5 are in town.*'

Jack closed his eyes and steadied his breathing.

He imagined the flame that burned in the little room between life and death.

At its heart, he saw Lucy. Not the awful disguise she had worn. Her true face.

Jack reached his left hand out through the curtain of light to touch her cheek. A golden tone filled the room. He gently stroked the air before him and the tone dipped and rose and dipped. A stillness gripped the room and Jack knew his instrument was casting its spell.

Tum, tum, tum, ta-ta tum tum.

Tum, tum, tum, ta-tutter.

He stamped and scraped his feet and drums beat the song's hypnotic tempo.

Tum, tum, tum, ta-ta tum tum.

Tum, tum, tum, ta-tutter.

He raised his right arm and waves of organ swelled, rising and falling like a universal tide.

The audience sat forward in their seats.

They took each other's hands.

They heard the piper dancing in the tune.

Jack's feet unleashed growling guitars.

His body transformed. Feathers, scales, fur, shivered into being, in the rising, writhing, leaping form of his song.

And finally, he drew a breath that reached deep down into the part of him where the words he'd searched for waited – words born of visions, solitude and longing. Words awoken by the Piper's song. He now gathered them together, lifted them to the brim of his lips, and sang.

I know I'm not the only one
Sailing for that distant sun
Far, far, far across the sea.
But Jack, John, Voyager 1,
Michael and Xinjuan's son,
Is lonely as can be.

Press my face against the glass
Listen to the waves roll past
Deep, down in the heart of me.
Inside, out of sight
Music echoes in the night,
An ancient melody.

It's a song a'calling out to me.

It's a dance only the lost can feel.

Move up through the doorway in the sky.

Blind or lame, we'll make it if we try.

In a vision. In a dream.

I saw you and you saw me.

Where we're headed, I don't know.

Fast as light, our love can grow.

You know you're not the only one

Sailing for that distant sun,

Far, far far across the sea.

I'm Jack, John, Voyager 1,

Michael and Xinjuan's son.

Run away with me.

Jack, John, Voyager 1,

Lonesome child of Hamelin,

Music sets you free.

When Jack finished, he dared not look up. The room was utterly silent, like it was one great lung holding the same breath.

Jack looked down at his hands. They were trembling. His whole body quivered, like land through which an earthquake has just rolled. He felt the last notes of his song shiver along his big cat flanks and out the tips of his wings' long feathers. He stretched them to their full span.

On this cue, the audience erupted into applause. They hollered. They called. They sang his name. He did not know where to look. Their affection and their praise hurt. But it was a pain that made him feel more alive than he had ever felt before.

'Thanks,' he mumbled. 'Thanks very much.'

'More!' They yelled. 'Encore!' But Jack felt overwhelmed and he crossed his arms and the wings disappeared back into the folds of his usual shape: a thirteen-year-old's fantasy of a man.

He looked up to the right at the screen displaying his avatar settings. One by one he erased all the mods which for years he'd tinkered with so obsessively. He deselected the muscular limbs. He deselected the bright white skin. He deselected the thick black curls, and lastly the sharp Hollywood cheekbones. It must have seemed odd to see a person diminish themselves so by degrees, but when he was finished and stood before the room as himself, an awkward little boy with his mother's eyes, not yet grown into his father's lanky limbs, the crowd renewed their applause for a full five minutes more.

It took him over an hour to get out the door. Everywhere he turned, someone wanted to shake his hand or hug him. The forms of Elton

John, Robert Plant and Bono elbowed one another aside to tell Jack how much his song had moved them. Word had spread. Friends of Miles logged into The Club and begged Jack to play again what they had missed. *The Piper's Song. The Psychedelic Sea Shanty. The Song Only the Lost Can Feel.* All wanted to know how his instrument worked. They wanted to know how he'd learned to move that way and what it felt like to make music sing from every inch of his electric body.

'For a second there,' Miles told him, as he led him down the alleyway back towards the main street of Sandbox, 'you looked like something I've never seen before. Some cross between an animal, an angel and a dream. I don't know. And you kept changing. With each note, your avatar kept melting into different forms. Amazing, Jack. Truly amazing.'

'I didn't realise what I looked like,' Jack confessed. 'I was just focusing on the music.'

'That's the way it is when you're inspired,' the trumpeter agreed and Jack realised Miles was no longer talking to him as an adult does to a child, but as one man does to another. Miles took his hand, pulled him in close and told him solemnly, 'Don't ever lose that flow, Jack. You've got it in you. You really feel it, don't you, like it's calling to you, here?'

He put his hand on Jack's heart.

Jack nodded, then said, 'It's also calling to me from…' he looked for the words, 'out there.' He pointed upwards, beyond the simulated world of the Sandbox, and through the metal walls of *The Hamelin*. But to where?

Jack struggled to say more.

Miles turned his face upward to follow the line of Jack's pointing finger and smiled as though he could see what Jack could not. Then he looked back at the boy and said, 'You'll get there, kid. You're ready. But you've got to make your own way.' He sighed and looked around him. 'These ships, man, they're all mazes. It's so easy to get lost. But if you do, come find us.' He laughed. 'Or we'll come find you!'

As Jack pondered what he meant, Miles retreated back down the alley to The Club and he called back over his shoulder, 'See you soon, Jack.'

'I'll come tomorrow,' Jack called.

But the door to The Club had already closed and the alleyway leading to it disappeared, leaving Jack alone on The Boulevard, staring at the loud and brightly lit facades of the games played by his classmates.

Emerging from the shadow that shrouded The Club's secret network, a backlog of messages appeared on Jack's console. Most of them were from his parents, concerned that they'd not been able to contact him.

'Where are you?' his mother wanted to know. 'Class finished an hour ago.'

'Why can't I locate you in Sandbox?' his father asked more

ominously.

What was he going to tell them?

Then one more message popped into view. It was from Lucy. Jack's heart stopped.

'Hey Jack, I just wanted you to know I think your song is incredible. It really moved me. You have no idea how much. I want to hear it all. Max and Jen are such arseholes. Don't stay away from School. Come to History, Period Two. I've got a surprise for you. I think you'll really like it. L x'

X!

If it were on paper, he would have pressed it to his lips.

Maybe the meaning of that little cross had changed recently. It wouldn't have mattered. Lucy had written it to him.

She had seen him.

Because his music, his song, was real.

DAY 65

25. LUCY HEARS THE LIGHT

Lucy remembered everything.

Everything she had been told to forget.

Everything she had been told to believe.

These different realities were layered over one another in her mind's eye, confusing both.

She saw the cinematic action of her father's heroic death while trying to save his fellow crewmen.

This ghosted over the image of her father slumped in a chair, unable to speak, unable to save Lucy from being laid on the couch by her mother's hands, under The Admiral's spellbinding stare.

This too was superimposed with another image: her mother humming happily to herself while she piled pancakes on her daughter's plate.

That was what was actually happening. It was not a memory, imagined or otherwise. It was live. Lucy could tell the difference because she had found a light to guide her through the storm clouds in her mind.

She had heard Jack's song.

It was like the haunting whisper of the mysterious piper's tune, but given flesh, and purpose. It lived and breathed and danced with all the energy of the boy who sang it, for himself, for everyone. Especially,

Lucy felt in her heart, for her.

She'd only heard a part of it, yet that was strong enough to break the hold of The Admiral's spell upon her. Lucy didn't like the old fairytales, in which a prince's kiss awoke the sleeping princess. But this was different. Jack's song had only loosened the knot. It was Lucy who had to untangle herself and get free.

And there was so much to unravel.

Where was her father now? Was he already gone, just another rat down the drain? Lucy tried not to think about the snowflakes she'd watched spiral through the night, each one a rejected person, of no use further use to The Fleet.

As far as Fleet Command were concerned, their subordinates' exile meant certain death.

But then Lucy remembered what her father had shown her next, when he'd removed his helmet and sang golden light, and breathable air, into the cold silence of space. And she knew that there was hope of something beyond.

To find him, she would somehow need to get past her mother. She had betrayed Lucy's father, and now Hannah was working with the Admiral to hypnotise her own daughter, erase her memory, and use her as a spy, little more than a drone dropped in to see what was going on in Mr Pfeif's class.

'Thanks, Mum. That's heaps!' Lucy said, gripping her plate of pancakes with both hands, letting out her pain and fear as pretend joy, like steam through a whistle.

'Oh go on,' her mother cajoled. 'You need your strength. It's another big day for my little winner.'

How long would she keep this up, Lucy wondered. How long *could* she? Had she let the Admiral cloud her mind too? Or did she simply believe her lies because they were less painful than the truth?

'I only wish your father were here.' Hannah put down the pan and rested both hands on the kitchen bench. 'He would have been so proud.'

Lucy waited. She knew what she was expected to do next. Jump up and hug her mother, asking, 'Really, really Mummy, do you think so?' so that Hannah could reassure them both that indeed he would have been so very happy with how Lucy was turning out. But she didn't. She couldn't force herself to play along.

Under the table, her right foot started tapping.

Tum, tum, tum, ta-ta tum tum.

Tum, tum, tum, ta-tutter.

The song had awoken Lucy.

Tum, tum, tum, ta-ta tum tum.

Tum, tum, tum, ta-tutter.

Maybe it could free her mum.

Tum, tum, tum, ta-ta tum tum.

Tum, tum, tum, ta-tutter.

Maybe it wasn't too late.

Tum, tum, tum, ta-ta tum…

'STOP IT!' Hannah screeched.

Silence flexed around them like a fist, squeezing.

Ting!

'Schooltime! Yay!' Lucy cheered.

Her mother turned around from the kitchen sink with swollen eyes and a smile stretched broader than her face.

'That's my girl!' she declared.

Lucy brought her plate up to the sink, put it down and kissed her mother on the cheek. 'Love you, Mum,' she said softly, sadly, because, despite everything she had done, it was still true.

'Give 'em hell, Luce,' said the lieutenant commander feebly as her daughter left the room.

Lucy spent Period One, Physics, floating idly amongst her classmates. No one bothered her. Even Ms Turing seemed intimidated by her newfound glamour. For Lucy still wore her camouflage of blond curls and wide blue eyes. She knew The Admiral's gaze could be on her any moment of the day and she did not want to arouse suspicion, not yet.

Lucy had a gift for Jack. A way to make him feel more at home in School after the horrible humiliation he had suffered the day before. Mr Pfeif had allowed Max and Jenna to teach their class some hacking tricks. For a moment Lucy had started liking them, sensing some vulnerability and eagerness to be kind behind their masks of malice. Now the joke would be on them. She could not forgive the cruelty they had done to Jack.

Within only twenty-four hours, every cadet in The Fleet knew about their prank.

The videos her classmates had taken of Jack's onstage tragedy were shared everywhere. The raw footage showed everything, from Jack's entry to the stage, the opening bars of his song, the slow beginnings of his avatar's transformation, and the *dacking* that cut short the show.

Then the edits began. Most of them looped the moment Jack's avatar enhancements, his simulated biceps and chiselled features, blinked away, and the camera panned down to find him. They zoomed in on his face, at first innocent of the hack, then twisted in horror when he realised what had happened. Some videos slowed that moment right down, tagged with the subtitle 'Dead in 3 seconds' or 'Fail' or 'Hell' and left Jack in an eternal loop of joy and despair, joy and despair, joy and despair.

Then other, kinder edits emerged. A different calibre of mind, or perhaps even the same cadets grown bored of their cruelty, cut out Jack's *dacking* completely and instead focussed on the song and the strange details of the fabulous beast it hinted at. One kid on *The Dauntless* had a theory that the drum beat was a code, concealing a secret message. Another cadet, from *The Shiva*, catalogued all of the animal parts he could see emerging from Jack's human form. This was followed by hundreds of posts of pictures drawn by kids imagining what Jack's final shape might have been - Lucy scrolled through this gallery of angels and monsters, some beautiful and ethereal, others wild and brutal. But she had seen the true form of her friend, his pale skin, his vulnerable, courageous eyes, and that was mightier than any fantasy.

Then, finally, there had been the songs, remixed from the few bars Jack had played. An amateur DJ from the *Star of Russia* sped the tempo up into manic galloping beats. Another, from *The Heavenly Tower*, removed the drums entirely and produced a meditative, moving dirge out of the organ and guitar.

The Piper's song had become Jack's, and now it was everyone's.

And they had only heard the start of it!

Lucy's heart leapt at the thought of what the rest of it might tell her, what it might awaken in her. And where it might lead. It was strange to feel such optimism, while also knowing that her mother, and all the forces of The Fleet, were watching, and working against her.

But finally she had found an ally.

Someone, the only one, who could help her find her father.

She would not let him feel alone anymore.

She would let Jack know that she heard him, she saw him, and she was on his side.

Today she'd make the world pay for silencing her friend.

26. LUCY'S LOVING VENGEANCE

Jack woke with a smile.

He remembered, like it was a dream, his time on stage at The Club. His body subtly twitched under his doona, recalling the moves that made his music.

Then he read again, for the hundredth time, Lucy's message.

He got up and went to his mirror and rehearsed what he would say when he saw her.

Playful: 'Hey Luce!'

Suave: 'Cadet Gemini'

Cool: 'Wassup?'

But it all came out wrong. The old doubts came crowding back in. About his looks. About how weird he felt compared to everybody else, who seemed so comfortable in their bodies and their world.

In reply, the voices of the people who knew him and cared for him, declared,

I think your song is incredible.

Don't ever lose that flow.

Stand strong.

We love you.

Jack smiled at himself in the mirror and made a silent vow that he would never hide again.

A gentle knock at his door was followed by his mother's face, peering in at him.

The night before, Xinjuan and Michael had accepted their son's excuse that he was late home because he'd been mucking about in The Sandbox. That didn't explain why his Net Cop dad couldn't find him, but to see his son so flushed and happy was a relief to Michael, and rather than press him further, he'd simply tussled his boy's hair and said, 'Glad to see you're making an effort to fit in.'

Now Jack's mother moved silently across his bedroom floor towards him. He turned from the mirror to face her. She took his face in her hands and looked deeply into his eyes.

'What's going on in there?' she asked. He wanted to tell her. 'Are you ok?'

That was much easier to answer. He smiled up at his mother and told her, 'I'm really great, Mum.'

That was all she needed to hear. She could see in his eyes that it was true. She smiled back at him and said, 'Well, that makes me very happy, Jack. Your dad and I know how hard you've been working. But, you know, you shouldn't need to work at being popular as well. I can see you're feeling happy, honey. But you look tired.'

And she was right. Suddenly, Jack felt how tired he was, as though her calming, knowing words, had washed clean all the adrenalin from his blood.

'How about this?' she said. 'Get back into bed and have a lie in. We'll set an alarm for Period Two, and if you feel up for it, then you can get back to conquering the world.'

Without another word, Jack let his mother usher him back to bed, and within moments fell asleep.

Two hours later, Jack stepped serene and refreshed into the shower.

He fairly skipped down the torchlit halls of Fukuyama's labyrinth. No monster could frighten him today. He went unarmed and, for the first time ever by his own decision, unmodified, unadorned, *naked*.

Stepping from the maze into his teacher's simulation of a grey cobbled city, he instantly regretted his choice. From almost every eave hung a bright red flag with a white circle that enclosed a black-thorned cross, tilted like a rolling wheel. This was the symbol of evil. The worst of what humanity was capable. It was the Nazi *swastika*.

Jack flinched and took a step back towards the darkness of the maze. A hand caught his in a strong yet tender grip. It was Lucy's blonde and blue-eyed Hollywood upgrade. She stood a foot taller than Jack, who took another step back. He sensed another trick.

Lucy let go of his hand and piece by piece removed her disguise until her eyes, hair, height, complexion were all her own.

And so, for the first time in Jack and Lucy's lives, they faced each other as their true selves.

She took a moment to run her gaze along his true form, fixing it in her mind. Then she smiled, looked right into his eyes and said, 'There you are.'

'There you are,' he agreed and took her hand.

It was like they were back in their shared vision of the mountain. Jack was holding onto her, afraid to fall. Lucy was holding onto him, afraid to let him go. In that moment, a secret understanding passed between them, the knowledge that their destinies were linked.

'Do you see *this*, Jack?' she asked and cocked her head over her shoulder at their class. They had assembled before Fukuyama in a broad square surrounded by Nazi flags and columns of grey-clad soldiers marching in goosestep. Officers, dressed in black, strolled more casually about, like jaguars on the lookout for prey. On their lapels and their black hats glinted silver skulls.

Jack smiled nervously and nodded.

After a moment's silence, he opened his mouth to apologise for being *dacked*, then closed it. He opened it again to tell her about the song and the club, but stopped that thought too. On his third attempt, he asked, 'What's this surprise you promised?'

Lucy gave his hand a squeeze, said, 'It's over here,' and led him down to the others. Each of his classmates' impossibly handsome and muscular avatars stood at least a foot taller than Jack and Lucy's natural forms. As they drew nearer, Jack stopped. They had begun to notice him and nudge each other and nod in his direction. He felt small and the urge to run gripped him.

'Hey,' Lucy whispered, 'don't worry about them. They're either too scared to be themselves or too stupid to know it. Some even admire you.'

Their classmates were all aware of them now. Ben Endeavour laughed at something, stepped over and asked, 'When's your next single dropping, Jangles?' Jack could sense behind the condescending grin of the man-child looming over him some real affection and interest. He smiled and shrugged his shoulders.

Then he heard a deep, fiendish chuckle. The voice was a mod Max Mercury had imported to his School avatar from his dark elf character in Dragon Quest.

'Back for more, Jack?' he hissed.

'He's saved us the trouble,' Jenna chuckled into Jack's ear. 'He's *dacked* himself!'

'Silence!' commanded Mr Fukuyama. He was dressed in a black three-piece suit and a fedora hat. A silver fob watch hung from his breast pocket. She snapped shut its case and began his introductory speech. 'This is Warsaw, Poland, 1940. The army of Nazi Germany has invaded and they have begun hunting down every Jewish citizen to separate them from the rest of the population.' He pointed to a series of streets that had been blocked by high walls made from piles of broken masonry, topped with barbed wire. 'Behind those walls, the

Jews of Warsaw - men, women, children – have been left to starve.'

'But why, sir?' Evan asked. 'Why were the Nazis so cruel?'

'An excellent question, Mr. Apollo,' his teacher replied. 'It is one I hope we will understand better before the period is over. The German leader, Adolph Hitler, told his people they were supermen, superior to everyone else, and promised them a glorious future in which all their dreams would be fulfilled. He told them that the Jews were diseased vermin, rats, the enemy of healthy human beings. And so he offered them a simple yet terrible choice, between dreams and fears. The only way to achieve their destiny,' Fukuyama paused, 'was to get rid of the Jews.'

He looked over the simulation he had prepared for his students. 'But these are just words. You will not understand unless you live it. Today you will take turns being hunter and being prey. If you are a Polish Jew, try to avoid being found or you will be sent to the ghetto. If you are a Gestapo officer, a member of the Nazi police, you will use whatever tactics necessary to track them down. If you are a non-Jewish citizen of Warsaw, you must choose between your sympathy for your Jewish neighbours, colleagues, friends, and your fear of the all-conquering Germans. Begin.'

Fukuyama raised his hand and Jack and Lucy found themselves transported to a dark cellar. Their features and clothing were transformed. They wore heavy woollen coats over flannel pyjamas, as though they had fled from bed in the middle of the night. Through the floorboards above them they heard a metal bell chime, boot-steps and voices.

'Good morning, sir,' said the first man to enter the shop. 'I trust you are having a profitable day.'

It was Max, which meant that Jenna was the other set of boots. The shopkeeper, by whose quiet, even voice Jack guessed was Ben Endeavour 2, shuffled over to greet them. 'Now that there are no Jewish shop owners to compete with, things are easier,' he said. 'But then there are also no Jewish customers to sell to.'

'That sounds like ungratitude to me,' snapped Jenna, and Jack had to stifle the urge to correct her. But Ben could not.

'That's *in*gratitude, officer,' he said.

'You think this is a game?' yelled Jenna, relishing her role. She began toppling piles of cans to the floor. 'You don't appreciate the protection of Germany? Perhaps we should take it away from you? Send you over the wall to join the Jews you seem to miss so dearly, eh?'

'Of course not, sir,' rushed Ben. 'We are all very grateful.'

'Really?' said Jenna, suddenly calm again, as though her rage had been calculated to get this response from the shopkeeper. 'And how will you show your gratitude to us?'

'Is there anything in my shop you would like? On the house, of course. Some cake, perhaps? My wife baked it fresh this morning. Or some polish for your shiny black boots?'

'No,' Jenna purred, stepping slowly to stand before Ben,

directly over Jack and Lucy's heads, 'I think you know what I really want.'

There was a long moment in which Jack could feel Fukuyama's lesson sinking into Ben's heart. Then the trap door above them opened and in popped the black officer's hat and the Germanic features of Max's avatar.

'Why Mr Shopkeeper,' he laughed, 'it appears that you have rats in your cellar.'

On the street, Max and Jenna posed, guns drawn upon their prey, luxuriating in the dark glamour of their black uniforms, silver skull-and-crossbones glistening on their caps and each lapel.

'Enjoying yourselves?' Lucy drawled, feigning boredom.

'Let's just say we wouldn't mind kicking you off the ship for real, freak,' the bully replied and Jenna opened her eyes wide and put her hands to her throat.

It was strange, Jack thought, to hear the young voices of his classmates emerging from the mature features of their 20th Century characters. But any amusement he felt quickly disappeared as Max raised the pistol to Jack's forehead.

'What are you doing, Max?' his partner asked nervously and lowered her hands from her throat.

'Well, Fukuyama wants us to have the full experience. To really know what both sides felt like. Consider this an exercise in empathy.'

Max put his black gloved finger on the trigger. 'Don't worry. It'll only hurt for a second.'

Lucy giggled. The cruel smile slipped on Max's face. 'What?' he barked.

Lucy ignored him. She turned to Jack with a smile, raised her hand and said, '*Surprise!*'

She clicked her fingers and instantly, everywhere in the simulation, the students' avatars were stripped of their enhancements. Their muscles deflated. The stilts collapsed from under their feet. Their high cheek bones and angled eyes fell back down into place. For the first time they faced each other as who they really were behind their masks.

Only the costumes Fukuyama had programmed for the lesson remained. And so, instead of two tall blonde athletic Germans in black uniforms and swastika patches, standing before Jack and Lucy were the real Max Mercury and Jenna Pioneer, in boots as long as their legs and hats that covered their eyes.

Jack could hardly believe what he was seeing. His tormentor from day one of School was a plump little lump. His eyes were shaped just like Jack's. His skin just as pale. But the eyes were mean from being screwed up with so much spite. And his skin was stretched shiny by fat and covered in angry pustules of acne.

Jenna was his opposite. She was so skinny Jack felt sorry for her. Her cheeks were hollow. Her lips thin and cracked. Her eyes were dark smudges of running mascara. Jack thought of her alone in the dark of her Shower, sweating under a double mask of cosmetics and Shower Cap, and all the fear and anger he'd stored for years against her went right out of him.

Lucy looked at her and saw the monster her mother hoped she'd be.

Max and Jenna looked at one another and the hard, sharp looks of nasty delight they had been wearing just a moment before, sagged into puddles of blushing flesh.

'That's not fair!' Max yelped and stamped his foot.

Jenna tried to run away but her frail legs snagged in the tall black boots of her uniform and she toppled to the ground. Lucy offered her a hand.

Just as their fingers touched, a bell tolled in the distance, freezing them in mid-air.

Through the streets of the simulation paced Mr. Fukuyama. Slowly and deliberately, he chimed the little bell whose tone paused the program. As he made his way through the city, the bell stopped children dressed as Nazis, Poles and Jews in their tracks. Their teacher found them in various poses of fear and surprise. Some had cowered or run to keep their natural forms from view. Others embraced, happy to finally meet the friends they had spent years with, studying the same lessons, playing the same games, but never truly seen.

Once they had all heard their teacher's bell, they were

transported to the starting point of the simulation, across the street from the high, wire-topped walls of the Jewish ghetto.

Before he spoke, Fukuyama scanned the ranks of students. When he finally addressed them, he annunciated each word like a stone dropped in cold, still water, 'This. Is. Not. A game.'

He waved his hand and all the students' avatars reverted to their default settings. Their bodies were all set to the same height and build, without the distinctive shape of gender. Their faces all wore the same characterless and neutral emoji, distinguished only by the ID tag floating above their heads.

'You have too much *freedom*,' their teacher continued. 'You do not understand the *responsibility* you bear. You must *learn* from the past. If you do *not*, the monster will sleep inside you, like a stowaway. When we reach *Uroun*, it will awaken and destroy our next world' - he gestured to the Nazi flags and the walls of the ghetto, -'just as it destroyed our last.' Looking directly at Lucy and Jack he said, 'The monster has many names. One of them is Vengeance.'

At the utterance of that word, a deep booming sound came from beyond the ghetto wall. The class and their teacher all looked in that direction and saw graffitied in white paint across the vast façade, letters ten feet high which read, *HE WHO PAYS THE PIPER...* The ground shook again. The children struggled for balance and looked up to find the sentence completed, *...GETS TO CALL THE TUNE.*

A great horn sounded from beyond the wall, shattering the

windows. In their Showers, Jack and Lucy's hands went to their ears. Booming, as of giant footsteps, drew near. Fukuyama glared at Lucy and demanded, 'Is this *your* doing?'

She shook her head, but inside Lucy thrilled at Fukuyama's panic. She knew that, whatever was coming, if it frightened a teacher, it must threaten The Admiral too.

The air split with a sound like thunder. Bricks and masonry burst into the sky before a titanic force emerging from within the Jewish ghetto. The whole class was thrown to the ground by the blast. As the dust cleared, Jack looked for Lucy's glowing ID tag. She was still beside him. He turned to see what had destroyed the barrier the Nazis had erected to imprison what they feared and hated.

It was a giant, five storeys high. It had long thick tubes for legs and arms, simple clogs for feet and fingerless clubs for hands. Its head was half a sphere set flat side down upon the rectangular block of its torso. It had no ears, no nose, no eyes. The great cavern of its mouth let forth a mighty siren that quaked through Jack and Lucy's every nerve.

'It is a golem!' Fukuyama declared, 'the mythical man of clay.'

'Do you know how to stop it?' Jenna demanded.

The teacher's eyes glazed over, scanning internally. 'The simulation is being hacked. Someone outside of School. I have only basic teacher control.'

Lucy saw her chance. 'Let *us* fight it,' she pleaded. 'Give us control of our avatars and we'll stop it.'

Fukuyama stared at her, searching her eyes for the truth of her intentions. He opened his mouth to speak, but faltered. A sound like rain on tin roofs rose into the air, and a tittering, squealing babble. The history teacher's face paled. 'The Rats,' he whispered, 'they have returned.'

Through the gap blasted in the ghetto wall, flowed a river of fur, tooth and claw. It streamed over the twisted metal, splintered wood and crumbled brick and headed down the street towards the children. With another blare of its trumpet, the golem followed. Their teacher's gaze returned to the front of his eyes. He nodded at Lucy and said, 'I will get the children to safety. Go now. You have control.'

'Without any restrictions,' Lucy insisted.

'No restrictions,' their teacher agreed. 'If the person who is doing this is playing by the rules of his own game, you will find a piece of paper in the Golem's mouth. On that is written the holy words that give the monster its power. Remove that and the clay will lose its shape.'

With that, he dashed to gather the frightened students and herded them down the street away from the approaching pack and their supernatural guardian.

Jack and Lucy looked at the golem, the rats, then each other.

'Who keeps doing this to us?' Jack asked her. 'All these nightmares, the mountain of skulls, the rats of Hamelin, this...'

Lucy whistled a snatch of the piper's tune. Then she smiled and took him in her arms. Into his ear she whispered, 'Let go, Jack. Don't be afraid. Let's find out where we're going.'

With that, the girl turned herself into an eagle and took wing into the dust-choked air. Jack watched her fly straight for the golem's mouth.

'Let go,' he thought. 'Find out.'

High above, the monster waved the clumsy masses of its fists. Lucy screeched, unable to fly past its defences.

The rats and the golem came closer. From this distance, their squealing was like the sound of complaint the crowd in Guitar Hero made when you hit the wrong sequence of keys. Jack remembered the rapt faces of the audience in The Club. He thought of how the music took control over their bodies and made their faces open wide in smiles and singing. He thought of The Piper of Hamelin, and the magic he'd worked on his musical reed.

Jack looked up to the right and found his favourite playlist – *Intergalactic Funk Armada*. He punched the triangle next to track twenty-one, Jame's Brown's *Superbad*. Instantly, broadcast across the rooftops of Warsaw, horns cracked their whips over a galloping rhythm, and echoed up and down the cobbled streets of the simulated city. The golem stopped in its tracks. Its massive head stilled.

Lucy saw her chance. She circled about to take another pass at the golem's mouth. As she swooped between the buildings, she passed over the heads of the rats. They sniffed the ancient funk vibrating the walls, rose up onto their hind legs, and began to dance. What had seemed like a menacing horde, now took on the feeling of a carnival. Their tails swished. Their little fists punched the air to the beat.

Up above them, the golem too became caught up in the music. Its massive torso swivelled. Its fist smashed through a clock tower crowned with swastika flags. Lucy swerved to avoid the falling debris.

As the dust cleared, she circled round and saw another giant form, silhouetted in the haze. Then she realised who she was looking at and cawed with eagle laughter. Standing one hundred feet high before the monster was the legendary soul singer, James Brown, in a shimmering white sequin tuxedo, clicking his fingers and thrusting his crotch to the beat. The golem roared and Jack's giant version of the venerable Godfather of Soul sprang into action. He shot his right foot out in front of him and yelped. He spun on the spot and ended with his arms up in the air and a proud yell on his lips. Then he let the rhythm rock through his whole gargantuan body. His hips gyrated. His legs shook and shot in all directions. His arms punched holes and sliced and chopped but not one blow did he land on the monster before him. In reply, the monster did not seem to know what to do but leave its great mouth agog.

This was the opportunity she needed. Lucy's eagle avatar swept down from above and into the monster's mouth.

Then, to Jack's dismay, the golem began to laugh.

The sound was like a horn honking deep inside the golem's

belly. Its whole body jiggled. It held its fingerless hands to its stomach and spun its head around in circles on the axis of its neck. Jack did not know what to do. He danced harder, accidentally knocking over a couple of nearby buildings. The monster laughed harder still and all the rats below joined in, sending up an eerie squeaking chorus at Jack's glittering feet. He didn't care; as long as the golem did not close his jaw and swallow.

Lucy landed on the wet clay floor of the golem's mouth and turned back into a girl. From the back of the low room, the golem's laughter rose up out of a hole, like hot blasts from a furnaces. There she found a wooden chest, inside of which was a rolled up scroll.

In the city's main square, Jack strutted back and forth, trying to keep the golem distracted. His dance sent German tanks tumbling left and right like toys. The golem's whole torso rocked forward and backward with laughter. As its head tilted back, Lucy burst forth from between its lips, the scroll of holy words clutched firmly in her talons. The monster pressed its club hand to its mouth and gasped.

Lucy perched on the roof of a nearby apartment block and transformed back into a girl. She stood and unfurled the scroll before her. As the golem stumbled towards her, she read the parchment in silence. She turned to Jack, confused, and then turned back to face the golem and read aloud, '*Dear fierce Lucy, blinded by tears, it's time to dance to my mountain. Go now! The lame boy will get here in his own time. Fond regards, The Piper.*'

With that, the spell was broken. The gallons of clay from which the golem was made collapsed into a torrent of mud that gushed through the streets. It flowed over the rats and transformed them. It washed away their fur and whiskers and revealed who they were within. Crewmen and women. Grey and grizzled. The exiled elderly. They stared silently up at Lucy.

Jack leapt into the air above the rooftop upon which Lucy stood. As he descended, he shrank back down and landed beside her in his natural size and shape. Struggling for breath and understanding, they looked deeply into one another's eyes.

Lucy was about to speak again, but over Jack's shoulder she saw Fukuyama appear, escorting the rest of their class.

'Well done Lucy,' their teacher began, yet he did not seem pleased. 'Tell me, what were the words written on the golem's scroll?'

She paused for a moment before answering, 'It was a line from the Torah, what Moses said to Pharoh,' and she turned to Jack and said, '*Let my people go.*'

'Oh, Lucy,' Fukuyama said, shaking his long white beard, 'Have you learned nothing? Only the truth will set you free.'

Their teacher opened his palm and the scroll disappeared from Lucy's clenched fist to reappear in his. Silently, he read the message from The Piper. He then tucked the parchment into the fold of his robe, closed his eyes and breathed deeply. The students called this his Buddha face, the one he wore when seeking the serenity and wisdom he needed to deal with either their misbehaviour or their incomprehension. This time he seemed to Jack to be especially in need of guidance. His face was grim. His lips were pressed white. His eyes moved left and right behind his eyelids as though he was reading some complex set of instructions on the screen inside his mind.

The children squirmed within the close vibrating air of their Gravity Showers.

Jack and Lucy looked at each other. The longer Fukuyama remained silent like this, the more trouble they felt The Piper's message had gotten them into. But they were heroes, weren't they? Hadn't they just saved their classmates from The Piper's hack? The children took advantage of their teacher's trance to walk their faceless avatars over to Lucy and Jack to congratulate their saviours.

'Thanks Jack,' Max gushed. 'That thing was going to eat us.'

Jenna, who had always followed Max's lead into cruelty, now followed him into humility. 'Yeah, really, like, thanks,' she told Lucy.

'Next time we're in Dragon Quest,' Max continued, making Jack flinch, 'I've got your back. OK?'

Embarrassed, Jack muttered, 'Yeah, OK. Thanks.'

Jack and Lucy were the only two avatars wearing their own faces in a crowd of children bearing the featureless uniform guises of the School program. Jack knew he should be happy, but he felt more keenly than ever like an outsider, as though these congratulations were bidding him farewell, not welcome. Lucy kept her eyes on her teacher, and waited for the sting in his still, poised tail to strike.

Fukuyama opened his eyes and tolled his little bell. His students turned obediently.

'What have we learned today?' he asked solemnly.

'That Lucy's amazing,' Evan called out.

'And Jack's an awesome dancer,' cried Breanna.

But their teacher was not amused. He closed his eyes again and waited for the students to quiet down. When they had, he opened his eyes again and asked, 'What have we learned today?'

There was a nervous silence. No one wanted to displease him. It was Ben who answered first, 'Fear makes us do things we don't want to.'

Their teacher nodded.

'And love gives us the courage to be good,' added Jack.

Their teacher nodded more deeply.

'And he who pays The Piper, gets to call the tune,' said Lucy.

Fukuyama closed his eyes again and kept them closed for an uncomfortably long time, so long the students began to whisper amongst themselves and look over the edge of the roof at the strange and frightening faces staring up at them from below.

'Children,' their teacher said without opening his eyes, 'prepare yourselves for guided meditation.'

The students arranged themselves cross-legged in three rows of nine atop the Warsaw rooftop. Jack and Lucy sat side by side, closed their eyes and felt for one another's hand. In the distance, they could hear the wartime simulation continue. There were the sounds of people running on cobblestones, of authorities shouting after them and brief bursts of gunfire.

Their teacher's voice sounded close to their ears. 'Empty your mind,' he said. 'Free yourself from the outside and go within.'

Jack felt his shoulders relax in the Shower and the little eddy of resonating atoms that remotely entwined his fingers with Lucy's.

'Concentrate only on the sound of my voice,' Fukuyama continued. 'See what I see. See a swastika, the symbol of the Nazi party. See only the symbol. It is ancient. With its spikes facing right and turning this way, clockwise, the swastika means eternity. This is why the Nazi's took it for their flag. They intended their rule to last a thousand years. But the swastika has a sister. Its spikes point left and its wheel turns counter clockwise. This symbol means change. See it turning to the left. To the left. To the left.'

The eye of Jack's mind sank through the centre of the anticlockwise spinning wheel, deeper into the meditation. His grip on Lucy's hand loosened.

His teacher's voice seemed to be speaking directly into Jack's ear, echoing down into the deepest part of his mind. 'The Nazis ruled for twelve brief years. They survive now only as a memory. We could choose to forget them. We could choose to forget. Choose to forget.

Choose to forget, Jack. Choose to forget. Choose to forget, Jack. Choose to forget.'

Deeper, Fukuyama's voice rumbled down through Jack. Deeper and wider through his mind, like the sounds of the words were fingers gathering all the strings of Jack's thoughts in their grip, and snapping them, one by one.

'Forget, Jack. Forget the message you read today. Forget everything you know about The Piper. Forget the instrument you made for him. Forget the song you play upon it. Forget the girl for whom you play it. Forget. Forget. Forget, Jack. Forget Lucy. Forget.'

Jack let go of Lucy's hand and sank all the way down into the Shower's fathomless pool of echoes.

27. LUCY IN THE SKY

Lucy woke up on the floor of her Shower. The tiles were still warm with Fukuyama's voice. Her shoulders were sore. Her feet were bruised. Her left side ached as though she had fallen from a great height.

Or jumped.

Stranger still, her right hand was clenched, as though it gripped something she could not see. A sword? A torch? Another hand?

She stared at it, trying to remember, trying to call an image from the emptiness in her grip. Her blood throbbed beneath the skin. A deep boom from far away within. The rhythm of a song…

Light split the darkness of the shower. Hands reached in and grabbed her by the arms and pulled her into her room.

'Oh sweetie. Oh my Lucy. I'm so sorry.'

Lucy's eyes adjusted to the light and she looked up into her mother's harrowed features. 'Mum?' she asked. 'What's going on?'

'We haven't got long, Lucy. You have to get changed. Here,' her mother thrust a Maintenance uniform into her lap and began to fit a helmet over her head. 'Lucy, hurry; they're coming!'

Her fingers, like talons, dug anxiously, impatiently into Lucy's flesh, stuffing her into the uniform, and Lucy remembered. The morning drills. The sparring. The bruising lectures about all the evils waiting outside their cabin, when all she knew of pain and malice lived within.

'Stop,' she told her mother and took her by the wrists. Lieutenant Commander Gemini squirmed in her daughter's grip. Lucy shook her again, 'Stop!"

Hannah's eyes pleaded with her daughter's not to ask her who was coming and why.

'It's all my fault,' she whispered, trembling. 'I tried to fix things. I tried to get you the best start in life. But I've only made it worse.'

Lucy looked around. 'Where's Dad?" she demanded.

The outer door sighed and Lucy leapt to her feet. 'Dad!' she called.

Hannah tried to catch her, crying 'No!'

But where was there to go? Back into the Shower?

The inner door parted before Lucy's beaming, expectant face. She blinked. Who was this man? She knew his face. His red beard and bright blue eyes. She had seen him before, in a picture, in a frame, on a bookshelf in someone else's life. He had been smiling there. He was not smiling now.

'Lieutenant Commander Gemini,' he addressed Lucy's mother over her shoulder, 'I am here...'

'I know why you're here, Mike,' Hannah muttered. 'She sent you.'

'You know why,' Jack's dad stated. His eyes flicked from her to Lucy and back again.

Jack's dad!

Jack Voyager!

'You're Jack's father,' Lucy whispered.

The Net Cop stared into her eyes, softened for a moment, and from behind the military glare her friend's features appeared.

'You poor kid,' he sighed, and from behind him in the corridor, two ensigns appeared and each took Lucy by an arm. She was so shocked, she didn't begin to struggle until they were in the corridor. She flailed from side to side. Jumped up and down and tried to pull them with her to the floor. But their hands were so well practiced, she could not slip their grip. They evaded her kicks and did not lose stride, carrying her and marching her in step past their fellow crewmen, who ducked their eyes, pretended not to see, or muttered curses under their breath, like 'Murderers.' 'Jackboots.' 'Fascists.'

Her mother trailed behind, pleading with Lieutenant Commander Voyager, 'She can be good! She can be trained! It's an *advantage* that she knows, that she's used to it *early*. She can be one of *us*. A Net Cop. Undercover. She could help us.'

Michael stopped. 'Enough, Hannah!' he barked. 'Do you think I'd risk letting her get Jack into *more* trouble? Do you think I would let *anything* threaten my boy?'

Lucy did not hear her mother's reply. Her escort had turned a corner, plunging them down, left, down, left, deeper into the bowels of the ship. Her thoughts spiralled down with her. She tried to trace her way out of the whirlpool of memories turning within her. She had been with Jack, on a rooftop. In a simulation. A time in the past when people had to choose between saving themselves and helping others. What was the lesson? That there was no real choice? No. There must be. There must be a way. But she did not know it yet. She hand't yet got to the end of the song.

The music bloomed in her mind. It sent tendrils of melody throughout her body, smoothing the panic out of her limbs, harmonising her senses. She stopped struggling against her captors, whose hands were trained to meet force with greater force. She let herself fall, slipped like water between their fingers to the floor. They leapt at her and landed on each other in the space where she had been. Yet she went the way they had been taking her. She fled towards her fate. Away from her mother. Away from her home. Away from School and Sandbox.

Soon, there was only one doorway left before her. Someone had scrawled on it in red paint, 'THE DRAIN'. She punched the lockpad. The door panel slid to the right with the grinding hiss of metal on metal.

All was dark within. She felt her way forward, slowly, trusting her fingers and her toes to guide her. To either side of her she the rhythmic bite of cold metal grills. A cage. A sieve. A shredder.

And then there was nothing. Only space around her. She took another step into the black and nudged something soft yet firm with her toe. It groaned. She knelt down next to the body and felt along what seemed to be a leg, up the torso to the shoulders.

'Hey,' she whispered. 'Who are you? Do you know Chiang Zu Gemini? Have you seen him?'

'Lucy?' the body croaked in reply.

'Dad,' Lucy breathed and lifted her father's head onto her lap. She stroked his face. 'What have they done to you?'

The man moaned. 'Nothing I didn't deserve, for getting you into this. Your mother was right. I should never have told you. Should never have shown you.'

'I would have found out eventually,' she assured him.

'You would've been older. You'd have had a path, Medicine, Comms. You could have made a choice.'

'I've made my choice. I don't want what they're offering. I want to go with you.'

'And just where do you think you're going, young Gemini?' The Admiral's voice drawled in the shadows.

'To The Piper!' she declared. 'He's calling us.'

'Do you think that makes you special?' The Fleet Commander asked. 'Isn't he calling everyone?'

'Yes,' Chiang Zu said, struggling to his feet, 'but how many hear him? And how many answer?'

The Admiral sighed. The sound echoed around them, like they stood within her mouth.

'Thankfully,' she said, 'for all our sakes, only a very rare breed do. If your kind were more common, The Fleet would fail. We would drift, *singing*, into oblivion.'

'You don't know that,' growled Chiang Zu. 'There is *something* out there. There is *someone* out there.'

'Someone willing to put all our lives at risk,' The Admiral seethed. 'Someone like *you*.'

Lucy's father hung his head. 'Perhaps, but not like my daughter.'

'No? You were so willing to recruit her before.'

'She is too young!' His words rang in the metal mesh.

'I'm afraid it is too late. She is older than you think. Certainly older than her peers. Her friend, Jack, he can still be saved. He can still be of use to his fellow man. This selfish, damaged little woman knows only how to disrupt, to disturb, and only for the sake of chaos.'

Behind father and daughter, the outline of a coffin, drawn in red light, appeared in the darkness. The shape of it emerged into the room. The light turned green and the chamber opened.

'NO!' her father roared.

Lucy took his hand. 'It's alright, Dad,' she whispered. 'It's what

I want.'

She could now make out his face in the green glow. There were cuts and bruises on his temple. His cheeks were gaunt and stubbled. 'Whatever it is, it must be better than here,' she told him.

He opened his mouth to speak.

'Save your breath,' Lucy said and led him through the doorway into the airlock. 'We're going to need it.'

The inner doors closed behind them. Father and daughter began to sing. A lullaby. From a simpler time. When love was all they breathed. When the outer doors began to open, the night flooded in and encircled them. But when it met their upraised voices, it did not drown them. It glowed like a golden tide, and swept them out to sea.

DAY 177

28. VOODOO CHILD

When at first you wake, and your eyes open, there is a moment before you remember who you are. There is only the still warmth around you, and the weight of your head, your legs, your hands, and your torso, on the bed.

Each morning, Jack would savour this silent stillness. It was his one brief portion of solitude, before the day-long dash of classes and homework sessions began.

Voices would creep up into his head, calling him 'student' and 'son' and 'loser' and names far worse, but he knew how to keep them at bay.

He would hum. That gentle vibration would purr from his lips along his flesh like a second skin. Inside of that he was safe. Inside he was a private ocean, dark and immeasurable. None of the names could reach him. None of them could put a hook through him and yank him out into the light.

Only the savage buzz of the School alarm could interrupt his wordless song. Like depth chargers dropped from a battleship above, each blast of sound would detonate in his head and drive him, explosion by explosion, up to the surface.

On this morning though, the first bomb had not yet detonated, and in the early darkness Jack swam alone and free. His limbs were abuzz with the thrum and grumble his breath made from his throat into his belly. He rolled this sound around in him, like a whale singing in the deep, like *The Hamelin* rumbling through the long starry night towards *Uroun*.

'Rrrrrrrrrrrrrrlllllllllllllllllllllllloooooooooooooo…..,' he murmured, and imagined their ship being drawn through space towards *Uroun*'s distant gravity.

'Oooooooooooossssssssssssssssssssss…'

It was bliss to surge across the intergalactic sea.

'Lllllllllllllllllllllllllloooooooooooooooooooooosssssssssssssssssssssssseeee eeeeeeeeeeeee!'

Jack opened his eyes, sat straight up in bed and opened his mouth to cry the word that had been forming inside of him.

What was it? A name? Yes, it felt like some*one*, not some*thing*.

But who?

In the silence that followed, he listened for the name to come again.

But it was gone.

The dream had moved through him and departed, taking the word with it.

Jack looked at the time. 06:47. He still had a little time before the maths exam.

The maths exam!

A predatory, feline face loomed up into Jack's mind.

Jack pushed the image away with a long exhale of breath, and pulled his doona around him. He emerged from his bedroom like an emperor in ill-fitting gowns and shuffled across the lounge room floor. When he reached the shelf where the ancient record player sat under its hood of unbreakable glass, he plonked down onto the floor so that his eyes were level with the long shelf beneath. Along this metal plank his father's precious collection of vinyl records was arranged. Their coloured cardboard spines sheathed in plastic were tilted slightly so he read their titles more up and down than left to right.

Jack had heard these albums played so many times, he knew them all by heart. As his eyes traced along their spines, their guitars and keyboards and drums and voices leapt out at him like he was moving along a corridor and briefly opening doors into rooms where each band was playing. But in none could he hear the name.

He traced back down the rainbow until he got to his favourite record, *Electric Ladyland* by Jimi Hendrix. He let the vinyl slip from its sleeve, carefully positioned the hole at the centre of the black disk over the record player spindle and brought the arm with its needle down onto the third ring in from the record's edge. After a brief crackle from the speakers, the first notes of the immortal bluesman's guitar, sounding like a cross between a lion's growl and a bird's warble, filled the air of the Voyager 1's tiny cabin. As Jimi's voice rose through the groove, Jack turned the volume knob right up to the little mark his father had drawn, two thirds up the dial at 8 o'clock.

With the snap of a snare, drums joined in the rhythm.

Jack turned around inside the sound. This music did what the Gravity Shower only pretended to do. It lifted him up on waves of harmony and transported him where he needed to be, not some prefabricated fantasy, but his own inner world of feeling.

The sensation that had risen up in him just before waking seemed to drift towards him once more. It flirted in and out between the snarls and wails of Hendrix's voodoo blues.

He turned the volume past his father's mark all the way to 12.

Hendrix hollered and his guitar declared all of Jack's secret yearning.

Jack knew why the mark was there on the stereo. Their cell was wedged between four others – one to each side and one above and below. Life onboard was all about taking the comfort of others into consideration.

So: no loud noise.

So: no child was allowed to leave its rooms until graduation.

So: Jack would need to keep quiet and do his sums for another three years.

But the word was so close, he could feel it on his lips. The word that was the name of someone, someone who might tell him, might show him, what…?

'Argh!' he screamed, yanked the knob and sent the volume right past midnight. He threw his arms wide and hollered up at the ceiling. His whole body was an instrument in search of the music it was made to play.

He growled around Hendrix's solo, ducking and weaving through it, trying different sounds on his lips, looking for the right combination. He turned words around in his body, twisting them wildly this way and that, up and down scales, dancing them around the maestro's wailing guitar, until the clamouring bells of the School alarm finally drowned out Jack and Jimi's duet.

But this did not end his dance.

He did not drag his feet.

He strutted towards the shower in time to the music still rolling through his head. He pulled the Shower Cap down like a tango dancer would his fedora hat. He drew the door shut and turned the Shower dial like these were steps in a choreographed routine.

Jack didn't know what he was looking for, but he liked being on the hunt.

Jack emerged in the First Period examination room in his usual guise. His default settings kicked in as soon as he logged on: thick, blonde curls, muscular arms and legs bulging to the permitted limit and eyes as round and as blue as an ancient movie star's. Yet he did not wear his usual attitude of fear, the downcast expression and slumped shoulders that cancelled out his best efforts to impress the other supermodels in his class that he was just like them. Instead, there was a smirk on his lips and a swagger in his walk that his classmates could not remember seeing there before.

It didn't take them long to remind him that he was a sad and awkward boy whom no one liked.

As he moved down the illuminated aisles of the virtual examination room, past desk after desk of students of every nationality in The Fleet now aged 15.56 years, each of them tried to distract themselves from their anxieties about the mathematics exam by dumping an insult in his inbox. They appeared in the top left of Jack's vision, some conveniently auto-translated from Russian, Chinese and Hindi.

'What are you so happy about?'

'You look like a chicken, walking like that.'

'A male chicken's a cock.'

'Pretty cocky, aren't ya, cock?'

And then the memes began. Image after image snapped of him moving down the aisle of the examination room, altered to exaggerate his features into a rooster's and captioned with slogans all riffing on the same theme: 'LITTLEST COCK IN THE GALAXY!'

By the time Jack got to his seat, he was no longer strutting. He was walking heal to toe with entirely straight legs and arms. He had tucked his smile away and stuffed all the music he felt back down into his guts along with any more thought of the magic word from his dream.

He didn't know why he couldn't just emerge in School at his

desk, but he imagined his teachers programmed the interface like this in order to shame latecomers and encourage prompt attendance. All it really succeeded in doing was add an extra layer of dread to the thought of coming to School at all.

In Jack's opinion, that did not help The Admiral's new initiative. It only made it harder. Recently, though he could not quite remember when, their commander had ordered that the School day be extended from nine hours to twelve. Between 0700 hours and 1900 hours, the cadets laboured to learn all they could in readiness for service to The Fleet. What was worse about this for most students, was that this meant Sandbox privileges had become extremely limited. The one consolation was that after twelve hours of classes, most students were too tired to enjoy their free time, and instead opted to get to bed early. Only the most motivated students, like Jack Voyager 1, used the final hours before sleep claimed them, to revise the work they'd done that day and prepare themselves for tomorrow.

Jack wondered if The Admiral and her squads of teachers understood how tired and stressed their cadets felt. They claimed they wanted to help their students achieve greatness. They claimed that

Jack's generation knew more than any other in human history. They assured them that, if only they pushed themselves to their limits, any one of them could be the one to crack the puzzle of light-speed travel. Any day now they could bridge the distance to *Uroun*. Then they would be free of their prison cells and play in *Uroun's* forests and fields.

Like The Admiral, the teachers loved to make big promises and rousing declarations of encouragement. But they never once asked the students what they thought about any of this.

Or how close they felt to falling over the edges of their limits.

These thoughts were interrupted by the voice of his jailer, Ms. Cruikshank. In her deep, feline purr she announced, 'You may now commence the mid-year mathematics exam. Do not panic. We expect only your best.'

Jack was ready for the test. It was all he could remember thinking about for the past year. He'd promised his parents that this semester he would find out just how well he could do, and he was proud of all the extra hours he'd put into his studies. He was confident that he had mastered everything Ms. Cruikshank had taught them.

But for all his accomplishments, Jack could not avoid the fact that her equations, and the state of mind they put him, made Jack feel awful.

To untangle Cruikshank's numerical riddles, Jack had to be able to think along various tracks at the same time, crunching multiple lines of numbers until all the remainders cancelled out. In that state, Jack felt very removed from himself. All sense of his body fell away. All memory of his past too. All he was left with was the space between the numbers and a dull aching in his heart.

He imagined it was how a computer felt, if it could feel.

Thus, the next three and a half hours disappeared in a rush of calculation. When it was done, Jack felt dazed.

Yet compared to the brutal teasing he had suffered upon his entrance to the examination room, it was a relief to emerge into an atmosphere of calm.

Looking around him at the hundreds of rows of desks, he could recognise the same blank yet contented expression on the faces of students who, like him, had solved all the problems.

Only a few of them seemed worried. They tried to get their peers' attention to ask what they'd got for question x or y. It was like watching a frightened housecat trying to talk to a languid panther. The chatty kids seemed like another species to boys and girls like him. Jack didn't feel sorry for them, or pleased at their distress, even though so many of them were the worst bullies. He did not feel superior to them nor proud for his own sake.

He felt nothing at all.

He couldn't say which mood he preferred: the slow, steady rhythm his heart beat now, or the wild drum solo that had made him stand out and be teased when he first entered. He could not remember what had made him so happy in the first place.

But he no longer cared.

After three hours of calculation, Jack's body hummed contentedly, in tune with the deep rumbling of *The Hamelin*'s distant engines.

When Jack got home, his father was waiting for him by the stereo.

'What do you have to say for yourself?' he asked. Jack said nothing. 'Answer me, mister.'

Jack didn't know what to say. He looked at his father huffing and puffing next to his records and thought how like a bull he looked. That made Jack think of dinner and the phrase 'bulldust' meaning nonsense and 'bull in a China shop' which referred to people overreacting to delicate situations, and how all words stand in for other things and… Jack's line of thought was interrupted by his father storming across the room and yelling into his face, 'Do you think I'm kidding around!'

Jack looked up at him and asked, 'Kidding about what, Father?'

Michael grabbed his arm and yanked him to the stereo. On the player, the record was turning round and round. The arm of the player was suspended over the central part of the disk, the 'dead wax' where there were no grooves, only the label. This one read, *The Jimi Hendrix Experience: Electric Ladyland.* No music came from the speakers, just a low whooshing sound like wind in a desert.

'The volume dial on this stereo is like any control on this ship,' his father began, gathering pace and volume as he spoke. 'Any single unit out of place could cause disaster. What if the music kept Ben Endeavour's dad awake? Then he turns up to his shift in Engineering and because he's exhausted he makes a mistake and our sails lose their hold on the solar wind and without that we fall behind the rest of The Fleet? Then where would we be, adrift in the middle of space. Lost! Lost forever. All because one little boy didn't know how to play sensibly with his toy! Do you understand, Jack? Do you?'

Jack just stared at the shining, black, spinning record and listened intently to the swirling silence gusting from the speakers. He did not notice his mother enter, calling his name. He did not hear her explain to his father that on their son's mathematics exam he had placed third from all the students his age, across the entire fleet. He did not see her joyful expression turn to anguish at the sight of Jack's slack, drooling mouth and vacant eyes; did not feel her pull him into her arms, crying, 'Jack, oh Jack. What have they done to my boy?'

He just stared at the dead, black, spinning wax and listened.

But for what, he could not recall.

DAY 180

29. TOKYO ROSE

'La, laaaa, la-la la-la-la, way up high…'

The gentle voice lifted Jack to the surface of his eyes.

'Hmm, hmmmm, hm-hm hm-hm-hm, once in a lullaby.

Jack? Jack, honey?'

He felt a soft hand on his forehead.

'The fever's broken. Jack, can you sit up?'

Jack groaned.

'Jack, you have to eat something. Here…'

Steam crept up into Jack's nostrils and spread salty warmth through his face. He took a deeper breath and the soup's healing aroma travelled all the way through his body to his toes. He opened his eyes. His mother was smiling down at him. A bowl of broth was perched on her lap. Beyond her, at the end of the bed, sat his father. They were both out of uniform.

'What day is it?' he asked.

'Monday, but your father and I managed to switch our rosters around to be with you. You've been asleep for three days.'

'You had us worried, Tiger.'

His father only called him Tiger when he was very happy or very sorry.

'Dad,' said Jack, 'I didn't mean to leave the stereo on. I just got carried away with the music and then the alarm went off and I had to get to the exam and I just ran...'

'Without eating any breakfast, I know. It's a miracle you got through the whole test, let alone aced it,' his father chuckled. 'Who knew we had a math genius in our family? I'll be taking orders from you soon enough. But first, food. Can you handle some of your mum's soup?'

Jack smirked, pulled himself up to sit cross-legged and raised his hand in a salute, 'Aye aye, captain...'

His father stared at him, searching his son's eyes. Jack let him, but the delicious smell of the soup was too distracting and he requested meekly, 'Can I have my soup now, please?'

Xinjuan handed her boy his bowl. As he devoured its contents, his parents watched him in silence. When the bowl was empty, his mother took it and asked, 'More?'

'Yes please,' Jack gargled, the last slurp of soup still sloshing in his mouth.

Xinjuan left the room. Once she was gone, his father turned to him and said, 'Jack, you know that we would never let anything bad happen to you.'

Jack gulped. 'Yeah.'

'And you know you can tell us anything. We're always on your side. No matter what happens.'

Jack nodded and his mother entered with the refilled bowl. But Jack was not distracted this time. He was focused entirely on his father. There was no hint of humour or anger in his voice. It was like they were equals. Jack felt a twinge of recognition. They had spoken like this before, but exactly when or why Jack could not recall.

Michael went on, 'We know it's not easy. This life. Being cooped up all day. Never really *seeing* anyone but us.'

'But it won't be forever,' his mother added. 'This is only the beginning. You'll see. We just want you to be prepared for what's next. We want to give you every opportunity to be happy, to make something of yourself.'

'You and your classmates, you're the future, son.' Michael took his wife's hand and smiled at her. 'And we just *know* that you'll do a better job than we have.'

Xinjuan's voice trembled, 'You kids are so smart, it's scary.' Then she smiled. 'But we believe in you. We trust you. You see things differently, but that's what we need you to do.'

'You're the ones who are going to lead us to the promised land,' his father vowed.

'Uroun,' Jack breathed.

'Uroun,' Michael agreed.

'Uroun,' purred Xinjuan and kissed a streak of tear from Jack's cheek.

An hour later, it was with a great sense of pride and purpose that Jack stepped into the Shower. His parents had gone to work, reassuring him that he could take a day before returning to School. But Jack also remembered that he had a job too, a great responsibility to fulfil his parents' hopes for him and be the best student he could be.

Pulling the Shower Cap down over his face, he checked the timetable for the day. He'd missed the morning Mathematics session. He didn't mind, though he knew he'd soon have to face up to the heightened expectations of Ms. Cruikshank to maintain his number three fleet ranking. The afternoon session posed a whole other challenge: Human Sciences.

It wasn't that he disliked Mr. Fukyuama. He was as boring and unemotional as all his instructors. But the study of human history was not as neat and solvable as equations. On the one hand, you needed to see through multiple pairs of eyes, understand vastly different experiences of the same events, and on the other hand, not get caught up in the biases, the feelings of the people involved.

Now, as Jack felt the Shower's warm stream of quantum vibrations echo and flow around him, he was more determined than ever before to see humanity as Fukuyama wanted him to, from a sympathetic, God-like perspective.

The flash and gong of boot up filled Jack's mind. He stepped forward into the blinding, deafening brilliance.

At first, he felt nothing but the ground upon which he stood rise and fall, rise and fall. He looked at it: steel, painted grey and glowing blue in the moonlight. He smelt salt in the air and a chill that sent shivers right into his bones. He looked around him. His classmates wore light blue shirts, dark blue pants, white sailor's caps and orange life preserver vests over their shoulders.

'Welcome back, Voyager 1,' Fukuyama's grumbled. His teacher stood on a platform above Jack and his classmates, resplendent in the officer's cap and medals of a World War 2 era, United States Navy admiral. He continued his introduction, 'This simulation will be the last from our unit on The Second World War, 1939-1945 CE.' He gestured to the ship they all stood on and the ocean beyond. 'This is the USS Missouri, the most powerful destroyer in the United States Navy. In the distance, is the main island of Japan, Honshu, and the city of Hiroshima, home to approximately 200,000 people. At this time, most Japanese are still loyal to their Emperor. They will not accept that Japan's conquest of Asia is doomed to failure. More importantly, their warrior code, *bushido*, will not permit them to surrender and so they will fight down to the last man to defend the honour of their emperor.'

High above them, a large quad-propeller bombers flew across the deck of the battleship towards the horizon where the island nation slumbered.

Fukuyama continued, 'A decision has been made by the Americans, to strike such a savage blow to the heart of Japan that it will awaken from its ancient dreams of samurai glory and surrender without condition. This will end a war that could otherwise drag on for years and kill countless more.'

He gestured to the plane above, moving slowly yet steadily toward the western horizon. 'This bomber carries in its belly an atomic bomb. It is the most powerful weapon yet created by man. It is the first and only time it will ever be used in anger.' He levelled his gaze upon every student and intoned, 'This morning, August 6th, 1945, is the moment the human race will realise it has the power to destroy itself.'

With that, their teacher turned away from them towards the horizon and stared impassively. It was clear he expected the class to do the same. All twenty students turned to watch the plane grow smaller. They stood at uniform attention, with their hands behind their backs and feet shoulder width apart, but each face wore a different expression. Some were excited to see history's biggest and most destructive explosion. Others closed their eyes and waited for the horror to be over.

Jack knew that Fukuyama was observing and marking them based on their reactions, and he concentrated hard on the disappearing plane and its destination. He tried to imagine the mood of the American pilots. Were they frightened? Were they blood-thirsty? Were they trying not to feel anything, just keeping busy, concentrating on the complicated operations of steering the plane and readying their weapons?

'Was their action justified?' Fukuyama asked the ocean.

One by one, the students who were not overcome by the impending horror, answered.

'They were blinded by bloodlust,' opined the heavy-set Saul Columbia. 'They *hated* the Japanese.'

'The Japanese hated *them*,' sneered Max Mercury. 'What choice did they have?'

Always at, as well as on, Max's side, Jenna Pioneer added, 'The only way to win was to show the Japs how far they were willing to go.' She turned to her deadly Dragon Quest partner. 'Like any fight. It's about will. The Americans' will was stronger.'

'But what about the innocents? The women, the children? How could the Americans decide to kill them?' Saul countered.

'It was a small sacrifice: a few to save the many,' Max seethed. 'Otherwise the war would have dragged on and more innocent people would have had to die.'

'You're a monster, Max!'

'You're a child, Saul!'

The argument went on but Jack kept silent. He thought to himself about how the scientists and the generals and the politicians must have felt when they discovered they had the power to destroy whole cities. It would have been like discovering Zeus's thunderbolt or Thor's hammer. They would have been scared, but how could they resist the urge to see what it could do? How could they not take up the power of the universe in their hand and wield it against their enemies?

Jack's mind was racing. He was confused, but he felt like he was getting close to the heart of the lesson.

He looked up and saw that Fukuyama was staring at him. All the arguing children were asking him to tell them who was right, but he kept silent and looked directly at Jack. He gazed so intently, it was as though he could see in past Jack's avatar, into the darkness of his Shower and in the echoing blackness read Jack's mind. The faintest hint of a smile ghosted at the edges of the teacher's mouth. Jack couldn't return his gaze.

He thought about how the purpose of history was not to memorise dates and names, but to detect patterns and changes. What was the pattern that led to this moment in time? What was the change?

Jack looked up with the answer on his lips. But his teacher was no longer looking at him. He had turned to scan the horizon.

'Good discussion, students. Excellent,' he said.

The children raised their eyebrows at one another and shuffled their feet, uncertain what to do next. One by one they too looked at the horizon and waited for the monster sleeping in the bomb's shell to hatch. Jack told his insight to no one, but in his heart he knew that this was the moment, centuries ago, that technology took control of the human race.

Then, just as the solemn silence of the ocean felt like it would drown him, Jack heard music.

Speakers were stationed throughout the ship to issue orders

and raise alarms. On these the gentle sound of a bamboo pipe began to play. Its fragile, breathy sound haunted across the deck of the ship, quivered along the massive triple turrets of the cannons and vibrated up from the deck into their uniform soles. Following close behind the pipe came a voice, as deep and feminine as the ocean. Like the pipe, its accent was unmistakably Japanese. 'Ahhhh,' she cooed, 'you are all so excellent, you brilliant children of *Hamelin*.'

The students gaped at the speakers and each other.

'Nasty little Mercury, fierce Jenna Pioneer, clever Jack Voyager 1...'

'This is part of the simulation,' their teacher called over the music. 'She is Tokyo Rose. During the war, she broadcast anti-American propaganda over the radio.'

'But she knows our names,' yelled Pioneer, taking hold of Max.

'Yes, I do,' Tokyo Rose purred over the ship's PA. 'The dead know a great deal about the living, more than the living know themselves.'

At that moment, a great light, as bright as the sun, exploded over the land on the horizon and filled the sky. At the centre of the fireball, a woman appeared. She spread her arms until they were as broad as the island of Honshu. From her breast came the cries of the thousands of souls who in that instant were incinerated by the bomb.

'Remain calm,' Fukuyama intoned without a hint of fear or alarm.

This reassured some, but not many. The heat blasting at them from across the Sea of Japan felt as real as the wailing that assailed their ears.

Then, from the water, emerged an image that petrified them all and confirmed this was not part of the program. From the ship to the horizon, thousands of samurai in full battle armour surfaced and strode towards them across the water. Some bore swords, others bows and arrows, others spears, but all wore masks carved into the terrifying faces of Japan's ancestral spirits.

Max and Jenna were the first to recover from their fear. 'It's a hack!' Mercury called out eagerly to his classmates. 'So let's fight it. Come on, defend the ship. Fight!'

Replacing the form of an American sailor, Max loaded his favourite avatar, a dark elf warrior from Dragon Quest. He drew two long thin obsidian blades from the sheathes on his back and cursed at the approaching horde of warriors through his sharp, pointed teeth.

'Best class ever!' hollered Pioneer and transformed into a dark elf sorceress. She crouched in her long black gown and held her arms aloft in a fighting stance from which to hurl purple bolts of dark-elf magic.

The first samurai to mount the railing at the edge of the ship's deck was thrown back into the water by one double-fisted blast of her furious lightening. The next slammed like a squashed bug into the deck beneath Saul Columbia's orc hammer. But the samurai kept coming, rising from the water, up the sides of the hull, onto the main deck, pushing the students towards the upper levels. Desperately, valiantly, the children of *Hamelin* fought back those fearsome wraiths from the depths of time.

All the while, Tokyo Rose taunted them.

'When you fall beneath these toy swords,' she mocked, 'and wake safely in your Mediation Rooms, think well upon this. The children of *Hiroshima* did not get to reset and play again. *Their* parents did not greet them afterwards and clap them on the back. They were gone, washed away, like rats drowned in a river.'

Jack wanted to know more. He wanted to talk to Tokyo Rose, to understand who she was and why she was so angry with the children of *Hamelin*. But he was also afraid. He did not want to be pierced by arrows or pushed over the rail into the icy water by a samurai spear. He had no skill, or power or weaponry waiting for him in a Dragon Quest character.

So he ran.

Over the cannon on the upper deck he scampered, up towards the command tower. He thought perhaps in there he could lock himself away until the hack was over. For a second he was hopeful. Then a voice from below singled him out, *'Jack, John, Voyager 1? Michael and Xinjuan's son?'*

It was a girl's voice. Jack recognised it, but where from he didn't know.

He looked down. The most terrifying of the samurai was looking directly up at him. Its winged armour was painted in streaks of white and red. Its face was a laughing tiger. Jack ran. It sprang after him, leaping from deck to deck. 'Where are you running to, little lame boy?' it hollered. 'That's not the way to the mountain.'

The girl warrior swung up over the railing onto Jack's deck. Backing away, Jack tripped and fell against the opposite rail. The tigress's mask shook with laughter. 'You can't hide from me,' she said. 'This blind girl hears your strange little heart.'

She prowled casually towards him, drawing her long sword slowly from its scabbard. Its edge caught a flash of the light shining from the horizon and for a moment blinded him. With the other hand, she unfastened her mask. When the reflected glare of the goddess's light cleared from Jack's eyes, he saw the face of the girl standing over him.

Those eyes.

'I know you,' he breathed.

The girl paused. A smile gently, carefully, lit her face. 'You remember?' she asked.

Jack faltered. He reached in his mind to connect a name to the face, but a swirling sense of vertigo seized him, almost causing him to faint. The girl's smile soured to a grimace and she raised her sword with both hands high over her head. Jack raised his hands before him.

'I'm sorry,' he pleaded. 'I wish I knew. I think I do. But….'

A wave washed through his head, making him dizzy and nauseous.

The sword hovered above the samurai girl's confused expression. The voice of Tokyo Rose purred out of a speaker right next to the warrior's head, 'Don't torture the boy. Just deliver the message.'

With a heavy sigh and a shake of her head, she drove the sword deep into Jack's belly. The pain was like a bomb exploding in his guts. White heat coursed through his whole body until it felt like it was pouring out of his eyes.

On the main deck below, his teacher mounted one of the *Missouri's* massive cannons and swung all three turrets around to face the goddess glowing on the horizon. Behind her, a mushroom cloud bloomed over Hiroshima. He pulled the firing lever and three shells thundered from their guns, arched, screaming across the sea, and found their target. A second flash of light, more furious than the first, ignited the goddess. The massive boom of the explosion dug into the water, lifting it up into a wave as wide as the horizon and high as the stars.

As the tsunami loomed up over the ship, the samurai girl twisted the blade in Jack's abdomen, and leaned down close enough to whisper in his ear, 'You'll remember me now, Jack.'

With that, the massive wall of water slammed into the side of *The Missouri*, tipping it over into the cold blackness below. The water churned with the mixing currents of the rolling wave and the swiftly sinking battleship. Jack could not tell which way was up to swim for it.

For a moment, he thought he spotted Fukuyama. The teacher was submerged with them in the dawn-lit deep, watching serenely as his students, weighed with costume armour, sank silently to the bottom.

Jack felt a force pulling on his body. He looked towards its source and saw a swirling vortex had opened in the murky depths below. It turned *The Missouri* round in its whorls as though it were a toy. His classmates were dragged towards its centre and he too could do nothing to resist its pull. He was drawn feet first towards its centre. With his last look back he saw that his teacher was unaffected by the current. Fukuyama was twirling his index finger in the same anti-clockwise direction as the maelstrom, and watching it suck them all down. Jack's eyes remained locked on Fukuyama's until the very last moment, when the whirlpool swallowed Jack whole in its cold, black maw.

The next moment, Jack collapsed onto the floor of his Shower, dragged the Cap from his face and gulped in lungfuls of air. He could not remember where he had just been. Perhaps there had been an emergency, and he'd been ejected from class so he could get to safety.

He listened for the alarm. But none sounded.

He tried to stand, but immediately a piercing blast of pain ignited in his stomach.

A phantom pain? An echo of sensation. From Sandbox? Or

School? But an echo of what? Jack's memory of the day was all shadows and blur.

Groggily, he pulled himself up off the floor and with slow deep breaths made his way to the edge of his bed. Cradling his side, he gently lowered himself down onto the warm, soft covers, thinking, 'I just need to rest for a bit. I just need to rest. I just need...'

He shot back up onto his feet.

Agony blazed like a sun in his belly. It burned through all the darkness and fog in his mind.

The pain had a name, and it leapt to his lips.

Lucy!

DAY 181

30. PLAYING IN A TRAVELLING BAND

The next morning, Jack did something he had never dreamed of doing before. He skipped School.

He didn't want to. He was petrified of getting in trouble, and worse, falling behind in his studies. And he certainly wasn't looking for fun.

But the pain in his side would not let him concentrate on anything else. He had to find its source.

So instead of School, Jack climbed into his shower and loaded up The Sandbox. In a instant, he stood upon the main boulevard, amidst the countless facades of the gameworlds, social networks and entertainments, and went looking for his murderer.

He had only one clue to explain the aching wound in his side. Only one lead. It was a name that came to his lips whenever the pain rose to bite him. He shouted it down the boulevard, 'Lucy! Lucy, where are you?'

The effort made him double over and clutch the throbbing sore in his belly. It felt like a knife had pierced his side and lodged cruelly under his rib. He could not see the steel, but through his shirt his avatar bled bright red.

Jack reasoned that the pain was some kind of hack. Therefore, the hacker, probably Lucy, whoever she was, could end it. He decided to seek her out in the chat lounges and took a step northwards, up the boulevard towards the social networking precinct. Immediately, the steel twisted in his guts. He gasped and reeled back a couple of paces in the opposite direction. The pain subsided slightly. He turned south, towards the gameworlds, and took another tentative step. The pain eased a little further. Slowly, he stood up straight and limped forward. He felt terrible but he could move, as long as it was southwards.

Guided by the gradual easing of the pain, Jack stumbled down the boulevard, leaving a thin trail of blood as we went. He passed the colourful marquee of *Jet Racer*. The little green trolls who lived there poked out of the craters in the game's façade, fondling bombs, and teased him to come test his mettle. But Jack kept walking. All along the boulevard the programs beckoned him by name, but the call of his body to find Lucy was far stronger than the allure of any game.

At last he stood in a puddle of his own blood before the high gates of *Dragon Quest*. The very sight of them gave him chills. He tried to move past, but as soon as he did, the pain leapt up again.

Across the street, the facades of *Zombieland* and *Gangster's Paradise* played their theme music at him: to the left, a shrieking soundtrack of strings and horns; to the right, an angry hip hop track that was all gunfire and curses. Without thinking why, he closed his eyes and focused on the space between their separate rackets. In that silence, he thought for a moment that he caught the whisper of a guitar and a woman singing. He stood and stepped towards the sound. Pain immediately slapped him from his trance. As if aroused by his agony, the queen of *Dragon Quest* stirred in Her mountain lair.

'Jack Voyager 1, dare ye enter and fasssce me?' intoned the cavernous voice of The Great Red Dragon. 'Will you take up armssss and challenge my infernal power, rissssking all for glory?'

Her voice rumbled the blade in Jack's side and he knew there was no way forward but into the dreaded serpent's realm. As the heavy gates parted, memories of all the awful murders he'd endured rose up in his mind. He crossed the threshold into the game and remembered his earliest and briefest adventure, when his first footfall had been greeted by a bandit's arrow to his forehead. Such memories dogged his every step. As he trailed red droplets between the moss and mushroom covered trunks of the majestic oaks in Moorcock Wood, he recollected being crushed by rocks flung down from the thickly entwined branches by malevolent orcs. Crossing by raft the Emerald Lake, he recalled the snickering sound the dark elves made as they slid out of the water to slit his throat and pull him down into the icy deep. So many awful encounters, so many terrible ends, so much time spent there in fear and misery; *Dragon Quest* was where what little pride Jack won at School came to die.

Now though, as he moved deeper into this terrifying land, his bleeding stopped and the ache in his side subsided. By degrees he filled with warmth and strength. Yet he was not merely healed. The closer he came to the source of his injury, the more invigorated he felt. Energy coursed through him and with it an emotion he could not recall ever feeling before under *Quest's* sky of yellow and green.

Jack started to feel bold.

His spirits were so high that, despite the enduring niggle in his ribs, he bounded up the final rise to the thorny summit of Sorrow Hill. From there he looked East across the blue-grassed Plain of Tears. There, countless armies of children, light and dark, had fought and fallen. He looked farther, to the shadowy fringes of The Dark Forest where Max and Jenna and their scorched-black brethren held sway. Beyond that, the crags of The Great Red Dragon's mountain soared up to meet a black thunderhead of cloud. This perpetual storm boiled and rolled in on itself like a great wave that was always surging yet never breaking. Jack looked up at the highest peak, where the dragon made its nest, and hollered, 'I'm not afraid of you, you damn worm. I'm not afraid of anything!'

'I sure hope not.'

Spoken from right behind him, the words so startled Jack that he flapped his arms and jerked his legs away like he'd been nipped on the heel by a scorpion. This proof of his bravery was rewarded with a burst of bright, clear laughter. Jack tried to compose himself. He turned around with his hands on his hips in a show of cool composure that made the girl double over into gut-deep guffaws. Jack smiled and laughed too, as though it had been his intention all along to amuse.

When she finally stood up straight, the laughter stopped in Jack's chest. Dressed in the bright blue armour of an elfin warrior, the girl looked like a queen. Jack felt certain that he knew her. That crooked smile, those almond eyes, all seemed so familiar.

'Lucy?' he asked tentatively.

She did not reply. The smile left her face like the sun going behind a cloud. She narrowed her eyes, as though trying to penetrate past his avatar's default Hollywood features and superhero physique to perceive the boy within. He felt foolish. Seeing his discomfort, the girl grinned, raised her left hand and approached him. He panicked. Was she going to touch him, hug him, kiss him? He stiffened, raised his arms like a forklift, closed his eyes and tilted his head to meet hers. But instead of a soft touch on his lips, he felt a new ignition of pain in his side. He looked down and saw her hand buried up to the wrist in his midriff.

He watched in horror as her hand withdrew and the broken blade of a samurai *kitana* emerged from his torso. She held the fragment aloft and with her other hand drew a broken elfin sword from her hip. She brought the two pieces together. The metals glowed at the touch of their familiar and bonded as one.

She turned to walk away, then paused to tilt her grinning cheek back at him and say, 'Follow me, lame boy. Try to keep up.'

31. THE SHADOWS

For hours, she led him along the ridgeline of hills towards the northern Woods of Gibson. Though Jack had never made it that far into the game before, he knew Gibson's Wood was a safe haven for newbies. Long ago, a generous senior wizard had cast a spell of protection around it that barred entry to any characters who had been blackened by The Dragon's corrupting breath. By the time Jack and the elf girl finally passed under its protective canopy, the sky was bright with stars.

All the way there, the girl had been silent, refusing to answer any of Jack's constant questions. At first he asked, 'How do I know you?' and, 'How come I had your sword in my guts?' But after a long while staring at her silent back, he began to despair and asked, 'Are you angry with me? Have I hurt you?' and finally, 'Would you please tell me what you want with me cos I think I'm losing my mind!'

Now, in a pool of starlight framed by the tall white trunks of Gibson's Wood, the girl at last stopped, turned and answered.

'Yes, Jack! You have hurt me. *Yes*, I am angry.' She kicked at the ground. 'But not just with you. I'm angry with every child on the *Hamelin*. You're all so blind. You don't know who you really are, or what's really going on outside your snug little dreamworld.'

'Give him a break, Lucy,' a deep voice growled in the shadows between the trees. 'He didn't make the world the way it is.'

Jack looked about warily, trying to locate the spectral speaker.

'No,' she scorned, 'he just enjoys it. Look at him. How's he supposed to help us now? He's just a happy little zip drive, empty of everything 'cept what they've loaded. He's got no memory of his own. He's got no music to give.'

'We can help him remember,' purred the voice in the trees.

She turned to him with a tear in her eye and said, 'You were so brave. How could you forget? The streets full of rats?'

Jack stared at her blankly.

'The Golem? The message from The Piper?'

He shrugged hopelessly.

'Your *song*?' she cried desperately. 'You must remember *that*!'

'It was all taken from him,' the deep voice grumbled, 'stolen while he slept. I know you've suffered, Lucy. We all have, but at least you have your memories. What's he got? A hole in his heart where his soul used to be.'

Into the moonlight stepped a sleek black panther. Smiling and purring he circled Jack, letting his tail flick Jack's nose, bringing to it the smell of tobacco smoke. Where had Jack smelt it before? A name wafted up to him from the murk at the bottom of his mind.

'Miles?' he wondered aloud.

The panther chuckled, 'There you go, Jack. It's coming back to you already. Maybe you recognise some of these cats too.'

From the shadows, a whole menagerie of animals emerged, but unlike any Jack had ever seen in School. There was a tiger whose paws each beat a different drum sound upon the earth; a gorilla whose great black hands held a slender brass trombone; a rhinoceros whose horn was lined with a series of holes that hummed like a saxophone whenever he breathed; and a gaggle of ducks whose wings beat twangs of guitar whenever they flapped the air.

'They sure remember you,' Miles continued. 'That show you put on for us in our club is legendary. You damn near blew the roof off with that song of yours. And the way you worked your movements into music, dancing vibrations out of the air like a… Well, you looked like some kind of angel.'

'Or a devil, hey Jack?' rumbled the tiger at Jack's shoulder, tickling him with his whiskers.

Miles gently shook his great feline head. 'But that was the last show, Jack. We got raided the very next day. Imagine it: Mona was doin her best Nina Simone. Everybody was feelin it. Then we hear banging on the door. Before I can even get to the hatch to ask what's the password, The High Admiral herself comes storming in. That woman is strong. Just kicked in the door, marched right up to the stage and said, Listen here. This is an unauthorised use of Fleet bandwidth. We're shutting this place down. Clicked her fingers and poof, no more club.'

'But *how* did The Admiral *find* you?' Lucy asked Miles mockingly, pressing her hands to her chest. She turned her expression of pretend confusion to Jack. 'Could one of you have been *followed*? Someone perhaps whose daddy works in Communications and likes to keep an eye on his special little boy when he's playing in the Sandbox?'

Jack dropped his eyes. His dad was an honest man, a guardian, a decorated hero. And if The Admiral was against these people, then Jack wanted nothing to do with them. He didn't even remember ever being in their 'club'. He should just log out right now and tell his father what had happened.

As though she had read Jack's mind, Lucy softened slightly and conceded, 'He may just have been doing his job, but your dad helped The Admiral take something special from them.' She walked amongst the animal band. 'The Club was where they got to be themselves.'

'That's alright, child,' purred the panther. 'It was time for us to evolve. The Admiral gave us the nudge we needed.' He turned to Jack. 'But it was your instrument that really inspired us. We tracked down a bunch of these animal avatars in an old back up copy of the School. Meant to be for teaching how Earth's animals used to communicate. We've been adding our own grooves to the way they move. We're getting pretty good. Call ourselves *The Shadows.*' His tail swished the air. 'Wanna join?'

'Hang on, Miles,' growled the Pakistani gorilla. 'We have not agreed on *The Shadows* yet. I voted for *The Misfits.*'

'*Misfits*?' huffed the tiger. 'What happened to *The Unamericans.*'

'Here we go,' a Russian duck squawked angrily. 'Always the

Americans are in charge.'

'Hey, hey, hey,' Miles meowed. 'Jack's the frontman. Let's hear what he thinks.'

Jack was perplexed. 'Wait. What? That's what all of this is about? You want me to play *music* with you? Why all the secrecy?' He turned to Lucy. 'And why *me*? I know I know you from somewhere, and sure, I love music, but I don't know how to play anything.' The animals stared at him. 'Really. No one's ever taught me.'

'No one?' Miles asked, moving closer. 'You never had a teacher called Pfeif? Skinny dude? Wore a crazy coloured tie?'

Jack stared at him blankly but something in him, all the way at the back of his mind, began to stir. His gaze turned inward, and as he swam down into the gloomy depths of his memory, the panther purred in his ear, 'You remember, Jack. You woke each morning with a song on your lips. You didn't know what it meant, but you had to sing it. And The Pfeif, he heard you. He heard the song you have inside you. He saw what you are, a superstar, and he sent you straight to us.'

Around him, the animals began to play. It was a sad song, a dirge, but it spoke directly to Jack's heart.

Miles crooned in his deep baritone:

I know I'm not the only one

Sailing for that distant sun

Far, far, far across the sea.

The tiger and the gorilla joined the great cat in harmony,

> *But Jack, John, Voyager 1,*
>
> *Michael and Xinjuan's son,*
>
> *Is lonely as can be.*

The tiger's paw struck the earth in a slow soft rhythm. The gorilla took up his trombone and the rhinocerous raised his horn, and they eased mournful tones from out of the air. Now Lucy sang,

> *In a vision. In a dream.*
>
> *I saw you and you saw me.*
>
> *Where we're headed, I don't know.*
>
> *Fast as light, our love can grow.*

The music continued and Jack felt like he could almost hear another verse. Something in him struggled to rise up and sing it. But he was afraid.

When the animals ceased their playing, the clearing hummed with a profound stillness. Jack couldn't believe what he had heard.

'Who are you people?' he asked.

'We're players, Jack. Just like you,' Miles purred in Jack's ear.

'We sing what people are too scared to say. We remind them who they are inside, beyond their uniforms and their ranks.'

Miles then turned to the other bandsmen and declared, 'The Admiral made a big mistake, kicking us out of our club. Now we're out, on tour, bringin' our sounds to the people.'

The musicians all roared and squawked and beat their chests.

'Good music is like magic, Jack. It turns fear and hatred into harmony.' Miles looked around at the moonlit gameworld. 'You don't get many places more awful than *Dragon Quest*. So this is where we'll make our stand.' He put his paw on Jack's shoulder. 'And we don't just plan to play here, man. We plan to win.'

Jack cast Lucy a questioning glance. She nodded back grimly.

Miles pointed his paw up past Jack's face to the stars above. As he spoke, the constellations began to shift and stir. Lines connected their points of light, forming characters that came to life and performed an epic story.

'It's like this see,' the panther began. 'You and all the other kids in The Fleet are all battling it out in here, forming alliances, getting caught, having your fun make-believe murdering.'

Drawn in starlight up above, whole armies of orcs, elves, giants, dwarves and knights clashed.

'All the while,' Miles continued, 'The Great Red Dragon watches over you, making sure that you're too scared and distracted to go for the real prize.'

Up above, the stars realigned to show the Dragon in Her lair, coiled around a pile of jars containing jewellery, armour and coins of gold.

'The dragon's gold,' Jack breathed, frightened even to mention it.

'That's right, man. She guards that stash with all her might. Anybody who gets close, she breathes Her fire on and makes them Hers. She's got so many minions now she doesn't ever have to fight. She just sits up there in Her mountain, snuggled up to Her treasure.'

'But it's not actual gold She's hoarding,' Lucy seethed and took Jack's hands in hers. She looked deep into his eyes and declared, 'It's memories.'

Jack took a step back but Lucy held fast to his hands.

'That's what She's really got locked up there in Her cave: all the thoughts and feelings and experiences She's ever stolen from kids like you who don't think or feel or do what they're told.'

'But I've hardly ever played Dragon Quest,' Jack protested, sickened to think that there were parts of him he didn't even know about, kept secret from him in the databanks of a game. 'How could the Dragon have stolen from me?'

Lucy moaned, 'You think anything in the School or Sandbox is really separate? The Red Dragon, The Admiral, the teachers? They're all part of the same system. Different faces. Different tools. The same power.'

'And this isn't a game to us, man,' Miles added. 'If we can get into the Dragon's lair, we can steal back the children's hearts. We can free them from their prisons.'

Jack looked again at Lucy.

She stepped away to look up at the glowing outline of the dragon high above their heads. She drew her sword and stabbed up at its throat. For a moment, Jack imagined the beast turn upon her and he took a step forward.

'OK,' Jack said. 'How can I help?'

A trill of music shivered through the band of apes, drakes and cats.

'Well, it isn't open mic night, Jack.' the panther purred, 'but at this party, *everybody* has to play.'

Overhead, an eagle swooped. It dropped from its talons a pile of cloth that fell at Jack's feet with a heavy clang of bells. He picked the pile up and let it unravel into shape before him. It was a court jester's outfit. It was lined from top to bottom in stripes of every colour and to each sleeve and trouser cuff were sewn rows of golden bells that rang whenever the wearer moved. Crowning the whole costume was a hat with three cloth spikes that sagged like the branches of a willow tree. These were also rainbow striped and tipped with bells. Jack looked at Lucy. She barely disguised her glee.

'Try it on,' she said. 'I'm sure it fits you.'

'You want me to face Her wearing this?' Jack exclaimed.

'It's your instrument,' the panther soothed. 'We've modified it to work here in the game.'

Jack eyed the costume suspiciously.

'We made a copy of it back in the club,' Miles confessed and shrugged his broad feline shoulders, 'but none of us can figure how to play it.'

'Like a fish trying to play banjo,' said the gorilla.

'Or a snake on the drums,' the tiger snickered, wiggling his furry paws.

'You think *I* know how to play it?' Jack hollered.

The panther nodded, 'Only you can, Jack.'

Jack shrugged his shoulders and turned his palms out. The jester sleeves gave a little jangle.

'You know what to do,' Lucy offered. 'Just open your mouth and sing.'

Jack gulped and a little cough escaped his chest. He looked from the strange instrument in his arms, glowing slightly blue in the moonlight, up to the stars where the ancient war between light and dark was fought over dragon's gold.

He stepped into the fool's costume.

The animals ringed around him. The trees grew still, as though listening.

'OK, this is just a rehearsal, friends. Let's start it off easy and slow,' purred the bandleader. Then he turned to the boy and meowed, 'Listen to the music, Jack. Don't move until you feel it. OK?'

The jester gave one brief tinkling nod.

The panther counted them in, '1, 2, 1-2-3-4…'

MORNING, DAY 182

32. DRAGON'S GOLD (PT .1)

Jack dreamed he was singing in the shower. His voice echoed off the tiles. Hot water beat upon his back and steamed around him in a thick, sticky fog.

A knock came at the bathroom door.

'Jack darling,' his mother's sweet voice chimed, 'the villagers are complaining.'

But Jack kept singing.

Now the rapping on the door was firmer.

'Jack!' bellowed his father. 'Don't ignore your mother. Get out of the shower and go to your room this instant.'

But Jack sang louder still.

Now the door shuddered and quaked from the impact of some mighty force stalking beyond.

'JACK!' roared the voice of The Great Red Dragon. 'The children of *Hamelin* are fasssst assssleep, all cossssy in their bedssss. If you make but one more peep, I'll twisssst and pop your little head!'

Jack stopped singing and yet the tune continued. It was being played on a pipe. The sound was rising from the plughole at his feet. He watched the water spiral down past the rim. The piping grew louder and the water spun faster. Clockwise, round and round, Jack plunged into the sound, down amongst the notes of the piper's song, and felt fur and teeth and tails upon his skin.

When Jack woke, his tiny room was spinning. He held onto the bed while Lucy, the animals and their plan spun round and round his head.

Even though they had rehearsed for hours, Jack had managed little more than to jingle in time with the players' beat. He had tried to feel the music, to let it in and guide his body. But he either got so excited that he flung his limbs about wildly, causing an awful cacophony of jangles and clangs, or he froze and shuffled so timidly that the bells on his feet barely tinkled. Worst still, when he tried to open his mouth and sing, the voice that emerged was feeble and distant. Jack felt a cold stone lodged in his throat that kept all but a whimper from passing his lips.

The panther had assured him, 'You may not think you know the music, Jack, but your body knows it.'

Jack didn't feel reassured by Miles's words. He felt frightened. The thought that there was a whole other part of himself that he couldn't remember, another Jack lurking about inside of him, was disturbing. The only thing that made any of this make sense and seem true was that Lucy knew this other Jack, and she cared for him, as he cared for her. That was the one thing that Jack was certain he and his shadow self had in common.

The night before, Lucy watched Jack play, trying to see through him to his deeper self and his special power. But with each bum note Jack blurted from his costume, Lucy's scowl of fear and disappointment had only deepened.

Jack now sighed and put his feet on the floor beside his bed, swallowed and felt the cold nugget of fear in his chest grow heavier and harder. By the time the School bell sounded in his room, the weight in his chest was so heavy that he barely managed to drag himself to the Shower. Like a stone he dropped into the echoing darkness and sank all the way to the bottom to land with a thud in his seat at the rear of Ms. Cruikshank's class.

His teacher prowled between the desks. Each time she passed, Jack snuck glances around the room. How many of his peers were in on the plan too? Were any of them? Had anyone else been called by 'Mr. Pfeif' to join the shadow band?

'Eyes on your page, Voyager,' the school ma'am spat, and Jack took refuge from his dread in the long list of equations.

After an hour of silent calculation, Jack glanced right to the desk next to him where Evan Apollo sat. But instead of Evan's massively muscular avatar, he saw a small rat nibbling at his console. Jack looked the other way and saw to his left in the row behind him, Constance Columbia was gone as well, replaced by a long-tailed rodent who perched on her desk and sniffed at her paper as though it were working the problem. A squeak in front of him alerted Jack to another disappearing act. One by one, the students around him popped out of view, their faces replaced by wiggling whiskers, their arms and legs by furry paws. Ms. Cruikshank and he watched the whole class disappear this way until they were alone together in a room infested with squeaking animals. She levelled her gaze directly at him and inquired with menacing calm, 'Is there something you'd like to tell me, Jack?'

The white room went blood-neon. A siren barked like the whole ship was about to explode. Before his eyes Jack's teacher transformed into the almighty form of The Admiral. Her crest of grey hair and fortress of medals towered over him as though at any moment they would all come crashing down on him with the entire weight of The Fleet.

'Did you allow this infestation on my ship, cadet?' she asked.

Jack felt a tingling in his Shower Cap that told him he was about to surf into another stream.

'Your ship, Ma'am?' he said, and as her face disappeared, he showed her his middle finger. '*The Hamelin* is Australian.'

He emerged on *Dragon Quest*'s Plain of Tears with his finger still up, face to face with the terrible maw of The Great Red Dragon Herself. The enormous serpent was crouched down with Her head at ground level. She chuckled - a noise like heavy machinery churning in the belly of some vast and mighty engine.

'Not ssso easy to give usss the sssslip, little Jack,' the beast grumbled.

Jack backed away with a tinkle of bells. He looked down and saw that his jester's outfit had loaded automatically. Now he felt ridiculous as well as afraid.

'Nicessssuit,' the dragon chuckled, and Jack's trembling caused the bells to chime in waves that jangled from head to toe. A tremor of laughter raised the serpent to its full height. She spread her wings and spewed fire into the air. Jack turned and bolted for the high ground.

As he ran, he saw where his classmates had been transported. They were all there on The Plain of Tears in their *Dragon Quest* forms, doing battle amongst thousands of other characters. From the fringe of Dark Forest to the crest of Sorrow Hill, their heaving mass of slashing, ducking, dashing forms filled the whole blue field.

Ahead, Constance Columbia gave out a savage battle cry as her dark elf lashed its venomous whip at a stone giant whom Jack didn't recognise. To his right, Evan Apollo's white wizard traded bolts of magic with an unfamiliar warlock. Over the ridiculous tinkling of Jack's jester bells, he heard their battle banter.

An orc behind him boomed, 'You kids should go play somewhere else. This is the deep end of The Sandbox, boy.'

To his left, three dwarves had a dark knight surrounded. They swung their axes over their heads, making their blades strike and spit sparks at their foe, chanting, 'We're gonna chop you down to size, senior. We're gonna chop you down to size.'

Passing them, Jack realised what Miles had accomplished: a

fleet-wide, whole-School hack. From all seven ships, every student of every age, thousands and thousands of children, had been scooped out of their classrooms and poured out onto the same battleground.

Jack looked over his shoulder. The dragon had recovered from Her fit of laughter and was scanning for Her prey amongst the hordes making war upon the blue grasses of the plain. Jack ducked his head and threw himself towards the top of Sorrow Hill, hoping that somehow he might make it down the other side, through the brambles, across the Emerald Lake, to the relative safety of Moorcock Wood, and there wait out the battle.

'JACK!' the dragon roared over the din of battle. Jack looked back through the swinging bells of his hat, to see the smiling serpent aim Her gaze at him. Jack's legs buckled under him and he sank to the virtual dirt. Pinned down by the weight of fear in his chest, he watched as the dragon stalked towards him. He closed his eyes and felt the boom of each dragon steps quake through him from foot to skull.

Then, from further up the slope of Sorrow Hill, a different sound thrilled through him, cascading down from his scalp to the tips of his fingers and toes. A thunder of hooves was descending. Jack opened his eyes and turned to see a group of knights in radiant white armour drive towards him in chevron formation. They vaulted over Jack and around him, straight at their monstrous foe. The dragon did not shrink from their charge. She reared on Her hind legs, drew a breath that sucked the clouds out of the sky and exhaled a thunderhead of flame into the path of the riders, engulfing them.

Jack roused himself and ran to the summit of the hill. There he turned, certain he would see a V-shape burnt into the grass. Instead, the same fifteen knights sat atop their steeds in the same arrowhead formation, but with lances now pointed back up the slope at Jack. Their horses and their armour had been scorched black by the dragon's breath. Under her spell, their purpose too had darkened.

'Ssssee how futile thissss fighting issss?' boomed the dragon, and spread Her arms to encompass the thousands of children, light and dark, playing war upon the field. 'CHILDREN, HEARKEN TO ME!'

The fighting paused. All turned to regard the unassailable might of the greatest power they had ever encountered in School or Sandbox.

'I am the fear you will never conquer,' She roared. 'I am the death that awaitssss you all. See me and dessspair!'

Jack looked down at his hands. They shuddered each time the dragon spoke. The sound of Her voice was everywhere, in everything, seeding everyone with dread.

For a moment there was silence, a beat in which even the wind seemed to lay down its arms.

Then, from the other side of Sorrow Hill, rose a babble of squeaks and honking, a clatter of drums and base. The panther form of Miles Sinclair stalked into view, leading a grand orchestra of animals, hundreds strong. At the summit, he stopped at Jack's side and roared to the left and to the right. The animal musicians peeled off to either side and arranged themselves along the rise: to the right, a brass section led by the trombone wielding gorilla and fluted rhinoceros; to the left, a rhythm section packed with wolves and big cats whose paws beat percussion; above them hovered a great flock of birds - eagles, storks, ducks, starlings and hawks - whose flapping wings stroked the sound of violin, guitar and cello from the air.

The players Jack had rehearsed with had numbered no more than ten. Here was an army.

'Where have they all come from?' Jack asked his feline friend.

'*The Shadows* have fans everywhere, Jack,' the panther purred.

From south to north, the dragon cast Her serpentine eyes along the row of musicians and then brought them to bear on the panther.

'Have you come to play a sssong of praissse?' she sneered.

'We have,' called Miles, 'but not for you.'

He let out a roar and the whole orchestra struck up and played the same note. The noise was extraordinary, like a door had opened in heaven, letting the music of the angels flood out upon the world. The dark elves, orcs, warlocks and sorceresses closest to the band swooned under the blare. But they were not in pain. They closed their eyes and smiled like they tasted something delicious. By the time the wondrous chord of music had expired and their eyes opened again, their skin and clothes and armour had been restored to their natural colours. They embraced the warriors of light they had been fighting moments ago. A cheer spread across the field and the liberated fighters ran up the hill to stand beside their comrades in the musical zoo.

The dark forces skulked back under the wings of their lord, until no one was left on the bluegrass field between the dragon's claws and the panther's.

Staring directly at Jack from the front row of the dark elf archers, Max Mercury raised his black sword and struck up a chant, shrieking, 'Dragon! Dragon! Dragon!'

The malevolent chorus behind him bellowed, wailed and screeched in reply, 'OI! OI! OI!'

'Dragon! Dragon! Dragon!' Mercury squawked again, roaming up and down in front of his master's ranks, enjoying his role. Louder this time, they answered, 'OI! OI! OI!'

'Dragon!' he screamed, pointing at the dark knights to his right.

'OI!' they thundered, striking their lances against their shields.

'Dragon!' he roared, pointing at the ice giants.

'OOOOIIIIII!' they moaned, bringing their massive clubs down on the ground.

Max turned, arms raised, smiling, and shouted up the hill at Jack, 'Dragon! Dragon! Dragon!'

And all the monsters at his back cheered, 'OI! OI! OIIIIIIIII!'

Once their awful noise petered out, Miles turned his gaze up to the birds hovering above and tapped his paw four times on the grass. The sound rose like a snare drum and overhead an eagle swooped and twirled through the air, winging a blues guitar melody. The bird repeated this rolling trill three times. On the fourth repetition, the geese beat a base rhythm with their wings and the big cats stomped and their brother wolves panted. Soon the whole army of light began to clap and strike swords against shields in time to the funky beat.

'*Come on,*' Miles meowed for all on The Plain of Tears to hear, '*Shake your bones. Come on.*' and the gorilla's trombone blasted, '*At the Red Dragon!*'

The beat was infectious. All across the Plain of Tears, the warriors began dancing.

In the darkness of their showers, the children of *Hamelin*, and all ships of the fleet, suspended between a home they never knew and a future world they would never see, danced too.

The music travelled through the air and rumbled along the ground between the two armies. The front lines of the dragon's force began to tap their toes and shuffle side to side.

The dragon paid them no attention. She kept Her eyes on Jack.

The panther pointed to a dwarf down the line from him. The stocky warrior pointed at himself and shook his head. But Miles just smiled and his rising whiskers lifted the young warrior's spirits and when the next bar began, so did he.

'*Come on,*' he bellowed and seemed surprised that so deep and sonorous a sound could come from his little frame, '*Stomp your feet!*'

The dwarves around him cheered at his bravado and the song went up and down the line.

'*Come on,*' they joined in, '*Up and down the fleet.*'

Now the whole army of light took up the song, *'Come on, clap your hands. Come on, children, take a stand.'*

Down the hill, the dragon's dark warriors grew restless. Some became so infected with the music raining down upon them that they bobbed their heads and shook their feet in time to the beat. Their generals tried to pull them into line but soon so many were waving their swords and tapping arrow heads together that nothing could prevent them from skipping and dancing across the field, up towards the party on the hill. As they climbed, their armour grew lighter in hue until, by the time they had reached the summit, they were restored to their true lustre. Their eyes and skin wore their colour again. They were welcomed back with high fives and hugging.

The Great Red Dragon lost one third of Her army to the song, yet still She did nothing. She watched the mass defection of Her horde with little more than a smirk.

Jack turned to Miles and asked, 'Why is She letting us do this?'

Miles leaned over and whispered, 'The dragon knows She can blow away all the good we're doing with one breath. What She doesn't know is we're not trying to win the battle. We're only playing for time.'

'Lucy?' Jack asked and the panther nodded.

'Right now she should be about half way up the mountain,' Miles confided. 'By the time we've finished our concert, she'll be in the dragon's cave.'

Jack looked across The Plain of Tears, over The Dark Forrest to the mountain beyond. He imagined Lucy, in her elfin garb, scaling the jagged cliffs that were home to the dragon. When she reached its lair, she would steal back from Her all the memories She had robbed from the children of The Fleet.

As their song came to its end, the orchestra of thousands cheered.

In reply, the dragon's voice purred thickly through the air, 'Your friendssss play prettily, Jack, but I think my musssic is more fit for making war.'

'Maybe,' Jack yelled back, trying to sound brave, 'but you're running out of kids to play it.'

'Ha!' the dragon scoffed and with one paw swept a whole class of seniors from the ground beside Her. Their screams of fear and surprise echoed across the valley. 'I don't need thessse infantsss.'

Inside Showers on every ship of The Fleet, children fighting in the dragon's army bowed their heads. There was nothing they could do. They had been touched by the dragon's flame. They were Her servants until She was defeated.

In the darkness of her tiled cubicle, Jenna Pioneer raised her right arm and screamed, 'Oh great lord, I will defend your honour!' In the game world, her avatar raised its staff of twisted oak and the sorceress charged up the hill.

Thousands followed her. It was not against the will of the dragon to attack its enemy. But this was their chance to be free, to have the curse on them beaten by the panther and his band's joyous song.

Miles turned to Jack, gave a wink of his great predatory eye and growled, 'Show time, kid. Let's rock.'

33. DRAGON'S GOLD (PT. 2)

The panther launched himself down the hill. His paws played a drumroll that mustered all the other instruments behind him to strike up and charge into the fray. They thundered down the slope like an impassioned host of angels, trumpeting, beating and strumming from their instruments a majestic harmony.

Jack stood agog, uncertain how to add to this resounding chorus. From behind him, the gorilla bounded forward, swept Jack up onto his back and huffed, 'Just keep time, Voyager. Just keep time.'

Diving downwards, towards an army armed with swords, clubs and all manner of hard, sharp and heavy things, Jack felt the fearful stone thudding in his chest. He heard his jester's costume meekly tinkling. But he took the ape's advice and shook his fist in time to Miles's thumping charge, making the bells on his hat and sleeves and cuffs jingle-jangle, jingle-jangle, jingle-jangle.

They passed through the front lines of their foes, into the shadow cast by the dragon's wings. All about them, green orcs swung their stone hammers and thrust their crooked spears. The gorilla swung this way and that, parrying sword thrusts with his trombone and blasting forth shocks of booming brass from the shining instrument. Each blast knocked a dark warrior to the ground and washed the dragon's black corruption from their armour. But there were so many to heal. For every one they saved, ten more took their place.

Soon they were surrounded by a ring of club-wielding ice giants and dark elves brandishing blades dipped in poison. At their head was Max Mercury.

'You never learn, do you Jangles?' he spat. 'You must really love dying.'

'Hold tight, my friend,' the trombonist grumbled.

Jack closed his eyes, but not to surrender. He'd been in the midst of so many battles from Earth's awful history and been killed by Max so many times, he was top of his class in being dead. Yet he had never seen a use outside of Human Sciences for Fukuyama's training. Now, as the dark elves and ice giants closed in, Jack imagined a flame in his belly. With each inhalation, he felt the flame rise and heat the stone lodged in his chest. With each exhalation, the stone gradually softened.

After three breaths, each longer and deeper than the last, he forgot the battle din. It was a distant buzz. Instead, he felt the muscles of the gorilla's neck flexing beneath his fur. He felt the blood pumping in the trombonist's veins, a mighty pounding answered by Jack's own small heart's rhythm. He noticed the little skip his drum made every other beat. He listened to it, let it echo in all the deepest parts of him. He felt the spaces between his joints and the vertebrae of his spine. They were humming. The cavity of his rib cage felt as wide as an auditorium. That too, Jack sensed, was full of sound. From his toes up to his skull, Jack thrummed and whirred with a strange yet familiar tone.

He opened his mouth to hear it better. The stone, melted down to a pebble, dropped free, and from its prison his voice rose up and out for all to hear.

The line of monsters closest to the Jack and the trombonist staggered back under the force of the sound. They fell to their knees and dropped their weapons. When Jack had expired the whole breath, a moment of silence descended upon the battlefield. The circle of players came to their feet - dark elves, cleansed white, ice giants, thawed - and turned to form a protective ring around their saviour.

'Jeez, Jack,' laughed Max as he watched the black stain drain from his elfin blade, 'you coulda spoken up sooner,' and took guard before his classmate.

Across the field, the cats of prey roared and beat their paws upon the ground. Above their heads, the birds beat their wings into a storm of strings. And all about them, the army of darkness moaned and spat and screeched Jack's name.

The battle renewed, and it was savage.

Jack stood high upon the ape's broad back and kept belting out a rambling melody, more sound than words, yet full of heartfelt purpose. The more clearly the notes sprang from him, the more richly tolled the bells on his costume until they pealed like great cathedral gongs in complex harmony.

He swung his arms to and fro like a dancing kung fu master, and waves of sound flung from his fingertips into the seething sea of warriors. These deep chords washed whole rows of dragon's men clean of their loyalty to the red serpent, and they joined their voices with *The Shadows'* orchestra.

At last, with a yawn, The Great Red Dragon decided to act. She gathered onto Her haunches and lunged across the field, straight at Jack. Her claw lifted the trombonist gorilla high off the ground. Jack fell from his back and hit the earth with a clang. He could only watch as the dragon's breath engulfed the ape in flame. Her exhalation spent, She opened Her talons and there on Her palm the trombonist knelt, bowing to his master. The dragon leant it close and whispered, 'Tell me, my new friend, what isss the purpose of thisss battle? Sssssurely the cat knowssss he cannot defeat me.'

'You are right, My Lady,' the gorilla uttered, casting his trombone aside to topple down onto the dirt at Jack's side. 'It is a trick, to distract you. One of them is right now climbing up Your mountain to Your lair. She intends to steal Your treasure.'

The dragon smirked, tossed the flailing ape back over Her shoulder and looked down at Jack. 'Ssssneaky,' she snarled and leapt into the air, beating Her vast wings towards the mountain.

Across the battlefield, Jack caught the panther's eye. Miles had seen the dragon launch Herself towards the mountain. He roared and Jack knew exactly what he meant.

He must help Lucy.

34. DRAGON'S GOLD (PT. 3)

Jack looked down at his rainbow-striped jester clothes. The bells were glowing like molten glass ready to be sculpted.

He closed his eyes and inhaled.

This time his breath was so long it reached down past what he knew - what School, Sandbox and the window screen taught - into the deepest part of him.

When finally he exhaled, he did not let it all come forth in one great yell. He passed the air slowly over the strings of his voice box. The breath radiated through him, vibrating every bone of his skeleton, echoing in every blood-cell, humming along every sinew, shooting fire through every nerve.

He opened his eyes to find his arms had spread into wings. He pushed down upon the air and they raised him up into the music's spell. The warriors ceased their battle to watch him ascend. With a cheer, the army of light struck up their instruments and added their many tones to his. On their vast harmony he climbed, higher and higher into the air, until he drew level with the winged shape of his enemy.

Now the song arising from Jack's belly took more definite shape. The melody firmed into a pattern. The notes sharpened into words.

Jack, John, Voyager 1,

Michael and Xinjuan's son,

Where do you run?

Into the sun,

To catch the tail of a dragon!'

Jack fixed his eyes on the serpent slumping heavily through the air towards Her mountain and his friend, and with a beat of his wings thrust himself mightily towards his quarry.

The more confidently Jack sang, the faster he flew, and the more fearsome grew his body. His legs thickened into powerful bear-like haunches. From his feet, long, sharp talons sprouted. His head broadened to make room for a massive, roaring lion jaw that filled with glistening harp strings. His wings expanded to support this formidable frame, and sprouted streaks of rainbow feathers imbued with guitar sounds that spanned from notes of tenderness to savage electric snarls.

By the time Jack's transformation was complete, the dragon was almost at the mountain, and Lucy was only metres from Her lair. She was shivering against the icy blasts of wind whipping about the mountain peak but her spirit was fierce. Hand over hand, she reached and grasped at the cold, forbidding rock. She needed only a few moments more to reach the top.

Too late.

With a triumphant cry, The Great Red Dragon swooped down

to seize her.

Jack mustered a fresh chord of rich harmony from his stomach and hurled himself at his foe.

'Dragon!' he sang. '*Winged worm, whose word*

Pollutes the air and sickens hearts,

My song is sharper than your sword.'

With that, he gripped the serpent's tail in his talon. The dragon howled and spewed fire. Jack held tight and sang, *'Face the music. Hear my art.'*

The dragon's claws snatched the air above Lucy's head, yet the colossal worm was unable to shake Jack's grip and reach Her prey. She had no choice but to turn and face Her enemy.

'Boy,' She growled, 'you ssshould know better than to keep a sssserpent from Her ssssupper.'

The Great Red Dragon inhaled the air about Her. Her lungs drew snow from the peaks and lightening from the thunderclouds into the dark, swirling vortex of Her cavernous gullet. Once full, She spewed Her molten bile upon Jack with the all force of an ocean tipped from a bowl. The heat sucked the air from Jack's lungs. His voice faltered and he felt the feathers wither and fall from his wings. He felt his tongue start to shrivel in his lion maw.

But the song in his belly would not die.

It was the warm deep tone his body knew so well, the refuge he kept secret and safe against the strangeness and sorrow of the world.

His talons bit deeper into the serpent's flesh. His voice pitched up against the dragon's rain of noise and fire, his tongue launched wordless lashings of melodic trills and his wings beat wild blues wailings that would have made the ancient Hendrix cheer.

Against this onslaught of music, the dragon had no reply.

Her breath exhausted, She despaired.

Shrunken, deflated, She feebly flapped Her frail wings, looked up at Jack and pleaded, 'Please, pleassse have pity. Do not let her sssteal my gold. I am not evil. I am but a force, like gravity. I wassss created to test the courage of you children. Now Jack, you have proven yoursssself the bravesssst in The Fleet. Let ussss pretend that you have sssslain me. You will have every child from every sssshhhhip begging to be friendsss with you. You will never be alone again.'

Jack's winged avatar flinched and roared at the offer.

'Yessss, I know,' the dragon purred. 'I have seen you on the boulevard of Sssandbox, too sshhy to enter the sssocial clubsss, too timid to ride the rollercoasterssss, too kind to play at murder here in my quest. Let me go and I will make you a realm of your very own, Jack. What would you like? A concert hall? All your friendssss could come and play with you? Or your own band? You can live your Voyager dream: a tour throughout the universsse, playing concertsss to alienssss from civilissationsss right across the galaxsssy. You will be a sssstar, a god amongssst humanss. All this I can give you but you must let me go! She is almossst at the door!'

Jack kept his eyes fixed on the form of Lucy as she climbed the final yards to the narrow lip of the cave.

The dragon played another gambit. Jack felt the scaly flesh turn to silk in his grip. He looked and saw the tail was now a long stretch of fabric that ended in a cloak. Wearing it was Mr Fukuyama. Smoke curled out of his mouth as he intoned, 'Jack, my most talented student, you have passed the test. You have learnt the most important lesson of history: to change the world you must begin with yourself. But these people you want to help, they are terrorists. They want to do harm to The Fleet.'

'They want to help!' Jack bawled through his lion harp.

'Help?' his teacher inquired calmly, 'Help how?'

'*To remember what you took from us,*' Jack sang, '*the memory of who we are.*'

Fukuyama closed his eyes and shook his head. 'Oh Jack,' he grumbled, as though genuinely saddened. 'We need you to be better than that. We need you to become what we are teaching you to be.'

Behind Fukuyama, the mountain rose into the night. Above it shone *Uroun*. The star gave off streams of light. Jack's eyes filled with their radiance. The star turned so slowly and shone so brightly, Jack felt his grip loosen on the teacher's hem.

'Let go of the past. Reach out for *Uroun,*' his teacher goaded.

Jack's talon let the tail slip a little further. The fabric changed again. It had become the stiff material of a military uniform.

'We need you to take us there,' The Admiral's voice drawled from her grave and noble features. 'Will you do that for us, Jack? Will you lead us home?'

Over The Admiral's head, *Uroun* revolved its carousel of light. Jack sighed longingly and closed his eyes. The star still turned in his mind. His talons retreated into fingers, the fabric slipped from his grasp and the black well of his Gravity Shower dragged him under.

Jack fell.

'Jack!' a voice wafted to him on the wind. 'Jack, wake up!'

He opened his eyes. Far above him, Lucy was looking down at him from the cliff edge. She had reached the mouth of the dragon's cave. She had made it and she was safe. Relief coursed through the body of his fabulous beast. He gave it voice and winged his downward fall towards the rocks into a roaring rush back up the mountainside. He rose up above the entrance to the dragon's cave. Below, he saw the icy rock that Lucy stood upon was bathed in rainbow light. The Admiral stood over his friend, casting upon her the same stupefying spell of starlight.

'We were wrong to expel you, Lucy,' the mother of The Fleet crooned. 'You are extraordinary. If only you would work with us. We need you. We need your best. Can you give that to us, Lucy? Can you?'

Lucy swayed on her feet. Her eyelids fluttered. 'Can Dad come too?' she asked. 'Can we both come back to *The Hamelin*?'

'Of course, child,' The Admiral soothed. 'Come home.'

'Lucy!' Jack called. She turned and her elfin eyes flickered open.

'Lucy,' The Admiral intoned. The girl turned back to her.

Jack sent the whole volume of his heart at the bewitching star pulsing over their heads. 'LUCEEEEEEEE!' he cried.

From Jack's mouth, her name was a word powerful enough to break any enchantment. Into a great cloud of coloured dust, the star of *Uroun* burst like a cheap glass Christmas bauble.

The spell lifted, The Admiral lunged for Lucy. Her eyes glowed red and she growled with the voice of The Dragon, 'Get off my mountain, you pessst!'

But before she could catch her prey, the glittering glass from the fallen star rained onto her grasping arms. Instantly, their enemy's form disappeared. In its place, a red raven squawked and flapped its little wings, struggling with all its strength against the icy wind to lay hold upon Lucy. The girl watched the pitiful bird flail, until the next strong gust from the mountaintop swept it away into the night.

Jack glided on these gusts down to the cliff's edge. As he descended, his magnificent wings returned to pale and skinny arms and his talons withdrew into black Fleet sneakers. He landed and looked at Lucy with his own eyes and smiled at her from his own face. She smiled wryly at him and remarked, 'So, the lame boy kept up after all.'

Jack shook his head.

'You'll understand in a second,' she said and they turned towards the entrance of the dragon's cave. A golden light glowed from within.

'Will I remember?' Jack asked.

Lucy smiled, nodded and looked away. For a moment, she stared into the deep distance, holding the breath of a question. Finally, she sighed and tugged free from her tunic a slender necklace. On its chain hung a small golden key, glowing with the same lustre that shone from inside the cave. She pressed the key into Jack's palm, closed his fingers over it and whispered, 'Come find me. We have an appointment to keep with The Piper.'

With that, she stepped across the threshold of the dragon's lair, into the dazzling light.

Over the sound of the wind raging round the mountain, Jack heard shouts and cheers of victory rising from the Plain of Tears. He walked to the edge of the cliff and gazed out over the world he had liberated. He looked at the key in his hands and then his skinny arms and realised with practiced panic that he was 'naked'. Yet he resisted the compulsion to load up a new form to mask his own. Instead, he closed his eyes and listened to the weird drum of his heart stutter its unique rhythm. He grasped the key tightly and hummed along to the beat, finding a tune that sounded like how Lucy made him feel.

Sandbox had disguised the cadet control room as the Great Red

Dragon's mountain lair. The details were impressive. The rocky grotto was cold and wet, yet shimmered in the light that glowed from the glass jars of data. Was this The Admiral's vanity, Lucy wondered? On the off chance some kid made it this far, did she still wanted the illusion to seem real and frightening?

Lucy saw through the illusion. She wasn't frightened anymore.

She had stepped off the edge of the world, died, and returned. And now she had seen her friend wake up from his own oblivion, and rattle the cage of forgetting in which he had been locked.

Now she would set him free, and he would remember.

Now everyone would remember.

She picked up one of the jars in which the memories of her peers were stored. The metaphor was fantastical, but what it represented was practical, brutal. The Fleet transmitted a signal which helped fix the hypnotic trance The Admiral used to suppress memory. Smashing the jars meant stopping the insidious broadcast frequency, thus 'releasing' the cadets' memories.

She raised the jar above her head, whispered, 'Remember me,' and dropped it. The crash echoed out into the night like a pealing of bells, a jangling, tinkling, crashing torrent of sound that resounded across The Dark Forrest and The Plain of Tears to every corner of the gameworld and tolled in the Shower of every last child in The Fleet.

It called them all to wake up from their parents' captive dream.

And Lucy knew they'd fight to never fall asleep again.

AFTERNOON, DAY 182

35. WHEN THE LEVEE BREAKS

Jack pulled the cap from his face. His eyes were no longer full of fabricated imagery. He stared into the darkness, and remembered.

He remembered Lucy. The first time he had seen her, his first fateful Induction Day, she was the only one, of all his classmates, who didn't laugh at the alarms set off by his random heart.

They had stolen that memory from him. Without it, he had no ally in this world. He was alone, and defenceless.

Without his memories of days spent loving her but not having her, of being near her yet feeling so distant, without all that pain, he was robbed of his passion.

He remembered the vision he and Lucy had shared, each child reaching for their own personal *Uroun*, tiptoed on a mountain of skulls.

He remembered his father's gift, a toy meant to distract him, but one Jack had mastered and used to make The Piper's song his own.

He remembered the shame of his debut performance, of being exposed. Then his joy on stage in The Club, the revelation, of knowing himself.

He recalled the strange episode of *Stars of Uroun*, the rats streaming through the streets of Hamelin, and in Warsaw too where the Golem had delivered The Piper's invitation:

All of these things had happened to another Jack, who now stood within the same body as this one. Two souls superimposed. Or the different elements of a single song, playing in stereo through his left and right hand speakers. On one side, the driving tempo of his loving heart. On the other, the rising fury of a lead guitar.

Jack drew back the door of his Shower and stepped into his room. What had been his whole world now seemed so small, like a miniature, the model of a stage set for a sitcom.

He looked up at the posters on his wall. The Admiral pointed at him, asking, 'IF NOT YOU, WHO? IF NOT NOW, WHEN? Beside that hung a framed photograph of *Uroun*, the swirling rainbow world towards which all their hearts were trained. Above that a bright pennant proclaimed Jack's loyalty to Team Blue.

He reached up, snatched the pennant from the wall and tore until it was nothing but ragged confetti on his bed. He reached a hand out for the image of The Admiral yet stayed his fingers an inch from the paper.

Jack stared into her printed face.

He remembered how like the Mayor of Hamelin The Admiral looked. What had The Piper's price been? He'd rid the town of rats if the Mayor promised her first born would become his apprentice. When the Mayor broke their deal, The Piper tried to steal the children of Hamelin. To 'instruct' them. Jack knew that he and Lucy were not the only two who had answered The Piper's call. Miles and *The Shadows* knew him too.

'So who are the rats?' Jack whispered to The Admiral's face.

His breath made the poster move, and The Fleet commander's image seemed to shake its head.

Jack heard the muffled thump of something large and heavy on the other side of the wall.

He imagined cadets on every ship of the fleet, rising out of their bedrooms to demand the truth from their mothers and fathers. He thought of his parents, Michael and Xinjuan, how they pampered him and praised his hard work, all the while aware of what School was doing to him.

He looked at the model of the *HMAS Hamelin* on his desk which his father had given him and they'd assembled together on his seventh birthday. Jack picked it up, ready to hurl it across the room. He held it aloft, feeling like a fool for trusting him, and also mourning the boy who had trusted.

His eyes caught on a little red dot his father had marked on the hull. That dot showed where their cabin was located, halfway to the port bow, two decks down from the bridge where his father worked, six decks up from where his mother worked in the algae farms. Below that were the engineering decks that led down to the keel.

Jack scanned his eyes over all the other portholes of the tiny craft. He'd been told *The Hamelin* was home to 12,000 souls. How many of them stared out those windows and longed for escape? Perhaps all of them did at one time or another.

If not you, who? If not now, when?

Jack felt a warm glow in the right-hand glove of his uniform. A key shape shone at the centre of his palm. Lucy's gift to him. He gripped it in his fist and whispered, 'Me. Now.'

In ten steps Jack reached the edge of his world.

He paused at the doorway and realised that, until this moment, he had never once questioned his confinement. He had accepted it as a fact of life.

He raised his right palm to the lock beside the door. The code in his glove communicated itself to the console. It chimed politely and unlocked the mechanism, allowing the door to slide back on its track with a whisper. He stepped through into the entryway. Its patch of carpet bore the fleet insignia: a ring of seven stars around a larger central star. Only one step separated the inner from the outer door and he made that step now, raising his palm to the final lock.

Jack paused. He had no plan for what he would do once he was through the door and into the world of his parents. The lame boy and the blind girl had followed The Piper's song.

He listened. He heard nothing.

Nothing from outside of himself.

He waited a moment longer, and then, from deep within, a melody swelled up softly and broke upon his lips:

'Safely tucked within its bed

The seed won't ever flower.

Underneath a video *sun*

Watered by false showers,

Jack, John, Voyager 1,

Your sweet fruits ripen sour

Michael and Xinjuan's son,

A rotting, wasted power.

He lifted his palm up to the console. For what seemed like an eternity the door thought about his request. Jack faltered. Was the charm Lucy had planted there wearing off? Almost relieved that the choice to risk it all had been taken from him, Jack lowered his hand and took a step back. In that instant, the console chimed and the outer door slid open.

36. STANDIN' ON THE OUTSIDE, LOOKIN' IN

The corridor was silent, dimly lit, and stretched into gloom in each direction. Going left would take Jack towards the bow of the ship, pointed towards *Uroun*. Right led towards the stern and *The Hamelin*'s engines. He looked at the doorway directly across from his. Beside the key pad was a little plaque. Upon it were printed four lines, Jack assumed, addressed to the parents of *Hamelin*:

THERE IS NO PIPER.

THERE ARE NO RATS.

IF YOU HEAR MUSIC,

TELL YOUR COMMANDING OFFICER.

Jack looked along the corridor. This same warning was stamped next to every single door. Jack knew his parents agreed with the first two edicts, but the third? They listened to music together all the time. It was the thing that bound them. And they knew he sang. Surely their gift to him of Guitar Hero put them all on the wrong side of The Admiral's law.

Above the plaque was another upon which the name of the

family dwelling within was stamped. The cabin directly across from Jack's was inhabited by The Mercurys. Jack shivered. All this time, his tormentor had lived only metres away. All those years of living in fear, thought Jack, if only he could have taken a few steps starboard and seen Max for who he is: the short plump goon Lucy exposed in the Warsaw Ghetto.

'If *he's* here…,' Jack breathed, and his heart beat faster.

He turned to the right and stepped down the passage, checking each sign as he went. To his frustration, the cabins were not assigned alphabetically. There was no outward distinction between each plaque, save the name and the relative freshness of the plastic upon which it was printed. Some seemed brand new, others soiled with age.

Growing desperate, Jack paused and in the gloomy stillness listened. From behind the door closest to him, The Apollo 11s', he heard raised voices muffled by the double layer of steel. He pressed his ear to the outer door and heard one high voice and a deeper one. The high one he recognised as Evan Apollo's. He assumed the other was his father's. The man had a lot of explaining to do. Yet from the barking tones, Jack could tell that Evan's dad was instead yelling importantly over all his son's protests.

Jack crossed to the door opposite, The Pioneers'. Inside he heard Jenna screeching and crashing about. On a whim, Jack pressed his palm to her door. Lucy's code worked there as well. The door slid back. The crashing inside the Pioneers' flat halted. Jack reached across the brief entryway and pressed the panel to the inner door. It opened to reveal Jenna. She was alone, clutching a busted table leg above her head. It was a pose Jack recognised from her formidable sorceress avatar in *Dragon Quest*. Her emaciated limbs and painted face he recognised from Warsaw. She recognised him too.

'Jack?' she asked, and dropped the improvised club. 'Oh, Jack. What have they done to us?'

Jack didn't know what to say. He was no longer thinking, but reacting. He beckoned her to follow him and moved back into the corridor. He showed her the glowing patch of e-fabric in his palm and pressed it to her neighbour's key pad. As the door slid open he took Jenna's hand and copied the Lucy's digital key to it. Then he walked past her to the next door astern, leaving her to stare wide eyed at the golden key aglow in the glove of her uniform. With a chuckle, she turned to her port-side neighbour's door and opened it to reveal a mother kneeling at her daughter's feet as her child slowly tipped all the contents of their refrigerator onto the kitchen floor.

Jack only opened the doors of cabins where he sensed there were no adults within. He knew that as soon as they learned there were children loose, the bridge would be notified and right afterwards the parents would all arrive banging their pots and pans and shoving toys and dress-ups under their children's noses.

By the time Jack found the door he was looking for, the corridor was abuzz with liberated children. Each of them was given a key and they copied it to each cadet they freed. Jack ignored their angry cries and wild hoots of victory.

He had found what he was looking for.

He stood before a door graffitied to look like the jaws of a wolf. Next to it was a plaque marked Gemini. Jack slowed his breathing. He had once dreamed that his feelings for Lucy had been so strong that they had split the hull of the ship and scuttled everyone aboard *The Hamelin* into space. In the dream, Jack had held his breath long enough to float through the confusion of broken fuselage and furniture and flailing bodies to find her cabin and free her from her room. They had embraced and in that pose frozen, drifting, slow-dancing for eternity.

And all this time, she'd been but fifty steps away.

He lifted his hand to the lock.

Inside, the cabin was still. Everything was neat and orderly.

A soft whimpering sound drew Jack to the second bedroom. To the door was pasted a little pink love heart with 'Lucy' written in her hand in silver glitter ink. Jack knocked lightly and the whimpering paused. After a moment, a whispered, 'Yes?' emerged. Jack entered.

A woman was slumped face forward over the bed. Between her pale, lank arms, her long blonde hair swirled across the bedclothes like a sea of milk in which her face was drowning. Jack knelt down beside her.

'Mrs. Gemini,' he began, 'Where is she? Where's Lucy?'

After a moment she quietly sobbed, 'Taken.'

'Taken?' Jack pressed. 'Taken where, by who?'

The woman's face rose to meet Jack's. Her eyes were raw, riven with sorrow and pain.

'Down with the rats!' she spat. 'Where everyone who hears that damned music goes.'

Her eyes softened and she reached her trembling hands out to touch him.

'But you don't hear it, do you?' she cooed. 'You'll stay here, won't you?'

Hannah looked up at her daughter's narrow desk and plucked from it the first thing that came to hand.

'Look, here's a pony,' she sighed, pawing a dusty *papier mache* horse Lucy must have made when she was much younger. 'Nice pony,' she said and pressed it into Jack's hands. She rose and grabbed more things from the desk with which to weigh him down - pencils, paper, a slide rule, a sharpener. 'Here, you can colour in. Make it all perfect. Your own perfect world.'

Gently, Jack put everything Hannah handed to him onto the bed. She tried to pick them up again but Jack held her hands and pulled her gaze up into his. They stayed like that and Jack opened his mouth to ask where exactly Lucy had gone 'down with the rats', when a voice erupted in the silence. It was The Admiral.

'ALL HEAR THIS. ALL HEAR THIS. THIS IS A FLEET-WIDE EMERGENCY,' she bellowed. 'ALL CREW WITH

CHILDREN REPORT IMMEDIATELY TO YOUR CABINS. WE ARE CODE DELTA. REPEAT, CODE DELTA. THIS IS NOT A DRILL. ALL PARENTS, ALL SHIPS, TO YOUR CABINS. CODE DELTA IS IN EFFECT.'

The voice sobered Lucy's mother. She took Jack's face in her hands and seethed, 'Run, Jack. Before they make you forget her. Go! Don't let them take her from you too.'

Jack pressed his hands to hers. 'Where is she?'

The woman took one trembling hand from Jack's cheek. It quivered in the air between them. She dipped her index finger onto the bridge of Jack's nose, tilting his face downward to stare at a drawing on the floor, sketched by Lucy's more mature hand. From her mother's perspective, the V-shape represented a pit. Near its bottom, a jagged waterline crossed the V like a row of jagged white teeth, waiting to mash the two figures tumbling headfirst towards it.

'The Drain,' Hannah whimpered fearfully. 'The Drain.'

From Jack's perspective, the V was an A. The crooked white line was the crown of a snowy mountain peak.

And the boy and girl were climbing.

37. DANCING IN THE STREET

The air in the corridor outside was thick with alarm. The loudspeakers continued to declare, 'CODE DELTA! CODE DELTA!' over a constant, ear-splitting clanging. Cries of fear and protest rang like gunshots. Shouts of anger and command burst the air like bombs.

Jack looked left and right. In each direction, children of all ages crashed and dashed amongst their parents. The smaller ones were far easier to catch. Many of them stood timidly outside their doorways, uncertain which way to go, or bawled until their mothers and fathers gathered them up in their arms and carried them inside the comfort of their cabins. Others stumbled about, trying to catch the attention of the bigger kids to ask them what they should do next. The older children didn't know, but they were close to graduation, close to being adults themselves. They were taller, stronger, faster, and they felt like a fight. They pulled free from their parents' hands. They pushed back, yelling, 'Bully!' 'Liar!' 'Fraud!' and 'Cheat!' They broke through the doorways of their cells and set off into the gloom; not towards something - they didn't know what they wanted – just away, away from everything they knew.

That left the middle year students, the thirteen, fourteen and fifteen year olds, smart enough and angry enough to want out, but not sure enough yet of their limbs to do more than to dart to and fro, just outside their parents' reach.

Jack was one of them, but he had his father's long limbs, his mother's grace and a bold desire burning in his chest. He saw a break in the chaotic crowd and bolted into the darkness. All the mothers and fathers were focused solely on their own children and ignored him. All but one. He grabbed Jack's wrist, yanked him to the floor, sat on him and pinned his arms to the dank carpet. It was the father of Evan Apollo.

'You! You did this,' he screamed in Jack's face. 'Michael-bloody-Voyager's son. I knew he couldn't be trusted. He was a weirdo in School.' He leaned down so the sweat dripped from his forehead into Jack's eyes, 'But your mum was worse. So bloody superior. Thought she was too good for the rest of us. Now look at you. Look what you've done. We should have gotten rid of your lot when we had the chance.'

'Hey dad!' a voice from behind Jack yelped over the din. With a glimmer of hope in his eyes, Mr. Apollo lifted his face and a small pale hand slapped it so hard that he fell off his perch on Jack's belly, onto the oil-stained carpet.

Evan looked guiltily from his father to Jack and helped him to his feet.

'Go!' Evan told him. 'Go find Lucy.'

As Jack sprang away, Evan's father cowered under his son's furious glare.

Up and down and side to side, like a Jet Racer between

asteroids, Jack flew down the corridor, past endless tableaux of children grappling with their parents. They gripped the edges of doorframes whilst their mothers and fathers pulled at their waists. Some kids barricaded themselves inside their cabins and refused to let their parents back in. Some adults knelt like penitents and wept silently as their offspring rained down upon their heads all the judgement they had earned.

'You let them get inside my dreams.'

'You let them steal my memories.

'You let them hurt me.'

'…work me.'

'…enslave me.'

'Why, Mum?'

'Why, Dad?'

'Why?'

Through these scenes Jack vaulted and ducked and began to feel like he might actually make it out, that there might be a way through this gloom, and at the end of it he would find Lucy waiting for him where she'd always been, one step ahead.

A rectangle of light appeared at the end of the corridor: an open doorway. Jack picked up speed. The doorway filled with the silhouetted forms of what looked to Jack like Ancient Roman soldiers. Their heads wore tall helmets. Shields, as wide as their shoulders, covered them from neck to knee. They began to jog in time towards him and Jack realised that they were adult crewmen in riot gear. Their shields bore the insignia of seven stars in a ring about the central star of Uroun. The visors of their helmets concealed their faces. They held their batons aloft, ready to answer conclusively any child's hand still raised in doubt.

The senior kids retreated back down the corridor. They'd spent enough time in Fukuyama's classes to know what happens when unarmed civilians meet armed police. From the other end of the corridor, more security personnel were approaching, driving the children back towards the centre of the passageway. Jack was caught between the oncoming waves of feet stomping in military time.

He closed his eyes and tried to think.

He listened past the thud of marching boots, the random, panicked rush of sneakers.

He tuned through the shouts, screams and sirens.

He heard a whisper of song.

It was coming from his right. Jack opened his eyes and saw nothing but the metal wall between two cabins. He leant down closer and pressed his ear to a panel between the doorways of the Challengers and the Endeavours. The metal hummed warmly. Jack ran his fingers along it until he found a seam. He dug his nails under it and the panel came loose in his hands. He pulled it free from the wall and stared into the dark space beyond. From deep within the darkness, he clearly heard the gently warbling rivulet of The Piper's woodwind call.

'Jack,' a voice intoned behind him.

Jack turned with the panel in his hands, preparing to use it either to shield himself or swat away any attempt to grab him. The guard's face was covered entirely by the helmet's visor. Jack imagined that behind that screen the world looked like a movie or a video game, and right now Jack was the target. But the guard did not raise his baton to strike Jack. Nor did he make any move to lay hands upon him. He just looked down at him, breathing heavily.

'Dad?' Jack asked.

The guard made no response. He simply turned away from the boy, took a step back and crouched, holding his shield out before him, concealing Jack and protecting him from the thresh of flailing bodies.

Jack did not need further encouragement. He put his hands on the floor and pushed his legs behind him into the opening. When he was in up to his shoulders he reached out and touched the leg of the guard. The man tapped the wall impatiently with his baton. Jack picked up the panel and drew it up into place, enclosing himself in a murky hollow that quivered with distant piping.

38. ROAD TO NOWHERE

Jack followed the song, feet first through the darkness. He feared electrocution from the wires and circuit boards lining this narrow space between the cabins, but with every thrust backwards into the dark, he put his faith in the beckoning sound of the pipe, and carried on into the unknown.

He heard the opening in the floor before he saw it. He stopped. From below, the music was rising like spring water, clear and sweet. Jack carefully lowered his sneakers into the hole. There were metal pipes. He used them like rungs on a ladder. As he descended beneath the deck of living quarters, he tried not to think of what awful fluids might be flowing through the thin tubes passing directly before his face. He concentrated instead upon the trilling thrill of song that rose louder and clearer with each downward step.

A sudden release of steam from a valve at his shoulder scalded his cheek and he lost his grip. Through long black shadows he fell and landed with a sharp, bright burst of pain in his knees. Unsticking himself from the metal grate, he looked around. This tiny space was slightly lighter. The source of the luminescence lay a short crawl away. It was a grill through which Jack could hear a babbling of voices and electronic jingles. He edged over to the vent and looked through.

Beyond was a space Jack did not recognise from any of the virtual ship tours Ms. Turing had taken him through. It seemed to be some sort of recreation area. There were video screens everywhere, suspended from the ceilings in banks of five. Beneath each screen stood a bar flanked with stools. The banks hung in three rows down the whole length of the cavernous hall. The screens were all broadcasting various stages and forms of competition between Team Red and Team Blue, representing all that week's online activity. But no one was there to watch it. The hall was deserted.

Jack pushed on the grill until it came loose and he pulled himself into the room. His eyes and ears were assailed by the hectic racket and the kaleidoscopic glare pouring from the speakers and screens.

The next thing Jack noticed was the smell.

It was soaked into the carpet and now stuck to his hands and knees. It was a stench he had once or twice detected on his father on Fleet Day. It was like sweetened engine grease and metal and it burned Jack's nostrils. Here, concentrated, the fume was like an alien atmosphere, syrup thick and heavy with anger and sadness.

Jack wandered between the banks of screens and noticed taps were built into the bars beneath. He sniffed at one. These were the source of the stench.

'Uh uh, not til you're graduated, mate,' a gruff voice cawed behind him. 'Stunt your growth.'

Jack turned to see the back of a grey and grizzled crewman sitting at one of the bars. A halo of frizzy grey hair surrounded his pale bald pate. Above the elder's scruffy head a game of cricket was playing. Without looking away from the match, the man raised his tinkling glass and motioned to the stool at his side.

Jack froze.

'Kid,' the man muttered, 'if I wanted to turn you in, I'd a done so already.'

Jack glanced at the helmet perched next to the man on the bar.

'Why aren't you helping the others?' Jack asked.

The man shrugged and sipped his drink.

'No kids,' he confided. 'What's the point?'

Jack was unsure whether the man meant there was no point in helping catch his shipmate's children or in being a parent. He edged closer, calculating how near he would need to be to snatch the man's helmet and run.

'So, why no kids, mate?' Jack said, trying on the familiar term with his elder.

The man didn't answer. Jack came closer still, until he could see the man in profile. He was unshaven. His bloodshot eyes sat heavily in the cups of his cheeks. Yet something about him defied his age. Something eternal.

Jack's question hung in the air between them as he shifted his gaze back and forth between the man's distracted stare and his fingers inching closer to the helmet.

With unexpected speed, the man shot out his left hand and grasped Jack's forearm. He turned and pulled Jack's face into his invisible haze of drink. 'Why no kids? Because they're trouble. Because they're born knowing nothing and raised to know even less. And because I wouldn't give The Admiral the satisfaction of having one more moron to salute her as she leads us all to Hell.'

The man set his drink down and used the free hand to move his helmet to the opposite side of him, away from Jack's nimble fingers. With the other hand, he forced Jack to sit. Once he was satisfied that Jack would remain still, he let go of him and resumed watching the game over the rim of his glass, reaching regularly under the bench to refill it from the tap.

The game was entering the final overs. It was a close contest. Blue had three wickets in hand and needed fifteen runs to win from twelve balls. This was the kind of finish Jack's dad hoped for each week. The kind of game in which it almost didn't matter who won. In moments like these, the story was all that mattered, the feeling that fate could be decided by the slightest error or stroke of daring.

The Red's star bowler, Rick Mercury, steamed in. The Blue batsman swung wildly, trying to lift the ball out of the stadium. He missed. The ball smashed the wickets, sending the simulated Red fielders into a laughing, back-slapping huddle around Max's dad. As the next batsman emerged from the dugout, the man turned on his stool to face Jack and sized him up.

'You're a sneaky one, aren't ya?' he began. 'Can't say I've ever heard of any of you punks getting off the Family Deck before.' He chuckled and turned away as he sipped, 'Where is it you think you're headed to?'

Jack repeated what Lucy's mother had said, 'Down the drain, with the rest of the rats.'

The man put his drink down, turned and leaned towards him as though seeing Jack for the first time.

'Really?' he smirked, 'You want to go down The Drain? Well, that's definitely one way off the ship. You'll never get there, though.'

He motioned to the arched double doors that were the only way in or out of the hall.

'They'll catch you within thirty paces of those doors,' he cautioned. 'And even if they didn't, how would you find it, little rat? Follow your nose? The Drain's stink is everywhere on this ship. It's on everyone. It's in your cabin, on the bridge, here in the casino, everywhere. No, to find The Drain you'd need some kind of map.'

He put his hand on his helmet and thrummed his fingers.

'Yeah,' he went on, enjoying his tease, 'you'd need some kind of heads up display with a detailed ship navigation app. Where would you come by one of those?'

Jack couldn't stand it any longer.

'I'll bet you for it!' he blurted.

The man laughed, 'With what? You've got nothing I need,

mate.'

Jack looked up at the screen. Blue had just lost another wicket. It was down to the wire, the best of all possible endings. Blue needed to hit a six off the last ball of the match.

'If Blue hits a six this ball,' he began, 'you give me the helmet.'

'Yeah,' the man snickered, 'and if they don't?'

Jack stepped out of the man's reach.

'You can turn me in,' Jack said with a sigh. 'I may not make it far on my own, but I don't imagine it's going to look too good for you, being here while Fleet Command is Code Delta. Maybe you won't be allowed in here for a while. Maybe they'll take away a bunch of your privileges,' he said and pointed at the drink dispenser. The man stiffened. 'If you turn me in,' Jack continued, 'you can say you tracked me here to catch me.'

The man filled his glass and drained it down with one gulp. 'Show's what you know about this ship, boy,' he muttered and filled his drink again. 'It's not as clean and tidy as School and Sandbox. No one knows I'm here and no one's going to ask. But I do like a bet, and it wouldn't hurt to look like I'm still worth something. Might even win me a couple more years before…'

With his index finger he made a downward spiralling motion and a whistling sound that ended with a splash in his drink.

'Alright,' he grimaced, 'you're on. This ball, Blue hits a six or you go back to your room.'

If Jack was not already sweating on the outcome of the final delivery, when the next Blue player at the batter's crease turned to face the bowler, Jack and the man both gasped. The batsman avatar wore Jack's face.

The simulated crowd clapped their hands and stomped their feet. Red Rick Mercury descended on Jack from his long run. The bowler brought his arm over and flung the leather with all his might.

Jack closed his eyes.

He heard the roar of the crowd. He couldn't tell for whom they were cheering. He couldn't look. The announcers were screaming, 'The greatest finish in the history of Red versus…'

The sound was muffled by the helmet squeezing over Jack's ears. He looked up through the visor at the man.

'Go Blues,' he mumbled at Jack and raised his glass.

Jack lifted the visor and watched a replay of the game's final ball. In slow-motion his avatar moved like a dancer through a crouching, swooping motion that brought his bat into perfect connection with the ball to reverse its trajectory and lift it back over the bowler's head, soaring across the green grass, over the upturned faces of the fielders and the simulated crowd and out of the stadium into the unprogrammed darkness beyond. He turned to the man to speak. Before he could, the screens went silent and an announcement came over the ship PA.

'All hear this. All hear this,' it declared. 'Code Delta is over.

Repeat. Code Delta is over. Return to your stations.'

The man grew serious.

'You know what that means,' he growled. 'It means all your classmates are being made to take a Shower. Right now, they're washing away the memory of that filthy little rebellion you've all been rolling around in. It also means that all the parents will be rushing back to their posts. And any who aren't on duty will be coming in here to do a little forgetting of their own.'

He tinkled the ice in his glass and lifted it to his lips. He closed his eyes, gulped and turned back to the boy.

'Now, Jack, what you want to do is this. When you step out those doors, do not, under any circumstances take this helmet off or lift the visor. You're lanky. With this on you might pass for a young woman. The map's voice-activated. Just ask for The Drain and you'll be guided all the way. Well, go on. What are you waiting for?'

'Would you have really turned me in?' Jack asked.

The man rolled his eyes, turned away and filled his drink. Without looking back at Jack, he told him, 'I work in statistics. Red V Blue. A whole lot of points came in for Blue from *Dragon Quest* today. That's what I call down-to-the-wire.'

Jack was stunned. The man sighed, looked down at his drink and said, 'We need some kind of hero to shake things up out here.' He smirked into his glass. 'If not you?'

Jack finished the Admiral's motto. 'Who?' He wanted to say

more, to thank him, but the volume of the jingling music and the baritone commentators of all the other games between Red and Blue resumed their deafening pitch.

The doors opened and in streamed a hundred adults, pulling helmets from their heads and sighing, slumping onto the benches and reaching under them for a draught of the noxious brew. Jack slammed down his visor. He walked between the benches, listening to the crewmen's conversation:

'Damn kids, I don't bloody know.'

'Tell me about it, mate. Don't they know how lucky they are?'

'The sacrifices we make to keep them happy... Ungratitude it is.'

'What's going on in that School? That's what I want to know?'

'Unbelievable, right. I ask you, isn't it their job to control them?'

'You get no argument from me mate. It's unbelievable.'

'Unbelievable.'

'Un-bloody-believable.'

39. DOWN AND TO THE LEFT

Down the passageway Jack went and in every face he met he saw anger, fear, but most of all fatigue. The adults of *Hamelin* were tired. They trudged past him in uniforms that were patched and re-patched, taken in and let out, time and time again by the generations who had worn them before. Why did Jack's parents' clothes seem so well-preserved? Was there a cupboard in the entryway to their flat in which they kept a change of dress, a costume they wore to reinforce the illusion they performed for him around the dinner table, that everything on board *The Hamelin* was wonderful and going according to plan?

Through his visor, Jack scanned the walls and saw for himself that things were certainly not going as intended. Many panels were missing or in disrepair, exposing the rotting innards of the ship. Everywhere, burnt out circuits, re-welded joints, and cavities filled with plastic cement, spoke of sickness and decay. It was as if the ship were dying.

Jack pushed aside these thoughts and concentrated on how to find Lucy. He engaged the helmet's interface.

'Helmet on?' he ventured.

The device responded by projecting an array of graphics and text on the inside of his visor, augmenting his view of the corridor. In his vision, text-boxes appeared above the heads of each crewman he passed, informing him of their name, rank, assigned section and current ranking in Red Vs Blue. 'Ignatius Endeavour, Lieutenant, Engineering, 2,315th Blue' bumped into Jack and walked on without a word and Jack realised that he was in little danger of being detected. Everyone with a helmet on was too involved in scanning their interface to bother with him, and everyone whose helmet was in their hands was off duty and too exhausted to care.

'Maps,' Jack said and his current location appeared.

'Destination?' a female voice inquired in his left ear.

After a moment, Jack ventured, 'The Drain.'

The helmet went silent, as though holding its breath at the mention of rats and rivers.

'Did you mean, Human Resources Re-Allocation?' it finally suggested.

'Y-yes. Human Resources Re-Allocation. How do I get there?' Jack spluttered.

Projected onto the screen before him, a glowing arrow appeared in the passageway. It pointed ahead and to the left. Jack took the turn and the arrow straightened, only to bend again to the right at the next intersection. In this manner, Jack proceeded through the decomposing innards of the ship, against the flow of a constant stream of human misery.

After many turns and downwardly spiralling stairwells, Jack lost his sense of which deck he was on and which direction he was headed in except that it was down and to the left, down and to the left.

In one particularly dreary corridor, packed with slouched and hapless humans, Jack sensed a presence, weaving through the throng, slithering just out of sight.

He heard the being before he saw it.

'Ssssomeone'ssss sssssomewhere they ssshhouldn't be,' the dreadful voice oozed through the speakers of Jack's helmet. 'Took me a while to find you, Jack, but here you are.'

Jack said nothing. He quickened his steps, turning side on to squeeze past the bodies lurching around him.

'How do you like it out here, Jack? Issss it everything you hoped it would be?'

Jack pushed more insistently through the crowd, desperate to avoid coming face to face with his nemesis. But it was too late. The Great Red Dragon had found him. Its serpentine form emerged from the crowd, fresh flames licking from the furnace of its smirking maw. Jack stopped and tore off his helmet. There was nothing before him but human traffic. Realising his folly, he pulled the helmet back on and there before him in the corridor crouched the rebooted ruler of the virtual realm.

'Do you understand now, Jack?' it intoned. 'Do you sssee now why we lie to you? Look around you. Do you think the children would ssstudy ssso hard if they knew the fate that awaitsss them after graduation? We need you to hope. We need you to believe.'

'You need us to keep out of the way.'

'Jack. Oh, Jack. All of thisss isss for you. Every watt of energy not needed to keep usss alive and moving forward isssspent powering the world you inhabit. Ssschool and Sssandbox are the sssoul of The Fleet. But the body isss dying. We cannot make it much farther before we exsssspire. We need you to learn, to think, to find a quicker path to *Uroun*, fasssster than light itsssself.'

'Then tell us straight!' Jack seethed. 'Don't twist us up in fantasies.'

'Better a dream than a nightmare, Jack. Reality isss… terrifying.'

'Then teach us to be brave!' Jack yelled and took the helmet from his head.

He held it at his side and pictured where the arrow had been pointing before the dragon filled his vision. From the speakers in the helmet he could hear the dragon's small voice plead, 'Your yearsss in The Ssshower are the bessst of your life. Come back. I promissss, you'll want for nothing.'

Jack looked into the helmet in his hands, at the image of the dragon coiled within, and shook his head. Like a snake in a basket, the dragon writhed in fury.

'Very well,' she spat up at him, 'keep running. Down the drain to the river with you! Down, down, with the ratssss, to drown.'

Jack dropped the helmet to the floor, put his head down and pushed down the corridor, weaving through the throng of sullen crewmen. Down to the left, down to the left, until the crowd thinned out and he could lift his head and examine his surroundings more closely.

The passage he was in was illuminated by a soft green and blue glow. He rubbed at the wall. It was glass. Beyond the wall-length, ceiling-high panes, organic matter spread in swirling patterns. He had found the algae fields where his mother worked. That meant that he was near the stern, beneath the engines, about the bottom-most corner of the hull. Here vast areas of the fuselage were devoted to these narrow screens that collected solar radiation from distant stars to feed the vegetation that in turn fed the entire crew. From this stuff every edible substance aboard *The Hamelin* was made, shaped, textured and flavoured to trick the palate it was meat, fruits, vegetables, or spicy noodles.

Jack suddenly felt very hungry. He hadn't eaten since breakfast that morning, a lifetime ago.

A voice at his shoulder whispered, 'I know that look.'

Startled, he leapt a foot in the air.

'It's alright darling. It's me.'

Jack looked up into the eyes of his mother and fell into her arms.

As he wept, Xinjuan held him and cooed, 'I know. It's awful, isn't? The world. You've been so brave to face it. I know you're angry and you're scared. But you have to understand what's at stake, Jack. Come with me. There's something I need to show you.'

He lifted his head from her shoulder and let her lead him into the next chamber. It was immense, a tall glass dome, glowing blue and green with ancient grasses fed by starlight. It was rich with life, except for one section, down where the glass met the hull. There the crop was yellowing and browning and curling in on itself. At the fringes of this blight, the greens and blues of the healthy algae were fading.

Jack's mother pointed to them and said, 'Do you see that, Jack? It's happening on every ship of The Fleet. We don't know how to stop it. You understand, don't you? Without this crop, we're lost.'

She bent down face to face with him and held his shoulders.

'Without a cure, there'll be no more crew, no more humanity, no future on *Uroun*. We need you to study. We need you to be better than we were. If you don't, you'll suffer the same fate as the rest of us, wondering which day will be your last.'

She shook with the effort to control her emotions.

'So we lie to you. We tell you what you need to hear, so that you'll believe in yourselves and the future. We want you to do more than just survive here on this awful ship. We want you to thrive, on *Uroun*.'

Xinjuan rested her head on Jack's and encircled him with her arms.

From a doorway in the opposite side of the dome, a guard in riot gear emerged. Jack stiffened. His mother's hold on him tightened. The guard removed his helmet. It was Michael. He was panting. From the speakers in his helmet emerged the sound of Fleet Operations demanding to know why he wasn't at his post. Jack's father switched the coms button off and put the helmet and his shield on the ground. He took off his gloves, tucked them in his pocket and dragged his hand across his red beard, from his cheeks and moustache, down into a squeeze of his chin. The familiar gesture made Jack forget for a moment how angry he was with him. Michael raised his hands and approached his family, saying nothing.

Jack pulled away from his mother and flitted his eyes between her and her husband.

Finally, his father spoke, 'We're sorry son. We've hated it, every second of it. But this is the life that we've inherited. You think your mother and I didn't hate our parents when they told us?'

Jack didn't answer.

His father went on, drawing closer, 'But we'd graduated. We'd gone through School. It had prepared us. We saw things in their proper perspective.'

Inwardly, Jack recoiled from the idea of going back to School to be 'prepared'.

'It's do or die out here, mate. There's no getting off the ship. We're all in it together, to the end.'

Jack thought about all that he had learned in the last few hours. The Fleet was in trouble. The crops were failing. They still had so far to go to reach *Uroun* and yet so little time to do it in. And so, every year the children of The Fleet were being pushed, harder and harder, to solve the mystery of light-speed travel. He understood the urgency of the situation. What he could not fathom was all the secrecy and the fear adults had of being found out. Jack knew that there was still so much they weren't telling him.

'You're afraid,' Jack said.

'Yes,' his father admitted.

'And your fear makes you lie to us, to manipulate us?'

Xinjuan raised her hands to her face. Michael nodded.

'Then we *are* doomed,' Jack said simply. 'Fear brings out the worst in us. It's love that inspires the best.'

'It's the only way, Jack,' his mother pleaded.

Her son shook his head. 'It's not,' he replied.

Michael grew impatient. 'What else is there, Jack? You're a brilliant kid. What you've achieved, getting out, getting this far, it's never been done before. So great, tell us, what should we do? Should we let all the kids know that theirs could be the very last generation? That they probably won't grow old enough to have kids of their own? That in their own lifetime they could be the ones with their hands on the wheel as the ship goes down for good?'

Jack trembled under the force of his father's outburst. In the silence that followed, his parents stared at him, half in anger and half in hope that he might actually know the answer to the awful questions they lived with each and every day.

Finally, their son admitted to them, 'You're right. I don't know.'

Their shoulders slumped and they bowed their heads, but Jack wasn't finished.

'But I hear something, something better. It sounds right. It feels true. Lucy heard it too. She's gone to find it and I have to follow her. I have to hear it out.'

Though he did not know why, Jack knew that this is what his parents feared most to hear. They looked at each other. They took hold of each other's hands, stared into each other's eyes and spoke in the silent language they shared. The surface of their exchange was brief, yet it concealed the depths of a conversation that had been going on for years between them. Now, for the first time, they invited their son to join them. Michael and Xinjuan turned to Jack and spoke to him as equals.

'You think we don't hear it too?' Xinjuan asked.

The breath stopped in Jack's chest. His mother smiled.

'We knew he was calling to you,' she confided. 'It's not as loud or as clear to us as it is to you, Jack, but it tugs at our hearts every second of every day.'

'The Piper's call is what brought your mother and I together,' said Michael.

'So why didn't you follow it?' Jack demanded. 'Why pretend like it wasn't there?'

'Because we were afraid of where it led!' Michael roared and instantly regretted his anger. To calm himself he looked at his wife. 'We didn't know what we'd become when we got there.'

'That's why we gave you Guitar Hero,' Xinjuan continued, 'so you could find your own voice, answer with your own music. But safely, Jack. We never meant it to go this far.'

Xinjuan was frightened. 'How do you know you can trust him?' she asked Jack as though he were the parent. 'What if The Piper is mad, or evil? We can't tell what he wants.'

Jack regarded his mother and father. He saw how they were reduced to children by a terror they had never faced and so had never outgrown. He felt more certain than ever that he must go.

'You understand,' Jack told them calmly, 'that if I don't answer the call, the part of me that hears it will die. It's the most important part of me. If I don't have that, I don't want to survive, anywhere.'

His parents again looked deeply into one another's eyes. Though they barely moved, Jack could have sworn that they were dancing.

In that instant, the doors at either end of the dome opened. Two detachments of guards emerged, batons brandished and shields ready. Without another moment's hesitation, Xinjuan led Jack to a hatch in the floor. As she opened it, she explained to Jack, 'Water is recycled from throughout the ship. Ducts lead everywhere to and from this garden. Follow this until you get to…'

She gulped down against her fear of the words. Jack said them for her, 'Human Resource Re-Allocation?'

Xinjuan's features retracted painfully. 'You know about The Drain?' she asked, horrified.

Jack shook his head, 'Only that it's where unwanted people go.'

Xinjuan squeezed his hand and said, 'That's the way to The Piper, Jack. It's the only way.'

Michael turned from the guards and crouched down next to them, looked in his son's eyes and said, 'That Lucy's something special, huh?'

Jack nodded.

They embraced one last time.

'When you get there,' Michael breathed into his son's hair, 'you play loud, like a *voodoo child*, alright?' Jack nodded, and let the tears flow down his cheeks. 'Play so loud we know you've made it.'

'I will,' Jack promised and raised his eyes to meet his parents'.

Xinjuan pressed the tears on her cheeks to Jack's and whispered, 'Play so *everyone* hears it.'

With that, they let him go.

Down through the dark, Jack was chased by the sounds of jackboots stomping upon metal, loudspeakers yelling his name like a curse-word, and his parents singing in harmony the tune at work in his veins.

NIGHT, DAY 182

40. THE DRAIN

At the bottom of the chute that dropped from the floor of the nursery, Jack expected to land in a torrent of excrement, the accumulated leavings of the entire crew of *Hamelin*. Instead, he was sucked into a gale of hot air.

The circulatory system of the ship worked on the principle of convection. The hot liquids deposited in each toilet rose upwards through the pipes coiled round the inside of *The Hamelin*'s curved hull. The heat drove it along. As it rose, it cooled, and fell, collecting more waste from further along *The Hamelin's* decks. On and on, round and round in a corkscrew motion flowed the river of waste, along the whole length of the ship.

In the final stages of its course, the waste waters were sifted for their precious contents: minerals, salts, enzymes, chemicals of every description, and allocated throughout the ship to be put back to their numerous and essential uses. The water, thus purified, was directed to the crew's drinking dispensers and Xinjuan's fragile garden. Beyond that, the current, for a brief section, was empty of all but the force of suction generated by the rest of the rising, falling, swirling course. It was into this Jack's mother had dropped him.

The liquid might not have made it that far, but the smell of it did. After one whiff of that hellish odour, Jack closed his eyes and held his breath. As the out-pipe bore him along in its stream of putrid air, he counted the beats of his jazz drummer heart.

'…24, 25, 26-27-28, 29, 30, 31-32-33-34…'

Through the bowels of the ship he tumbled, with no light to guide him, and no handhold on the smooth intestinal wall to steady his fall.

As he reached the count of 56, Jack was struggling to decide whether it was more important to stop himself plummeting and find a way out, take another breath or let himself succumb to asphyxiation and so avoid ever tasting that smell again.

At 57, the decision was made for him. His body's momentum was stopped instantly by the impassable force of a grate that knocked the last gasp of air from his lungs. The noxious stream still passed Jack's scraped and latticed face, but through the gaps in the metal his body could not go any further.

He forgot to count.

He forgot to keep his sinuses closed.

He forgot the awfulness waiting to fill his mouth.

Shocked by the impact, he took in a long voluptucus breath, drinking the stench deep into him. Though his mind reeled at the stink, his blood sang with the oxygen that now flooded his veins. He opened his eyes and saw through the grill, farther up the pipe's curvature, dark deposits fall and whisk away around the bend on their long journey to be food again.

He shuddered and looked around him for a way out from this

abysmal condition. At his feet was a small door. It had no handle on the inside. Jack began stomping on it with his heel. After several sharp reports with no visible effect, the hatch seemed to come away of its own accord. A face squinted up at him. Jack recognised its features from his cabin's window screen. It was his rival on the field of Red V Blue and the dad of his Schoolroom tormentor, Rick Mercury.

'Hello, *rat*,' he chuckled.

Mercury's thick mitt grasped Jack's ankle and yanked him through the opening. Jack landed with a crash to the floor and gulped down lungfuls of clean air.

'Smelly little rodent, aren't ya, Jack?' Max's dad gloated over him. 'Oh yeah, I know you. You're the one that broke my winning streak. I was headed for a fleet record before you came along.'

Dazed, Jack spluttered, 'It's just a game.'

'Just a game?' Mercury bent down and clutched the font of Jack's shirt in his fist. 'What else do I have to live for on this hulk?'

Jack gazed back at the man who was the source of his classmate's twisted, sulky features and answered, 'Your son?'

Mercury senior's expression softened for a moment as he thought of his little boy. Then, with a grunt he shoved Jack back to the floor.

'That runt,' Rick muttered and turned his back on Jack. 'He's useless. Just like his dad. Thinks playing games is how you get ahead.' He sighed and his gaze turned inwards. 'That leads straight to one place

– right here, the arse-end of the ship.'

Jack saw his chance and ran in the opposite direction. The room was stacked with crates, all numbered and marked 'Personal Effects'. He ducked down into the rows of belongings. Max's father stalked after him, continuing his self-pitying rant, 'We can't all get great marks, can we? We can't all make it into Net Surveillance, can we Mr. Voyager? No. Someone's got to do the dirty work.'

He straightened a box back into place on its shelf.

'You know though, you've gotta hand it to the School program. It sure knows how to spot aptitude. Good at Physics, Maths *and* Human Sciences? Go right up to the bridge, my boy. Fail Fukuyama's little touchy feely lessons in empathy, but really good at killing elves in Dragon Quest? We've got a job for you, mate. Human Resources Re-Allocation. Down to The Drain with you. You're a rat catcher!'

Rick Mercury shoved aside two crates to reveal Jack's hiding place. He grabbed Jack by the scruff of the neck and dragged him along, keeping on with his mad monologue.

'It's a job no one else wants to do, but you're *supremely* qualified. Yep, we think you're our man. Here's an award, from The Admiral herself! Stick that on your wall.' He paused, as though listening to another voice, and answered it, 'What's that? Is it right? Is it moral?' He laughed. 'The question you want to ask is "Is it necessary?" and I can assure you, mate, it bloody well is.'

He continued dragging Jack at his side as though his jostling, kicking, punching form were no more trouble than a squirming puppy's. They entered another room, white-tiled and starkly lit. Jack could hear people murmuring.

'Help!' he called, but he received no reply.

'Help is what we need, mate. Yes, indeed. And you're the one to give it,' Mercury went on, incorporating Jack's cries into his rant. 'You see, here's the thing. We don't have enough room on this here ship for everyone. Thought we did, but we don't. So, we're gunna have to trim the fat. Don't worry. You don't have to pick who stays and who goes. We'll do that for ya. Thing is, none of us upstairs has the stomach for *doing* the actual *throwing away*. So, if you wouldn't mind, here's a special hat and a badge and your very own office.'

With that, he dropped Jack to the floor. Jack turned and scurried away on his hands and feet. Without looking back at Jack, Mercury snapped his fingers and pointed at him.

'Oi! Don't you move a whisker. You're not on my list, but if you interrupt a man at his work once more, I swear I'll give you a good belting. And believe you me, your parents'll thank me for it.'

Jack was shocked still. He leaned against the tiled wall behind him and watched the madman ply his trade.

Assembled in the room before his desk was a sorrowful cue of souls. One by one they filed past the 'rat-catcher', reported their name, which he ticked off his list, signed the form he offered them, and then shuffled on through the coffin shaped frame of an airlock. Through the gap, Jack could see that thirty or so people who had already climbed into the chamber and were silently awaiting their fate.

Almost every one of them was what Jack would call old. They were not grey and wrinkled, but the fatigue they wore on their faces was more pitiful than of anyone he had seen on his long downward spiral through the diseased body of the ship. Yet they could not have been more than ten or so years older than his parents.

'What have they done?' Jack wondered aloud.

'We got old, mate,' came a familiar voice. 'Gotta make way for fresh blood.'

Jack looked up over the executioner's back to see the man from the casino. He was smiling sadly back at him.

'Don't worry, mate. I've had a good innings. Made myself useful, for a while.'

'How come they didn't retire you earlier, Felix?' Mercury grumbled before his senior.

'My successor was almost as thick as you, Mercury,' scoffed Felix. 'It's taken 'til now to show him the ropes without him getting all tangled up in 'em.'

He winked at Jack.

Rick just grunted and pointed to a spot on the page, 'Sign here, Voyager.'

'Your'e a Voyager?' Jack gasped.

Felix nodded, 'Soon to be in deed as well as in name, kid.'

With that he stepped through the door into the airlock.

The next person in line was not of retirement age. He seemed only a few years past graduation. Of all the people whose fates had been decided, he was the least resigned to his. His hands were bound behind his back and his eyes were blindfolded. He did not struggle against his bonds, but with his last few moments aboard the ship, he invoked every condemned man's right to speak some final words.

'Out with it, then,' the executioner yawned.

The blindfolded man was uncertain which way to direct his speech. He settled for straight ahead.

'I was raised to be proud,' he began, 'proud of what we had accomplished. I was proud that humanity had broken free of the Earth. I believed what I was taught, that we had left our animal nature behind and amongst the stars we would discover our true potential. It was a promise to become all that was best in us. Then, upon my graduation, I awoke from this dream into a world that was as cruel and as brutal as the one our ancestors departed.'

The young man turned his blindfolded eyes back down the line of the unwanted and said, 'I have tried speaking out, but no one will listen. I have tried finding others whose hearts have not yet been extinguished by despair. But there are so few of them and they are distant, scattered throughout the ships of our armada.' He turned back to face forward. 'So I declare myself free. I will take no more part in

The Admiral's command. If I cannot inspire mutiny, I will…'

'What?' Rick bellowed and rose to his feet, 'Bore us to death? We've got jobs to do, mate. Got no time for your whining. Gotta get on with it, don't we. Got better things to do than wish things were better. This is the way things are. You got a better idea? Tell us! You got a way of getting to *Uroun* faster? Bloody-well do it!'

Jack was shocked at how like his father Mercury sounded; angrier, more spiteful, but their argument was the same.

The man said nothing.

'I didn't think so,' muttered Mercury and dragged the bound and blindfolded man through the hatch. Though there was space in the airlock for the dozens of people still waiting in line to sign their own death warrants, the executioner had grown impatient. He brought his hand up over the button that would bring closed the door between the rats and *Hamelin*. Jack looked past Mercury at his friend, Felix, waiting in the dock with glistening eyes and a smirk on his lips. The rat catcher then intoned by rote and without feeling the official declaration that legalised, formalised and sanitised the extermination of *Hamelin's* unwanted crew.

'As we have all learned from humanity's long history,' he droned, 'it is often necessary for the few to be sacrificed for the benefit of the many.'

Jack was shocked to hear a lesson from Fukuyama's class brought to such an awful conclusion. Had this been the point of all their years of instruction, a long preparation for this moment of horror?

The bored executioner droned on, 'Your service to The Fleet and to the greater cause of humanity's survival will never be forgotten. You are passing the torch to the next generation who will bear it as far as they can before stronger hands rise to carry it further still. In this way, we trust that in time, the hands of our descendants will plant that torch in the soil of *Uroun*, and around that eternal flame a new people will gather, there to warm themselves with the memory of the great deeds you have accomplished on their behalf.'

From the back of the group in the airlock, a voice rose, pleading, 'This isn't right. There's been a mistake. I'm still useful. I can eat less. I can share quarters. I won't be a bother. Please!'

The woman struggled to the front but could go no farther than the thick hand Mercury thrust into her chest.

To soothe her, Felix touched a hand to her shoulder and began to whistle.

The sound made Jack's heart swell. At first he thought it was because the man was being so brave. Then Jack realised it was gently twisting, turning melody of The Piper. The woman struggled to control her breathing and pursed her lips to join in. Others in the airlock picked up the song until soon Mercury had to shout to make The Admiral's pronouncement heard.

'So it is with great sorrow and gratitude,' he bellowed, 'that we accept your gift to the future!'

Unseen by the exterminator, Jack crossed to his desk and flipped back furtively through the pages of his long list of the departed. Finally, he found the names he was looking for: Lucy Gemini and her father, Chiang Zu, next to the words SPECIAL RENDITION. They had passed through this room three months ago, on the day Lucy and he had received their invitation from The Piper. That day Lucy had been expelled into space.

Yet he had just been with her, online.

Not a ghost. It was her.

Wherever she had gone to, beyond this place of execution, she was alive and waiting for him.

As Mercury's fingers flexed over the airlock's control, Jack burst from behind his desk with a yelp and elbowed the unsuspecting executioner aside. Before his Red adversary could recover, Jack depressed the button himself and leapt into the airlock to stand between Felix and the young rebel. Through the metal of the inner door, they could hear Mercury banging and screaming, but it was too late. A siren voice counted down their final seconds.

"Airlock doors will open in FIVE…"

Jack knew the cold vacuum of space was deadly.

"…FOUR…"

All his life he'd learned to fear it.

"…THREE…"

Now he was leaping into it…

"...TWO..."

..without a suit.

"...ONE. Doors opening."

The outer door of the airlock slid open. In flooded a silence more profound than Jack had ever heard. It sucked the air from the lock like water into a drain. It washed Jack away, twisting and spinning him, down into the fathomless black.

41. RIVER TO THE SHADOWLAND

The Voyager 1 probe was launched from Earth in the 77th year of the 20th Century. Its mission was to photograph Saturn, Neptune and Uranus. When scientists realised that its path through the outer planets would shoot it out past the limits of their solar system into the infinitude of space, they decided not to waste the opportunity. They sent a message to any civilisation 'out there' who might, like them, be looking for signs of life.

The scientists wondered what they should say about Earth. How should their invitation be expressed to inspire our interstellar cousins to travel the vast distance to meet us? The answer was obvious: music.

A search began for the singers, musicians and composers whose work best expressed the beauty and fragility of our world. From its oldest culture, Australia's First Nation peoples, and from the Eastern and Western classical traditions, folksongs, operas and symphonies were chosen. Even an example of one of the newest forms of music to be born at that time, Chuck Berry's rock n' roll hit, *Johnny B Goode*, was etched into the grooves of Voyager's gold-plated record.

Before *The Hamelin* and the other six ships of The Fleet embarked on their epic journey, *Voyager* was the only man made craft to have left the envelope of warmth that radiated from Earth's Sun. On its way past Saturn, it turned back and took a photograph of humanity's home-world. In the image, Earth was a mere speck of blue suspended in the vastness of space. The photo was both tender and terrifying. It showed what a delicate and rare place the Earth was.

More than two centuries later, another Voyager drifted through space and turned back to regard his own small, fragile world. He had only ever seen it from the outside in simulations. This experience was altogether different. He would not be shortly logging out and returning to his cabin.

This departure was final.

And would soon be fatal.

...34, 35, 36-37-38-39, 40, 41, 42-43-44-45...

The drummer in Jack's heart beat out its final solo. Jack held his breath as long as he could. He knew that once he exhaled, the difference in pressure between his body and the freezing void around him would burst every cell in his body.

...56, 57-58-59-60-61, 62, 63-64-65-66...

The bodies of his fellow deportees were like flecks of kelp swirling in the wake of a whale. Through tears that instantly became icicles, he watched the other discarded shipmates fall through the abysmal dark. Their legs and arms flailed in slow motion, bidding a long farewell to the only home they had ever known.

...86, 87, 88-89-90-91, 92, 93...

As the words formed in Jack's mind, his lips pursed, and with his final breath of recycled *Hamelin* air, he whistled.

The breath spent, Jack waited for eternal night to chill his flesh.

Then, in the deep distance, he heard a slender pipe reply.

His drummer heart leapt at the feeling.

And he took another breath.

Another breath!

Jack opened his eyes. A fragile golden aura shimmered around him, gently pulsing with the rhythm of the piper's song.

He breathed again. It was impossible but there was air within this luminescence. He laughed and the sound echoed within the cloud, heating it. It was like floating in the vibrating air of a Gravity Shower, but without tiled walls to echo and focus the waves of the signal. Nothing in Jack's understanding of engineering or physics could explain what was happening, but it was real.

This must be how Lucy had survived. For joy, he sang,

Jack glanced back at *The Hamelin*. His birthplace was shrinking into the distance. Jack turned to face his uncertain fate amongst the stars. Before him, the expanse of space seemed to drop away like an ocean strewn with sinking lights. Born into it on a current of song, he gave over to its pull and sang,

'Father, Michael,

Mother, Xinjuan,

It's me out here, your only son.

The night is clear.

And now I hear

The tune that's calling everyone.'

New lyrics came to Jack. He heard other melodies, endless possibilities for song. Clear of the interference of the ship and all its subtle droning confusion, Jack understood that The Piper's call had only ever been a slender river leading towards this ocean of music. Up and down the roaring waves of song, Jack rose and dipped and turned, drawn further from home, deeper into the night, glowing brighter and brighter, like a comet feeding on its own speed.

'Your setting sun's a golden coin,

Each day dropped in a slot -

Press the buttons of the great machine -

The song you paid for's what you got.

It's a funeral march. An elegy.

Made for keeping clocks in ticking time,

Treadmills turning day by day,

And thoughts in nodding rhyme.

But someone, somewhere else, is calling out my name.

Somewhere, someone else is calling out my name.'

The more he sang, the more momentum Jack made.

He was not the only one.

A hundred metres to his right, Felix Voyager's whistling melody wove in and out of harmony with the Piper's call. He still held onto the hand of his frightened shipmate, and coaxed her along. Her meek voice slowed him down, but he kept her in tune and together they waltzed down the shimmering stream of song. The rebel graduate also had difficulty keeping time, but his moans and grumbles found the base notes of the song and bore him onward in awkward sparking cartwheels. At different speeds, but in the same direction, those who heard the song reached out and pulled, note by note, like knots in a rope, towards an invisible shore.

Others were not so charmed. Those overwhelmed by fear, who could not grasp the music and did not sing along, spilled out into the cold and silent void of which they had lived their whole lives in terror. Jack watched with sadness two thirds of their company drift away. But he could not leave the stream to save them. He could only press on, singing upon the golden river.

'*Waves rise to meet you,*

Pouring out of screams.

A distant eye burns green-red-blue.

Tears fall like starlight beams.

In my heart beats a drum.

I am. I am. It's beating.

Not the same as everyone.

Though we're all repeating,

'*Someone must be calling out my name.*

Somewhere someone must be calling out my name.'

In the distance dead ahead, Jack noticed one of the stars behaving strangely, flashing red, green, blue, red, green, blue. The space about the flickering luminescence was empty of stars. Within moments, he perceived the light was artificial, some sort of beacon, pulsing at the tip of an enormous diamond-shaped silhouette lurking in the current. Eventually Jack could see that this dark form had its own lights, though dimmer, and it dawned on him that he was swimming towards a vast island in space.

Closer still, he saw the rainbow light was a neon sign in the shape of a dancing pipe player. Each step of his jig was represented in a different colour. Red, he was standing on the toes of his left foot, kicking his right into the air. Green, both legs were wide in a vaulting split. Blue, he stood, his right hand lifted off the pipe to wave in welcome at the flock of singing, whistling, astronaut refugees.

Within a few hundred metres, Jack could make out even more detail. The neon sign was dancing atop a mast that rose from a platform. This stage was joined by a narrow gangway to a slowly shifting line of variously shaped buildings: slender towers, low domes and blocks connected by archways, like the ancient skyline of Jerusalem, not the colour of sand and stone, but shimmering dark blue as though seen through deep water. Looming above them in the distance beyond was the mountain from the Piper's broadcast. Yet it was not made of snowcapped grey rock. It was dark glass whose facets pulsed from within with dark purple flame, as though the whole enormous crystal were alive and breathing.

Jack gasped. This city, he realised, was moored to a mammoth asteroid, of which the mountain was just a part. All of this was following along in secret behind the fleet of starships that bore the last vestiges of the human race toward *Uroun*. All his life, this place had lurked in their shadow.

And it was populated.

The people who lined the pier at the dancing piper's feet did not wear spacesuits. They were not protected by glass. They stood as though upon the opposite bank of a river, clapping and singing along to The Piper's tune, enveloped in a golden, glimmering haze.

And standing at their head was Lucy.

42. DUET

Lucinda Gemini, troublemaker, dropout, enemy of The Fleet, jumped up and down, and laughed. He'd made it. That awkward, beautiful boy had actually made it.

She'd been longing to see him for months. As soon as she and her father had arrived in *The Shadowland*, she had been working with her new friends to free him. All the weeks planning for their fleet-wide hack. All the hours writing the code. During that time her feelings had swung between fear for Jack's safety, frustration with the time it was taking to reach him, and a growing anger with him.

For going back so easily under The Admiral's spell.

For forgetting his instrument and his song.

For forgetting her.

But seeing him dive towards her through the frozen black of night, Lucy realised that who Jack was inside had never gone away. Not when they were in Seven, when he'd stood alone against those marauding bullies from the older level, and been shamed into silence. Not even these past months, when he had been asleep, held under a heavy blanket of confusion. After all, she had also been put under by that same power, and his song had awoken her. Now she'd returned the favour, and Jack was wide awake, calling her name across the night.

'LUCY!'

She called back to him, 'Come on Jack! You're almost there! Come on lame boy! What's keeping you?'

In reply, Jack sang out more loudly. 'LUCEEEE!' The extra force in his voice thrust him forward even faster.

'Look out, Lucy,' Miles growled. 'You're boyfriend's coming in a little hot.'

She glared at him. 'Don't be so juvenile. He is not my …'

Jack knocked her from her feet at a speed that was not convenient for graceful embraces. They rolled together through the shimmering air for ten yards, before landing with a yelp and a groan at the tips of a pair of pointed leather boots.

'What an entrance, Voyager!' cheered Mr Pfief with a hoot and a clap.

He helped his protégé to stand. The touch of the emergency teacher's hand was electric. The sound of the piping seemed to emanate directly from his smiling face.

Jack opened his mouth to speak. He tried to order the questions he had crowding in his mind. But what was more important, to understand how he had been brought here or the purpose, why? He turned to Lucy. Without realising it, he had been holding her hand. She had already noticed and now that her friend was facing her, she grinned and shook it.

'Very nice to finally meet you, Jack,' she laughed.

Jack blushed and floundered for words.

'Where have you been?' he finally blurted. 'What is this place?'

'Welcome to *The Shadowland*, Jack,' a familiar voice purred behind him.

Jack turned to see Miles. The leader of The Shadows swept his arm across the long vista beyond the pier. The domes and squares and minarets of the city seemed to drink in the starlight and glowed a spectral blue. They rose and fell upon the tide of an invisible ocean. The pontoon upon which they stood was lifted by a swell and Jack gazed across the luminous rooftops of the city. He saw the wave lift row after row of buildings, rolling towards the shoreline of the distant asteroid and the crystalline peak of the Piper's mountain.

Jack swooned at the sight and the sea-swell sensation of all that energy moving beneath him.

'Steady on, Jack,' Miles said, catching his hand. 'Our city coasts in the wake of The Fleet. It makes us a little seasick at times, but it's also why The Admiral can't spy on us. Too much interference. They know we're here, but we're invisible, like ghosts. *The Shadowland* is *Unamerica* to some, *Unaustralia* to others, *Un-China*, *Un-England*. We're from all over, but we're all in the same boat, if you catch my drift.'

Lucy turned to Pfeif and beamed at him, 'I told you he'd make it.'

'I never doubted it for a second,' said the teacher with a chuckle.

Jack looked him up and down - the multi-coloured tie, the

pointed boots and the slight mania burning within his eyes. He took a quick breath and turned to Lucy.

'Is he…?' Jack whispered, but dare not finish the question.

Lucy rolled her eyes. 'Catch up, Jack.'

The teacher's body seemed to shimmer, as though it were an avatar projected into the physical world.

'Are you really here, Sir?' Jack asked him sheepishly

The Piper considered his question for a moment.

'Firstly, Jack,' he pronounced and the words seemed more like the trilling of a bird than human speech, 'we don't call each other Sir and salute around here. Call me Theo. It's my name. Secondly, yes! As ever, you're very astute. I am *not* actually *here*. Where I *am* is about a hundred Ks that-a-way,' he said and pointed back over his shoulder, 'up the mountain.'

'One hundred!' Jack drew a deep breath. He looked around him at the people on the jetty. They wore the fabric of Fleet uniforms, but these had been recut and sewn back together into very different garb. Jack felt like he had discovered another tribe, so similar to his own, but which in isolation had grown strange and wonderful.

He looked past them at the city, floating in space, and beyond that, the shimmering purple rock rising into a mountain. And surrounding it all, a halo of golden light, humming warmly with music.

'How?' Jack whispered. 'How is any of this possible?'

The Piper smiled and nodded. 'For all I know, Jack, this

asteroid is unique in all the universe. The crystals it is made from react with music - any kind of patterned sound - to create atmosphere. It's a mystery. It's a miracle. And that's not all it can do. Oh my! What those rocks can roll when the right groover moves em!'

He leaned down and put a hand on Lucy and Jack's shoulders. 'So purse your lips and get whistlin', kids! There's a whole symphony's worth of music to go between you and my mountain.'

His face grew serious. He reached out to his two proteges.

The buzzing hands of his projection pressed pulses of electrical current into their shoulders, like the echo of distant drumming.

'Time is running out, 'he said. 'The fate of all this,' he raised his eyes at The Fleet, the city and the mountain, 'will soon be decided. So get here quick, Lucy and Jack! We *need* to *jam*!

A manic smile spread along his lips, yet his eyes remained fixed sternly on the two children of *Hamelin*. Jack gripped Lucy's hand more tightly.

She turned to him and asked, 'Are you up for it, Jack?'

Jack looked up at The Piper. This was the man the parents of *Hamelin* feared most - a boogeyman who wanted to steal their children. All Jack's life, he had been calling to him. How many had he summoned before? How many generations ago did The Piper make his deal to take the *Hamelin's* 'rats' in exchange for an apprentice?

Slowly, not taking his gaze from the mad piper's eyes, Jack

nodded.

'Ha!' exclaimed The Piper and pointed up at the stars, 'Take that, *night*! Take that, *fate*! Lucy n' Jack are coming to kick your butts!'

'Yeah, *death*, look out!' Lucy called into the starry darkness.

She looked back at Jack's sombre face and smirked. 'You're so serious,' she said. 'You'd think you were some kind of hero.'

Jack blushed. Lucy winked at him and they turned together to watch the last few outcasts from The Fleet arrive.

Each 'rat' that tumbled to them down the river landed gently amongst Miles' shadow band. By their voices, Jack recognised players from The Club: Ibrahim Riaz, the gorilla trombonist, and the Russian Blind Willie. *The Shadowland* was where all who lived for music came to die and be born anew.

Felix and the lady he had saved were the last to come aboard. The couple alighted and walked to Jack in a daze, marvelling at the welcoming choir and their floating world protected by an atmosphere of song.

'Do you hear it, Jack?' Felix asked him. 'No engines. No drone. What's keeping it all together is music. This place is made of songs.'

'I only dreamed it was true,' the lady whimpered up at The Piper.

'But you played along all the same,' tittered the magician. 'Ever since you were a girl, Carol. You knew.'

Carol laughed and years seemed to fall from her face.

'None of that matters now,' The Piper assured her. 'You're among friends.' His eyes widened as though seeing something terrible. 'But steer clear of the Grandmaster DJ and his Choir! Those guys will eat you alive!'

He yelped, shook his head, and laughed at the confused expressions on the new arrivals' faces. He slapped Miles on the shoulder. 'He'll tell you all about it, OK. OK? OK!'

He turned once more to Jack and Lucy. Though everyone's eyes were on him, he raised his left hand up beside his mouth in a gesture of secrecy, pointed through it with his right towards the mountain and mouthed the words, 'See you up there.'

Jack and Lucy nodded, and with that The Piper winked, spun on his toes and disappeared.

Miles coughed and led Felix away, leaving Jack and Lucy alone. The two friends walked to the edge of the pier and looked back across space to where The Fleet's ring of seven embers flickered around *Uroun's* beckoning light.

'Hard to believe, isn't it?' Lucy offered.

Jack shook his head. 'How could The Admiral have kept all this secret?'

'She didn't have to,' she said. 'She just told us a different story. It had enough truth in it to seem like it was all there was to tell.'

'Do you know now?' Jack asked. 'Everything, I mean? Do you know it all?'

'I know some of it,' she answered. 'not even Miles and his band know everything.' She cast her eyes back at the mountain. 'I'm not even sure if *he* does. He doesn't look it but he's very old. I think he was here from the beginning, from when we left Earth. He made all of this.' Her gesture seemed to take in The Fleet as well as the city behind them. 'But I think he's calling us to bring *him* the answers.'

Lucy brimmed with everything she had learned in the past few months. The dangers she had faced. The wonders she had seen. But she did not want to overwhelm her friend. She did not want to break this moment.

'Why ask me?' Jack said, dropping his head. 'It's only ever been *his* song I've sung.'

'To begin with, sure,' she purred. 'But you filled it with *your* words, *your* spirit.'

She took his hand and pressed it to his heart.

'Until you made it your song.'

Jack remembered all the nights and all the mornings he had spent at his cabin window, staring into the stars, listening.

He shuffled his feet.

'I sang it for you,' he said and waited for the next words. 'You've always been so brave. So strong. So…'

But the word 'beautiful' would not come.

The Shadows' music swirled around them.

Beyond their golden bubble, the universe was hushed and listening.

'I know,' Lucy said at last. 'I heard you,' she touched her heart, 'in here.'

Her mother's face loomed before her in the dark.

'But I had to fight…I…'

She shook away the image and leaned closer towards him.

'I still hear you, Jack,' she said, and looked her friend in the eyes. 'I think I always will.'

For a moment, they rested their foreheads against one another, closed their eyes, and breathed. They were closer than they'd ever been, but they still had so far to go.

A mountain loomed between Jack and Lucy.

And the first notes of a new song.

A ballad.

An adventure.

A duet.

End of Book One.